A Gentleman
and
a Scholar

Wings ePress, Inc.

Lynn Shurr

A Gentleman and a Scholar

"Where is my daughter, you blackguard, you cad?"

"Here and quite well after her ordeal. Do come in." He stepped back before the door hit him in the face and allowed the furious father to roar inside. "Would you care for some tea?—though you will have to drink it from a glass as the Russians do."

"What I care for is my daughter. Where is she? Naked in your bedchamber. I see her clothes spread on your chairs, Professor Lord Longleigh." He sneered the middle word.

Betsy, swallowed in the huge chair facing the fire, stood, carefully holding onto her blankets. "We are merely waiting for my dress and petticoats to dry. And I am not naked. I still have my undergarments and stockings on."

Her father continued the attack. "Simply because you are the son of a duke does not mean you can dally with my daughter, Longleigh. You will offer for her at once and marry her posthaste."

Justin envisioned his life of the mind slipping away. By acting the gentleman, he had thrust his foot into the parson's mousetrap. His father would have made the same demand about any of his sisters. The duke had come close to doing that at least twice. What would his life be like, wedded to a pretty and quite intelligent young lady he barely knew and living on an allowance for the rest of his days?

What They Are Saying About
A Gentleman and a Scholar

"Shurr is a wonderful storyteller."
—The Romance Studio

"Very easy read, well written, combined with conflict, believable plots and secondary characters that make the story come alive."
—Jane Lange, *Romances, Reads and Reviews*

"I love the picture the author paints of the town and the way of life, and the characters are strong and interesting.
—Joan Conning Afman
Author of *The Cheetah Princess*

"Lynn Shurr breathes life into the characters and allows each turn of the page to lead up to a pleasurable ending."
—Cherokee
Coffee Time Romance and More

"I love how deep well-written the characters are."
—Juliette Brandt
Paperbacks and Frosting

"You can count on Lynn Shurr to deliver interesting characters and great romance."
—A.C. Mason
Author of *Deadly Bayou*

A Gentleman
and
a Scholar

Lynn Shurr

A Wings ePress, Inc.
Regency Historical Novel

Wings ePress, Inc.

Edited by: Jeanne Smith
Copy Edited by: Bev Haynes
Executive Editor: Jeanne Smith
Cover Artist: Trisha FitzGerald-Jung
Images from Pixabay and Pexels

Wings ePress Books
www.wingsepress.com

Copyright © 2024 by: Lynn Shurr
ISBN 979-8-89197-989-5

Published In the United States Of America

Wings ePress, Inc.
3000 N. Rock Road
Newton, KS 67114

Dedication

For Dorothy Ann Faillace and Tia Ann Owens-Powers, super fans of the Longleigh Chronicles.

The progeny of Pearce and Flora Longleigh, Duke and Duchess of Bellevue, as recorded in the family Bible:

James Logan Longleigh, Storm Cloud, born in the Ohio Territory, April 12,1784?

Thalia Amabel Full Moon Woman Longleigh, b. March 1, 1785.

Iris Emily Doe Eyes Longleigh, b. October 16, 1787.

Twins, **Calliope Constance Corn Tassel & Clio Judith Small Turtle**, b. June 22, 1789.

Joshua William Big Paw Longleigh, b. January 24, 1791.

Jason Samuel Benjamin Rattler Longleigh, b. January 24, 1792.

Pandora Jane Black Wing Longleigh, b. September 15, 1794.

Euphemia Dorcas Little Dove Longleigh, b. December 31, 1795

Justinian Giles White Bull Longleigh, b. July 10, 1800

And all made the lives of their parents
very interesting.

One

Oxford University, 1822

Justinian Longleigh, youngest son of the Duke and Duchess of Bellevue and by far the Oxford don with the least years, strode through one of the smaller quadrangles of Christ Church College on a brisk but beautiful March day.

Hilary Term had just ended, freeing him from lectures and giving him a month to do reading and research before Trinity Term began late in April. A slight breeze flared his black robe faced with golden panels embroidered by his mother's own hand. Early daffodils showed off their bright yellow blossoms against the Gothic gray of the ancient buildings, making them far less grim.

They reminded him that his mother, Lady Flora, also beautiful and blonde, though she most likely remained that way through many feminine artifices the men in her family did not question, would be making her way from Bellevue Hall in the north to London for the start of the social Season. With his great, bearish father, Pearce Longleigh, reluctantly accompanying her on horseback and a retinue of servants and household items deemed necessary for their comfort following, she was on the march like the late Napoleon ready to conquer. He sighed. Once ensconced in the townhouse, she would demand his attention, prying him away from the life of the mind that suited him so well. He might as well submit by being there to greet her.

He knew his appointment as a professor of physics at the age of twenty-one had been controversial, but he had begun his basic studies at sixteen, learned all his tutors could teach him in such short time that he'd advanced to graduate studies and completed those with equal rapidity. He sought professorship immediately. The more traditional of the fellows of the college, and perhaps the more envious, opposed such an unseasoned lecturer. Those more forward thinking proclaimed him Oxford's answer to Cambridge's Sir Isaac Newton. Not to mention that having a wealthy duke for a father might shake loose some endowments for the university. Justinian doubted that. His father had hated his brief years at Oxford as much as he rejoiced in them. The doubters soon learned that his lectures were the most popular from the start, attended not only by students, but other tutors and in the far rear of the hall, a few young ladies who had asked to audit the class to the horror of the male participants. In thanks, they left him apples with pretty ribbons tied to the stems and their calling cards resting beneath. Dons were not permitted to marry any more than women could attend college, but they seemed to share a hope he might change his mind about his life's path.

Never. He pushed all that aside to enjoy this day, the burbling of a small fountain near his pathway, the anticipation of an excellent Lent meal in the grand old dining hall where the professors served by their own chef ate far better than the students.

The blast fairly knocked him off his feet. Shards of glass flew in his direction as he shielded his head from the tiny spears. Smoke boiled from the broken windows of the laboratory he'd been passing. Inside, he glimpsed a figure flailing at a small fire rapidly spreading.

Giving it not a second thought, he raced to the door blown open by the explosion and grabbed the leather fire bucket filled with water on the doorsill as if in anticipation of a disaster. Entering the room, he moved directly to the form shrouded by haze and dashed the water over it. Not good enough. What appeared to be petticoats were still afire. He slung this person in distress over his shoulder and made haste to the nearby fountain. In she went with one mighty heave. Surely, the water wasn't deep enough to drown a person, but she surfaced and appeared unable to stand. Ah, he saw the problem. Not only was she weighed down by a heavy leather apron tied around her neck, but she wore spectacles so begrimed by soot she must be blinded.

He found his pen knife and sawed at the straps tightened by the water until the apron fell away. Removing her spectacles, he cleared them with the edge of his robe and set them in place again over the largest pair of cornflower blue eyes he'd ever seen—yet they seemed familiar. Then, he offered his hand to assist her from the water. At once, he saw his mistake. Under the apron, she wore only a simple white frock made transparent to her undergarments by her dunking. He immediately lifted her from the fountain, whose spray had removed some of the smut from what appeared to be blonde hair turned gray by ash. It fell in strands down her back, all pins removed by her great splash. Stripping off his academic gown, he covered her at once.

A crowd had gathered. Some formed a bucket brigade from the fountain to the lab, putting out small fires within. Others merely enjoyed the disaster by making what they considered witty comments.

"Betsy Boom has done it again. Won't her papa be wroth with her."

"Second time in a month. I doubt the university will want to pay for new windows again."

"About time someone threw her in a fountain."

With his hands still resting on her frail shoulders, he could feel her body shaking. "Never fear, Miss Boom, I shall escort you to your home immediately."

Teeth chattering, she answered, "B-b-Barton is my name, Elizabeth b-b-Barton."

"Pardon my error, Miss Barton." He offered his arm for support as if they were about to leave a ballroom before he discovered another problem. Somewhere amidst the crisis, she'd lost her shoes. Her charred hems exposed a foot of white cotton stockings which somewhat preserved her modesty. "Perhaps I should carry you, if it isn't too far."

He was spared that by the approach of one of the fire brigade members who held out a pair of flat, black ladies' slippers. Recognizing the man as one of his more eager students whose eyes lit when he comprehended new knowledge, he asked, "Yes, Mr. Simpson. What do you have there?" A rather stupid question from such a touted scholar. Clearly, they were shoes.

"I found these in the laboratory and thought the young lady might be in need of them, Professor Lord Justinian Longleigh, sir."

"Of course." He accepted the slippers, turned them inside out to rid them of any glass fragments, and turned to Miss Barton. "If you will allow me the privilege of restoring these to your feet, please sit on the edge of the fountain." He knelt in the grass and placed one on each foot in the manner of a prince from a fairy tale his sisters favored in childhood.

"Why not push her in again and leave her there? Teach her a lesson," one of the onlookers quipped.

He rose with balled fists and an unexpected quickness that had the idler taking a step backward. Part of the Justinian Longleigh legend lived on from his very first term at Oxford. When still wearing the short gown of a new student, he'd been stalked by the hearties, those sporty athletes of the college who delighted in dunking the artistic aesthetes in the Mercury fountain. Not yet at his full growth, but well-schooled in fisticuffs at his father's gymnasium, he'd taken out his first attacker with a blow to the stomach, the second with a right to the jaw, and the last with a simple trip and shove that put the bully into the water, not him. Unfortunately, three more took their place and upended him into the pool. After that, however, they'd left him alone. In fact, he'd been asked to join various teams which he declined, though if he got word of an upcoming attack on another scholar, he did give them warning and escorted them about until the interest waned. His father had once defended the helpless, and so would he.

Later, when he told his father of his humiliation, the duke had replied, "What matters is how many of the enemy you took out before being overcome. You are not a saber but an epee whose slender blade kills just as well."

He had no desire to kill anyone, though he could fence with skill if necessary. Hence, no desire to join the military as many younger sons of the nobility did. As a professor, he did have other powers and much more dignity. Now, he eyed the loudmouth. "Mr. Simpson, take this boy and his cronies into the lab to clean up the mess. I will check on their progress later."

"Yes, Professor Lord Justinian Longleigh, sir." Simpson was a scholarship student who came of common stock and aimed to make his family proud, unlike the young louts who followed him back to the lab. He all but pulled his dark forelock in reverence. Most of the others would never graduate in any field at all but would fall back on family remittances for the rest of their worthless lives. Though, he shouldn't be so scornful. In addition to his stipend from the university, he still received a quarterly allowance from the duke.

"Where were we? On our way to your home, Miss Barton. Shall we go?"

He offered his arm again, and they set off at a pace the young woman could sustain. He tended to forget that having attained the family height of six feet for males, taller than most men and all women, but not the broad shoulders or the heft of his father, he often took long strides and outdistanced companions. They hadn't far to go into a recessed courtyard with a venerable building where some of the profs resided in their bachelor quarters.

"H-here," she said, not much warmed by walking.

"Is there someone to tend to you?"

"N-no. Papa must be dining now and will bring me my dinner later. I can manage."

"Hardly. You'll catch your death of cold." He sounded very like his mother when she'd caught him playing in the Triton fountain at Bellevue Hall before the water had properly warmed. "Come to my lodging. I'll start a fire to warm you and dry your clothes until your father is available. My intentions are entirely honorable, I assure you."

No young woman of his own class would accept such an offer, but this one did. Perhaps she was still stunned by her ordeal, because she followed him, docile as a pet pony. He hurried her to the Tom Quad, the greatest of Christ Church quadrangles designed by Christopher Wren himself. His quarters lay up a staircase above the massive gate and had a marvelous view of the large Mercury Fountain, the one where he'd been doused. Only two rooms, but both had large windows that let in light for study over his desk and into his bedchamber where it reflected in his shaving mirror, lessening the use of candles. He hurried his guest to the huge, worn armchair sitting by the fireplace, one of his father's that he'd purloined from the townhouse and where he did much of his reading.

"I'll ruin the upholstery I am so sodden," Miss Barton objected.

He had to laugh. His mother had been glad to get rid of the bedraggled thing his father loved so dearly. "I doubt much could harm it, but go into my bedchamber and take off your wet things while I start a fire. There are ample blankets in the chest at the foot of my bed to wrap around you."

Again, he expected her to object. His sisters, who went armed, would have had their stilettos out by now. Without a word, she agreed by entering his bedchamber and closing the door. He set to work raking up the coals from the morning fire, lit to take the chill off the rooms and carefully banked in his absence. He added some twigs and used a small bellows to start them afire. Once he gained a flame, he placed a small piece of wood atop them and nursed the fire to create a greater blaze. He added water from a jug to his tea kettle and swung it on an arm into the heat. She'd need to be warmed inside and out.

A wet mass of clothing landed outside the bedchamber door, which snapped closed again. He spread out the dress and mass of petticoats over the backs of the two wooden chairs by his dining table and moved them nearer the heat. In time, the kettle boiled. He removed it from the hook and poured its contents over the leaves in his teapot to steep. Whatever was taking her so long? He rapped on the door.

"Miss Barton, are you well?"

"Yes, simply cleaning up a bit."

Well, he'd missed his afternoon meal and hunger nagged at him. A cheese sat under a glass dome on his table along with a wooden bowl mostly filled with apples, some with the ribbons still on them. He put his pen knife to use again and cut some cheddar slices, cored and quartered a couple of apples, placing them on a plate along with crackers from a packet on a shelf. He had some rather good chocolate biscuits and added those. If he was peckish, his guest most likely was also. Politely, he waited for Miss Barton to emerge.

When she did, attired in two blankets, one tucked under her arms as if it were a gown and the other over her shoulders like a cloak, he noticed she'd scrubbed all the smut from her face and hair, which now hung down her back, golden as he'd expected, and neatly combed. Her spectacles were nowhere to be seen. Why, she was quite pretty. He banished that thought as unbecoming to a professor.

"Come sit in the armchair. I've made tea and prepared a small meal to help in your recovery." His hand hovering over the teapot, he asked, "One lump or two? I have no cream but can cut a slice of lemon if you like." He held up the single lemon residing among the apples.

"One lump. Lemon would be delightful."

He strained the tea into a mug since he had no delicate china cups and added the sugar and a lemon slice. After delivering the beverage, he made his own to the same specifications and brought the plate of food to rest beside her on his desk chair. She began with a slice of cheese on a cracker, moved on to a quarter of an apple, and then the chocolate biscuits in quite the proper order to this strange tea party. For lack of a chair, he remained standing but helped himself. Awkwardness set in, which he decided to dispel by asking about her experiment.

"Exactly how did you come to explode the laboratory?"

She didn't seem insulted. "Oh, I've been working for several months on a splendid idea for self-igniting splints to light fires far more quickly than blowing on coals or using flint and steel. I've been experimenting with various substances to coat the end of small sticks—antimony, potassium chloride, and sulfide paste— that would burst into flame when struck against the rough stones of the hearth. I had one previous mishap and was still unhappy with my solution when I decided to add a small amount of yellow phosphorous today. It worked rather too well. The first splint I struck blazed up so suddenly I dropped it onto the rest I'd coated and they in turn set the mixture in the bowl on fire. That's when the explosion occurred."

Truth be told, the idea horrified him. "Phosphorous is highly volatile."

"Yes, but not if handled properly. I've been watching my father teach chemistry for years and often helped as his assistant in the laboratory. You see, he is getting up in years, and I thought if I could perfect my splints and get them patented, we might make a fortune for his retirement from teaching."

"Your father and the university approved of this?"

"Well, no. After my first failure, I was banned from experimentation by both—but the idea was far too good to abandon. I knew Papa would be occupied by his lectures this morning, and he does like to take a long and leisurely meal afterward. This was my chance to prove myself." She gazed at her stocking toes just peeping from the covers. "I suppose that I did not." A charming blush covered her cheeks.

So many questions came to his mind, he did not know where to begin. He chose one. "Since the dons cannot marry, how did you come to live at the university with your father?"

"Being forbidden to marry does not preclude their having children. I have also studied biology." She offered him a faint smile. "But that was not the case with me. My papa was introduced to my mother through mutual friends and fell so in love with her that he gave up his position to marry. He became a private tutor for her sake. Within a year of their wedding, I came into the world—and killed my mother in the process."

He rushed to comfort her. "Many women die in childbirth each year. This is not the fault of the child."

"Logically, you are right, but Papa could not stand the sight of me and turned me over to my grandmother. He returned to the university and sent what money he could to support me, but seldom visited. I was fortunate that Grandmama's sister, who also lived with her, was a governess pensioned off by a wealthy family when she grew too old. She never lost her love of teaching and now had another child to form and educate. By the age of six, I read well, wrote, and could do simple sums."

"As did I. Much younger than my sisters in the nursery, I'd sit nearby playing with my blocks and listening in on their lessons. I often did their sums when the governess did not pay attention. When I was turned over to a tutor, he expressed amazement at what I'd already learned."

"My father had the same reaction when my grandmama died and left her small cottage to her sister. Grandmama had begun to teach me the domestic arts, but I did not complete my first sampler before she passed. Aunt Aggie had little patience with needlework. We moved on to learning French. Then, she, too, died, passing the cottage to me. The solicitor summoned my father, who arranged for the house to be sold and the money put in trust for me as a dowry. Then, he faced the choice of putting me in an orphanage or a school at a very early age. We'd run out of female relatives, you see. He asked the chancellor if I could stay in his quarters until he'd sorted out what to do. This was granted. Once Papa realized I was a tad precocious, I remained unsorted and apparently forgotten. He taught me himself at first, giving me an education reserved for boys. As I grew older, I slipped out and audited many classes, always quiet and careful not to be exposed."

"That's it! I've seen you in my lectures." He'd nearly spilled his tea in her lap he leaned so close. He stepped back closer to the mantle. "Before the apple ladies were done expressing their admiration, you'd gone. Even hidden behind them and their hats and furbelows, I noticed your blue eyes peering out, always intent on what I taught."

"Yes, your lectures are fascinating. I know I should have asked if I could attend but was afraid I'd be denied."

"Never. I allowed those ladies with little true interest to attend in hopes they might learn something other than hair curling and polite conversation out of respect for my very strong-minded mother and sisters. I do not believe that knowledge overheats the female brain and makes women useless for marriage as some do."

"Thank you for that. I keep a robe and a soft cap to hide my hair and wear my spectacles to enable me to move about unnoticed. This worked very well as I've always been slight for my age, but then I began to mature, which has caused some problems." She glanced down at the blanket covering her chest.

So did he, but immediately turned his gaze upward to her eyes again. "You don't need eyeglasses then?"

"Not for walking about, only for reading and close work. I am heartily glad I had them on today. I believe they protected my eyes from the blast."

"Those eyes would have been a great loss to both your beauty and your scholarship."

Her blue eyes blinked as if she'd never received such a compliment in all her life. He realized that might be the case. He snatched a piece of apple and filled his mouth with it before more elegant words spilled out.

"Um, Papa believes I've ruined my sight from too much reading in dim places. The librarians at the Christ Church library always pretended they did not see me slip into some obscure niche with several volumes purloined off their shelves. I made sure to put them back into place correctly. They were very kind, as are you."

"I was raised as a gentleman and will always remain so, as well as being a don."

"I am very glad of that, especially today, Professor Lord Justinian Longleigh, sir," she replied, imitating Simpson with another bowing her pink lips.

"Professor Longleigh is sufficient, Miss Elizabeth Barton."

"Considering that you saved my life, please call me Elizabeth or Betsy if you wish."

"Then I should be Justinian to you, or Justin. My name is far too long."

He gazed into her eyes, and she returned the glance, holding it fast.

Thunder sounded. Both looked out the window on a still clear day. Someone pounded on his door with great urgency.

Two

Justin approached the door with great prudence. In his two years as a don, no one had come calling in this manner. In a corner nearby leaned the sword cane his father had given him for emergencies. It had developed a coating of dust, but assuredly, the blade retained its sharpness. He pulled it closer as he cracked the door open a slit—and discovered a furious Professor Barton ready to tear it off its hinges if need be.

"Where is my daughter, you blackguard, you cad?"

"Here and quite well after her ordeal. Do come in." He stepped back before the door hit him in the face and allowed the furious father to roar inside. "Would you care for some tea, though you will have to drink it from a glass as the Russians do."

"What I care for is my daughter. Where is she? Naked in your bedchamber? I see her clothes spread on your chairs, Professor Lord Longleigh." He sneered the middle word.

Betsy, swallowed in the huge chair facing the fire, stood, carefully holding onto her blankets. "We are merely waiting for my dress and petticoats to dry. And I am not naked. I still have my undergarments and stockings on."

Her father continued the attack. "Simply because you are the son of a duke does not mean you can dally with my daughter, Longleigh. You will offer for her at once and marry her posthaste."

Justin envisioned his life of the mind slipping away. By acting the gentleman, he had thrust his foot into the parson's mousetrap. His father would have made the same demand about any of his sisters. The duke had come close to doing that at least twice. What would his life be like, wedded to a pretty and quite intelligent young lady he barely knew and living on an allowance for the rest of his days?

Before he could make the required offer, Betsy spoke. "Don't be ridiculous, Papa. This man saved my life and took care of me in the aftermath because you were not at home when we arrived there. He would not leave me to take care of myself, wet, cold, and chattering. I believe you should thank him instead of spewing this nonsense."

He looked on her with wonder. Many a society marriage began with a kiss being stolen and the culprit caught to be forced into marriage. He'd often suspected the ladies involved had witnesses waiting to discover them with lips locked. But this strange girl was letting him off her hook to swim free again.

"I believe I will sit and have that tea," Professor Barton said. Eyeing a decanter on the table, he added, "Or brandy, if you have it.

He removed the driest petticoat from a chair and moved it closer to where Betsy sat in the great chair again. Taking up the decanter of excellent French brandy, now readily available with Napoleon gone, and also a gift from his father who declared that even a don should have small luxuries, he splashed some into a glass and handed it over.

"Truly, nothing untoward has happened here, Professor Barton."

"Yes, I took off my own clothes in the privacy of his bedchamber and washed in there, also. As you can see, I am quite well-covered with blankets." Betsy offered him the cheese plate. "Because you've missed your dinner."

Professor Barton ignored the food and took a deep swallow of the brandy. He addressed Justin instead. "Do you see her there, the image of her mother and bound to become more beautiful each day if she doesn't keep herself disguised in this all-male world? She has turned eighteen, and the chancellor has ceased to look the other way about her lodging with me. After the previous blast, he made it very clear that she must be removed from the university immediately. When he learns she has destroyed another lab, I fear her time here is done. I have nowhere to send her." He studied the brandy as if answers lay in its rich, brown depths.

Barton took a deep breath. "Betsy, I have put your name out as seeking employment as a governess, companion, or nursemaid. I cannot think what else to do."

"And you did not tell me? I have no knowledge of children or how to teach them. I am sure I would be dismissed as soon as the family found out that I have no feminine accomplishments. I do not do fine needlework, paint watercolors, or play the pianoforte. Yes, my French is very good as is my German. I can offer Spanish and Italian as well, but I believe they'd have no use for my knowledge of equations, biology, chemistry, and now thanks to Professor Longleigh, some of physics. I may be better equipped to instruct boys, and doubt that would be allowed." She took a breath so deep it nearly exposed her bosom. "If I must, I will do my best, but where shall I stay in the meantime? A boarding house? Can we afford that?"

Her father avoided the last questions. "Marriage would be preferable, but you've had no proper way to meet suitable men in a place swarming with them. I thought Longleigh might be the answer to my prayers for you, but I see you will not allow me to force him to take you."

"Papa, that would be a dreadful way to repay him for his kindness."

Certainly, she could not stay with him. However, his clever mother with her many connections and love of matchmaking would arrive within days. He made a different offer.

"My brother, Joshua, and his wife live in the London townhouse with their two sons. I will speak to them about taking you in for a while. The duchess will soon be in residence and is very resourceful. She shall apply her mind to solving your problem. Return to your quarters and pack your belongings."

Startled, both faces turned his way.

"That is very generous of you after my verbal attack on your honor. I meant to do right by my daughter, but know what it would have cost you. I once gave up my calling for a woman and then lost her as well. I was able to return to the university only because she had died. If you had wed my Betsy and produced children, your fate would be sealed with no return to academia." Barton tossed down the last of the brandy. "Come, daughter, dress, get packed, and I'll be prepared to see you off tomorrow. You may wear my gown to keep off the chill."

"Do take one of mine. I have half a dozen."

"Perhaps only five if the stains I've made on the one you wore today won't come out. You are truly the most kind and gentlemanly person I've ever known," Betsy said. She made an expansive, wide-open gesture that caused the blanket covering her shoulders to slide down to the floor, revealing her small, white shoulders.

He tried not to notice. "It's a journey of fifty miles by coach. I suggest you go home and get your affairs in order. We will leave directly after breakfast. I will do anything to help a fellow scholar." And he did mean Betsy and not her father.

Three

Hardly the way he'd planned to spend this extraordinary day. He entered his bedchamber and found he had to clean his shaving and bathing bowl of blackened water which he thew out the window. She'd used his soap to wash her hair and his comb to put it to rights. A few fair strands remained caught in the teeth. Her spectacles sat to one side, and he pocketed them. In an afterthought, he removed the colorful ribbons from the apples and shoved them in beside the eyeglasses. He had no use for them, but Betsy might. The *subfusc* of required dark clothes and a white shirt he always wore beneath his gown would do to go out into the streets with the addition of a gentleman's tall hat in place of his mortarboard and the cane quickly wiped down.

Now, he stood on a street corner just outside the university to hail a hackney coach for transportation to Bellevue House, which he'd planned to do anyway, hoping to have a brief visit with the family. With his general air of prosperity and nobility, he experienced no trouble in gaining a driver's attention. The second-hand conveyance offered enough room for him, Betsy, and her belongings, plus Professor Barton, who would certainly want to inspect the place where his daughter might stay. Justin laid out his plans to the driver.

"That's a far piece, milord. I'll have to spend the night and won't be home for me dinner." Yet, avarice lit pale gray eyes beneath dark brows.

"That's professor, actually. Professor Lord Longleigh. Just professor is fine. You will stay the night in my brother's carriage house and take your breakfast with the servants before returning. I'll have Cook make up a hamper for you filled with food for the return journey. You will have only one passenger on the way back and little baggage. I shall pay half your fare now and the rest upon arrival with a bit extra to rest your horse for today and feed it well before we begin."

"I takes good care of me 'Arry, but it will be oats tonight for me old boy," he said of a placid bay gelding with black socks switching its tail as it waited. The driver bobbed his head in agreement. "Barney Butts and 'Arry at your service.

One reason he'd selected this particular conveyance was the condition of the horse with some fat on its ribs and no sores to be seen and a coach exterior free of mud. "If I might inspect the interior, please."

"Go right ahead, your professorship. Me wife sweeps it out daily. Clean as a nun's habit, it is."

He sniffed the interior. Though the squabs were worn and flattened, it had none of the odors of sausages, garlic, and urine often found in public coaches. It passed his inspection. If he were going alone, he'd have rented a horse, stopped halfway at an inn, and completed the journey the second day. But traveling with a young woman and her father complicated matters and upped the cost. They could doze along the way and even if arriving after dark, he knew Josh's reliable Kate would make them welcome. He'd sent notice a fortnight ago saying he'd visit for a short time with them and Mama to give her time to prepare the room he kept at the townhouse. Two more bedchambers should be no great problem for her.

With all that settled, and a meeting place arranged, he returned to his chambers to assume academic dress again and line up by the professors' entry for an evening meal. At last, the men in their black gowns, flat hats tucked under arms, processed inside to the high table, stood for a prayer that could have been shorter, and sat down under the gaze of many portraits of famous professors, deans, and alumni. Below the fellows, students also took their places to receive a meal. The old Tudor hall sat beneath its hammered beam ceiling illuminated by stained glass windows. There was not a more beautiful place for a meal in all of England.

Justin had more appetite than usual. Perhaps the excitement of the day stimulated him, rescuing a young woman and caring for her in his quarters. Not that he would want to do that every day. He preferred his quiet studies and perfect location as Tom Quad also boasted its own library and an eight-hundred-year-old cathedral where pilgrims once came to pray at the shrine of St. Frideswide, and where he could worship if so inclined, which did not happen often. He'd found his perfect life at a very young age. Savoring the fine food afforded to the dons, his mind still drifted to the morrow and the long carriage ride ahead with pretty Miss Barton, who had more on her mind than marriage.

~ * ~

Directing the driver as close to the courtyard building that housed the Bartons as possible, he found them already waiting just outside the gate. Betsy had only one large box to her name.

She'd changed into a becoming white muslin dress sprigged with small blue flowers and drawn her hair back with a black ribbon. A lacy shawl covered her upper body, providing some warmth against the chill of the day. He knew little about feminine fashions and cared not at all, but where were her bonnet and gloves? He felt fairly certain his mother and sisters would never leave home without them—even the rebellious Pandora, who would have preferred pantaloons to skirts. One thing he did know was not to remark on a lady's clothes unless he could deliver a compliment. Instead, he offered his hand and helped Betsy up into the coach while the short, squat and brawny armed driver heaved the trunk on its top.

"Professor Barton, will you join us? I know you will want to inspect your daughter's new dwelling."

"Ah, yes, of course," the man said as if he hadn't considered the idea at all. He wore his academic gown and cap and climbed aboard rather awkwardly.

Justin gave the driver directions to an address in Mayfair.

"Knew you was quality, professor sir, but you will have to guide me once in the city. ''Arry and me don't know the way."

"That won't be a problem. Onward, Butts, onward."

'Arry set off at a walk until outside the boundaries of Oxford, then assumed a gentle trot at the urging of Barney Butts. Justin opened a leather satchel he'd brought along containing some papers he'd meant to read about Stokes' equations in fluid dynamics and settled in before he noticed that Betsy had taken a small book of poetry from her reticule to pass the time and squinted at its small print.

"Oh, I'd almost forgotten I put these in my pocket. Your eyeglasses, Miss Barton, and some ribbons I certainly don't need." He handed them over to her delight.

"I thought I'd lost them. Just another example of what it costs Papa to have me always around as I'd need another pair."

Her father did not deny it but continued to stare out the window at the passing scenery. Justin felt some anger toward the man who made his only child feel like a burden. "What are you reading?" he asked, to break the awkward silence.

"Poetry, *Hebrew Melodies* by Lord Byron. A shame he was hounded out of England."

That brought a reaction from Professor Barton. "For very good reasons, a seducer of women and always in debt. You should not be reading this."

"I hardly think he will seduce me from Greece, Papa. I have it on loan under your name from the library. You will kindly return it for me, I hope. Listen to this one. It's very manly, *The Destruction of Sennacherib*, all about war."

Justin noticed she did not choose *She Walks in Beauty*, a poem he knew because his brother Jason was an admirer of Byron's works and had spouted them often. While thought to be a tribute to a dark woman, he considered that fair Betsy might someday have a poem written for her by a smitten young man.

"Enough. Haven't we anything else truly worth talking about? Terribly stuffy in here as well." Barton fanned his face with a hand.

"Might I suggest you remove your gown? I assume you wear *subfusc* beneath it?"

"Of course, I do." Betsy's father struggled from his gown and joined Justin in looking like a cleric gone on holiday in his stark black with only the white shirt to relieve it.

"If you are not fond of poetry, would you care to hear about fluid dynamics? Stokes from Cambridge has some brilliant new ideas that make a nice corollary to Newton's work."

"Better than poetry, I suppose."

That engaged the man enough stop him from finding fault with his daughter. Justin also noticed that Betsy had shut her book, marked it with a red ribbon, and listened to his every word, never interrupting the two men as they exchanged opinions, but avidly engaged in her mind. That was how she'd come by most of her learning, sitting still and listening, he guessed.

They stopped about a quarter of the way to water and rest the horse, make use of an inn's necessary, and partake of light refreshment before moving on. By afternoon, Justin called a halt at another watering place he knew to be clean and capable of supplying a plain but hearty meal of stew and bread. Sending his driver inside to order their food, he checked 'Arry and found him with head hanging and sides heaving. Before he went to join the others, he made arrangements to trade the horse out for a stouter dray animal that would not be fast, but certainly have stamina for the rest of trip. 'Arry could have a nice rest before his owner picked him up the next day. Any other academic might not have thought of it, but when one was raised by the Duke of Bellevue, one did not run a horse into the ground. Butts had no objection as long as he didn't have to pay for it.

After dining, they proceeded to London with another short break along the way. When the great city began to encroach, Justin climbed aboard the box, the better to give directions amid the clamor of other coaches and the cries of vendors touting hot meat pies and baked potatoes to those on their way home from various professions. Soon night would fall and those practicing the world's oldest profession would be on the streets to earn their bread by lifting their skirts. He hoped to have his visitors at Joshua's door before they caught Betsy's pretty blue gaze.

Luck was with him. He jumped down to knock on the door of Bellevue House as dusk descended. A puzzled housekeeper, plump and neatly dressed in a black gown and white apron with a lacy cap pinned to her graying hair, answered, cautiously peering out. After a moment, a look of joy overtook a face so jolly it rarely achieved a stern demeanor.

"Ah, Lord Justinian, we did not expect you so soon. Let me inform Lord Joshua that his brother is here."

Before she could scuttle away, Josh appeared behind her, along with his wife Kate. Being as tall as all the Longleigh men, he easily looked over Justin's shoulder and stared at the hackney coach.

"Always good to have you visit, but in a hackney, all the way from Oxford? We could have sent the coach if you'd asked, but we thought you were riding."

"Why not a mail coach, which would have been faster?" his always acute spouse asked.

"Filled both top and bottom with students going home since the term ended, but really because I am travelling with a young lady…"

"You, Justin, with a young lady?" his brother questioned.

"And her father. Perfectly proper. She is in need of some assistance from the duchess, and I hope you will allow her to stay here for a short time until her predicament is sorted out."

"Her father also? How many rooms do you need?" practical Kate asked.

"Mine of course, one for Miss Barton, and another for the night for her father. Oh, and also a place for my driver, the horse, and the hackney overnight."

"Mrs. Crump, will you see to the rooms, perhaps the blue and the oriental, and send the scullery maid to alert our stable hand that he is about to have company?"

"At once." Mrs. Crump dropped a quick, bobbing curtsy and trundled off, but not before saying, "So good to have youngest Longleigh home again."

Why did everyone have to remind him of his placement as the last of ten living children? At twenty-one, he'd achieved a full professorship when at the same age, both Joshua and Jason were still attempting to cross the bar and become barristers, and the heir had gone off adventuring and seldom returned. He had to put those thoughts aside when Kate prompted, "Your guests, won't you bring them inside?"

"Oh, yes, certainly." He moved to the coach and helped both Betsy and her father, who had resumed his gown, down, waving them up the stairs to their hostess. To Butts, he said, "Drive around the back. The stableman will be watching for you and your rig in our mews."

He'd almost forgotten Betsy's luggage, but Barney had not. "Need a hand with the box, milord professor?"

"No, I think I can manage." He did but rather ungracefully. It proved more awkward than heavy. Once it hit the cobbles, Butts moved out to find the stable and a place for the night as promised.

"If you are waiting for a footman to help you out, you know we keep a light staff until Mama arrives." Joshua leapt to his aid and grabbed one handle of the trunk as if his little brother were too weak to move it. Between them, they transferred it into the hallway where his guests stood dithering and not properly introduced.

"So sorry about this. May I introduce Professor Eli Barton of Oxford and his daughter, Miss Elizabeth Barton. My sister-in-law, Katherine Longleigh and my brother, Joshua Longleigh. Somewhere, I have two nephews as well."

The usual bows and curtsies were performed before Kate replied, "The boys have gone up to the nursery for their supper and bedtime. We were about to sit down to ours as well. Simply give me a minute to tell cook there will be three more to dine. It's only a simple meal for now *en famile,* but once the duchess arrives, expect much more. Perhaps you'd like to refresh yourselves after your long journey. Here is Mrs. Crump again to show you to your chambers."

"Very grateful," the professor managed while Betsy remained tongue-tied. They followed the nearly out-of-breath housekeeper up a flight of stairs.

"Very pretty, your Miss Barton, but rather quiet," Kate remarked.

"Not mine," Justin was quick to say. "I simply saved her life and now feel responsible for her rather precarious future. If you ask her about science, you will see she has tons to speak about."

"Hmm," said Joshua in that annoying big brotherly way. "Dinner conversation should prove most interesting tonight."

"I gather Miss Barton is an unusual young lady," Kate added.

"Very. You shall see."

Four

Betsy stood in her assigned chamber listening to Mrs. Crump rattle on. "As soon as we get your trunk here, I'll send Lady Katherine's maid to assist you in getting ready for dinner. Hot water for washing should be along any time now. The linens are fresh and clean as we have been airing all the chambers for the arrival of the duke and duchess. If you need anything more, you have only to ask." She hustled away.

Betsy took in every detail of the amazing room, so different from the one she'd been assigned by her father. He had given up his study for her and asked what she wanted from her grandmother's house: the rocker where she'd been read a bedtime story every night, her narrow bed with its special canopy embroidered on the inside with butterflies and flowers done by her granny's own hand, the escritoire where her aunt did her writing, and Aunt Aggie's small collection of books, including the primers from which she'd learned to read and the fairy tales of Charles Perrault. There hadn't been room for much more other than a washstand with a mirror and a chamber pot behind a modesty screen. The rest had been sold along with the house. Her father assured her over and over that every cent had gone into a fund to provide her with a modest dowry of five-hundred pounds which might increase with interest paid. At the age of six, she'd had little interest in interest and would rather have had her aunt and granny back again.

But this bedchamber had been decked out in a Chinese theme right down to the blue and white bowl and pitcher set depicting willows and ponds and graceful ladies hidden by an oriental screen on which tiny people trudged up a mountain toward a temple at its peak with much scenery and wildlife on either side. She could have gazed on its details all day. Bronze sculptures, two stout horses with bobbed tails flanked each other on the fireplace mantle with two other objects placed in between. She examined them more closely and sniffed. Ah, incense burners that smelled like the Anglican church on high holy days.

The night table by the generously proportioned bed was chunky and painted black, but the bedposts were carved with dragons delineated in gold against the dark wood, each scale a masterpiece and every eye a tiny red stone. Flames shot from their mouths onto a canopy streaked with yellow and beneath that the underside was lined with red silk. The bed covers, black satin embroidered with red dragons facing each other, made her afraid to sit upon it, not because of the creatures but more out of fear of ruining the stitchery. She felt as if she'd fallen into a painting of the mysterious orient.

A thud outside her door announced the arrival of her trunk, followed immediately by the entry of a woman dressed much like the housekeeper and a lesser servant bearing the promised hot water.

"I am Clement, the lady's maid. Nan, pour the water and move on. You have two more chambers to service. Men!" she exclaimed. "Leaving your box outside the door."

"Oh, I am sure I can drag it inside."

"But you should not have to. Do it for now. Once the duchess is in residence, you need no longer lift a finger."

"That will seem very odd."

Clement threw open the trunk and rooted through it, finding little else than a couple of worn gowns, her clean undergarments, the rags for her monthlies, and a thick layer of books. "Have you nothing else?"

"This is my best dress, and I know it is dusty, but…"

"Then it must do for now. Go behind the screen, hand it out to me, and I will brush it while you wash. Do you need my assistance with your buttons?

"No, they are few and all in the front."

"Then go, hurry. The dinner gong will sound soon."

Clement had rattled her so badly that she needed to use the chamber pot first in an attack of nerves. Then, she scrubbed face, neck, arms, and hands with a soap that smelled of sandalwood. Her dress appeared, thrown over the screen, and clad again, she emerged to find the maid brandishing a hairbrush.

"Sit and allow me to brush your hair. Have you no other ribbon but this black?"

"A moment." She went to her reticule which she'd left on the bed and pulled out the handful of wrinkled ribbons Justin had given her. "Will these do?"

"They want ironing, but I shall put the two blue ones into a braid for a nicer look. You do have lovely cornsilk hair I would adore to make more fashionable. Lady Katherine has no use for style, always the same old thing, day in and day out. They rarely entertain or go visiting."

"I doubt I will have much need for fashion either," Betsy admitted as the maid deftly braided her hair, working in the blue ribbons. Done, she pulled them back from her face and pinned in the ends, the closest Betsy had ever come to wearing her hair up as a young lady her age should.

A loud bong that she assumed was the gong sounded. Clement shooed her out the door. "I shall unpack your belongings while you dine."

"Won't you be eating, too?"

"Servants dine before dinner, miss."

Having displayed her ignorance to this rather intimidating woman, Betsy fled down the stairs and discovered the three men and Lady Katherine awaiting her.

"So sorry to be tardy. Clement wanted to put ribbons in my hair."

"They are very nice. It is no problem. We dine informally unless the duke and duchess are in residence. Come, walk with me."

The men trailed them deep in conversation that she hoped did not reveal her predicament. The dinner table wasn't at all as grand as she expected. In fact, it was oval and resided in a rather small room with windows overlooking a narrow garden shrouded in darkness. In daylight, it must be very pleasant. Lord Joshua held a chair for his wife and Justin did the same for her while her father took a seat across from her.

A soup course was served at once, followed by a leg of lamb deftly carved and distributed by Joshua. They passed dishes of spring peas and a salad of early greens, new potatoes, and fresh bread, more than enough, but followed by cheeses, dried fruits and nuts, and a custard pudding. She'd eaten well enough at the university on what her father brought from the dining hall but was overwhelmed by this abundance and even more so by the need to converse while eating. She kept silent unless asked a question by Katherine.

"How was your journey?"

"Oh, dusty and long, but I am very grateful to be here."

"Is your room satisfactory?"

"So intriguing with all those dragons and the screen that made me want to travel all the way to China."

"Oh dear! Mrs. Crump was to put you in the blue room with the cornflower wallpaper, not the Asian chamber which is so masculine, James' chamber if he were ever here. The duchess keeps hoping to lure him home again and decorated it with gifts he sent from his journey along the Silk Road. Ever exploring is our James, the first son and heir."

"If he is expected, I will gladly change chambers."

That caused the three Longleighs to burst into laughter. What had she said wrong?

"James is never expected. He simply appears. Mother is ever hopeful of his return. Your presence does no harm," Lord Joshua explained.

"I suspect your late arrival had Mrs. Crump in a dither, and you were put in the first chamber she opened. The blue room is far more feminine," Lady Katherine commented.

"I don't mind at all. I spent much of my early years disguised as a boy in order to stay at the university with Father and received a masculine education, I am told, which is one of the things wrong with me."

All eyes stared her way, including her father's, not pleased at all by his expression. She clapped a hand over her mouth.

"Eat your pudding, child, and allow me to explain." Her father took a deep swallow of his second cup of wine. She hadn't finished her first and felt a bit tipsy, having never tried any form of alcohol.

Composed, he began to talk about her childhood. "When both of Betsy's female relatives passed away, I found myself faced with an undersized, frail, but very precocious daughter of six who still needed a great deal of raising. A boarding school or an orphanage, I thought, but did not believe she would survive either. She was so like her late mother I could not part with her, nor let her wander the campus, a little girl in an all-male environment. I made a space for her in my lodgings and taught her all I could at home, but she could not be kept in all the time. Dressing her as a boy allowed her some freedom, you see."

Betsy interrupted. "I thought it a wonderful adventure. Women in Shakespeare's plays often went disguised as boys as I learned from *Lamb's Tales* which my aunt read to me. I offered to cut off my hair, but Papa would not hear of it because it reminded him of my mother, so we stuffed it under a soft cap. I am not sure how many we fooled or for how long, but the other professors ignored my slipping into their lectures, and the librarians were especially kind, allowing me to linger in the library on rainy days reading whatever I liked so long as I was quiet and always reshelved the books. When I was older, I donned a first term student gown and went about like any student. Then, I became a woman." She ceased speaking and hung her head in embarrassment."

"Yes, that complicated matters. I made her my laboratory assistant to keep her near me."

"Did you enjoy that, Miss Barton?" Lady Katherine inquired.

She raised her head. "Very much. I particularly enjoyed making precipitates by joining two chemicals and then analyzing their properties."

"Interesting," Lady Katherine assured her.

"If I had the proper ingredients, I could show you how some of the simpler ones are done. I would not explode anything or start a fire."

"Enough, daughter. You are beginning a new phase of your life and must apply yourself to that. You can never be an academic, at best a governess." Her father paused for a moment before adding, "She does have a small dowry that I invested which has now grown to six-hundred pounds. Some men in the trades might find that adequate. Marriage is not impossible for her, but she lacks domestic skills, which is my fault. We both appreciate any efforts on her behalf, Professor Longleigh, but she must accept her fate and be kept from anymore experiments.

Well, I am sorry to have ended this fine dinner on such a serious matter. I shall leave early with the hackney driver and so will bid all of you a good evening as should Betsy." He rose, came around the table and helped her from her seat.

"Yes, I do want to be awake to say good-bye, Papa." She knew his real fear was that she might blurt out more about her peculiarities. Surely, the Longleighs already regarded her as a hopeless case.

They found candles already lit on a table by the base of the stairs. Her father entered his blue feminine chamber without another word. She went back to the Asian world and tried to sleep but did not.

Five

Betsy did awaken with the dawn despite the heavy red drapes being closed the night before when presumably Clement or Nan had turned down her bed and brought fresh wash water. It helped that she hadn't slept much. She washed, and never having taken the braid out of her hair, carefully brushed the rest of it. Her choice of clothes consisted of the worn, white gown with the ruined hem which she had no idea how to mend, and another of drab gray suitable for her work in the laboratory. No choice but to don her blue-sprigged best dress again. She put on her mother's lovely shawl against the chill morning air and to present herself slightly differently than the day before. Taking along the volume of poetry to read some more before it must be returned to Oxford, she made her way downstairs.

She followed her nose toward the room where she'd eaten the night before. The large buffet presented a series of covered dishes that Justin had already availed himself of as he tucked into eggs, sausage, and toast. A rack of toast and pots of butter, marmalade, and jams sat on the oval table as well as a teapot and coffee service. Unlike her, he looked well-rested. She'd seen the dark circles under her eyes in the mirror when she washed. He greeted her in a most pleasant manner.

"I see you found the breakfast room again on your own. Please, fill a plate and join me. I had to be up early to pay Butts and see your father on his way."

"Sorry to put you to so much trouble."

"None, none at all. There are kippers and kidneys, too, but I've never cared for either."

Before the situation of dining alone with Justin grew more awkward, Lady Katherine arrived in dress of green the color of the new buds now visible in the garden on small closely clipped bushes and trees. Daffodils bloomed at their roots, and tulips pushed their tips out of the soil. The sun glinted off a small statue on a plinth, all beautiful like the gown. It possessed long sleeves with a frill on the cuff and puffs on the shoulders. A modest neckline rose into a high collar that showed off Lady Katherine's neck. Her thick, brown hair was rolled in the same manner as yesterday but now bore some small ornaments shaped like golden leaves. The leaf pattern continued on, embroidered beneath the pinched in waist.

Her hostess placed toast on her plate and poured a cup of tea. She sighed. "I wish corsets had not come back into style, though I suspect after bearing two children I do need one."

Lord Joshua appeared behind her and kissed her nape. Did married men do that? They must.

"Nonsense, you are perfect as you are, so curvaceous." He helped himself to the various offerings and sat beside his wife.

"Truth be told, when we have no guests, we usually break our fast in my sitting area with both of us in our dressing robes, but I know the duchess is already on the march and will arrive today. This is what she would consider a suitable day dress, as does Clement." Checking about for servants, Lady Katherine continued, "I do wish Flora had not left her here. I feel very bullied. I did send her your way, Miss Barton, but you'd already gone down. She so wanted to play with your hair if you'd left the braid in to create curls about your face. She'll have you frizzled in no time."

"Oh, I don't need to be frizzled," Betsy replied, having no idea what that involved or day dressing either. "But your gown is so beautiful, as is the yard."

"Thank you. We must see to your wardrobe. Clement tells me you have no corset, but you are slim enough to do without. Still, you won't have the proper form without one. I do so hate fashion, but when the duchess is here, I can't disgrace her."

"You know Mama hates corsets, too." Joshua poured his coffee and doctored it with cream.

"Yes, but she is wearing them now."

This bewildering conversation ended with arrival of her father. "Good morning, all. I am ready to travel back to Oxford. Splendid day." He raided the sideboard for a hearty meal of eggs piled on kippers. He poured his coffee and appeared to be happily relieved of his responsibility to his daughter.

When Butts pounded on the door to announce his arrival with the hackney, all rose to see the professor off. Justin went ahead to press the final payment into the driver's hands. "Did Cook make a hamper for your journey?"

"Aye, a large enough one to feed us both and some left over for me family."

"Good. Here is some extra to feed 'Arry his oats. He did his best by us."

The driver returned to his perch. "If you be needing me in Oxford, look around that same corner where ye found me."

Her father took a deep breath. "Come here, girl."

Betsy moved into an unexpected embrace. The professor wasn't given to signs of affection.

"If I ever caused you to believe you were a burden, I am sorry. You did brighten my life, and I often thought if you had been born male, we could have carried on together. Still, I saw your mother in you every day and that was a blessing. Be brave. Make your way in life and do not forget your old papa." Releasing her, he hastened to the cab and waved from the window.

Betsy rushed after him and pressed the small volume of Byron's poems into his hands. "Please do return this to the library, Papa."

"Yes, my dear. One never wants to get on the bad side of the librarians. Onward, Butts," he shouted as she stepped back. Would she see him again? Somehow, she had doubts, but he had left her with the kindest of people, especially Lord Justinian.

Lady Katherine took her hand as the coach moved off. "Come inside with me. We'll visit the nursery before the day gets too complicated. I want you to meet my boys, imps that they are. Their first tutor is already gone."

The men parted before them, and they moved to a back staircase that led to the nursery under the eaves. Still in their nightclothes, Katherine's offspring sat at a low table with a boiled egg each before them, bowls of porridge, a plate of toast, and glasses of milk. They wore clean, white napkins around their necks. As soon as they saw their mama, they toppled their chairs and raced to hug her around her lower skirts.

"No, no," cried the nursemaid. "You will soil your mother's nice dress."

"Do not worry, Sarah. They are not sticky yet." Lady Katherine bent to kiss both their heads, one the same shade of brown as hers, the other black resembling Lord Joshua. Warm memories of hugging her granny and auntie the same way flooded back into Betsy's memory. She'd heard the nobility had little to do with the raising of their children, but not in this house.

"Enough now. Go eat your breakfast. But first let me introduce you to my sons, William and Richard. Boys, this is Miss Barton, who is visiting with us."

Both executed low bows that nearly exposed their bare bottoms beneath their nightshirts. "Pleased to meet you, miss," they parroted together before making a mess of decapitating their eggs. Katherine continued to watch them eat as if it were the most fascinating act in the world. She radiated love that spilled over onto Betsy like sunshine.

"I supposed you find me doting, but you see, for the first two years of my marriage it did appear I would be barren. Before Joshua took me as his wife, I suffered a period of captivity and starvation. Dr. Gudikunst believed my ordeal had impeded my ability to bear children and worrying about it made things worse. Time, he said, give it time. Then, in the third year, I conceived William and the next year Richard. They are six and seven now and the lights of my life. Of course, with James always gallivanting around in dangerous places, some say they will be Joshua's heir and spare one day. I do hope not. I want nothing to do with the ton and their vicious ways."

Betsy presumed this somehow tied in with her ordeal but didn't want to inquire. Lady Katherine seemed to have a secure and happy life. Who could ask for more? Well, she could—a laboratory and a husband who might kiss her neck at breakfast, too.

"Lately, I've had an urge to have a daughter," Lady Katherine confided. "All the other Longleigh ladies have at least one. I've been taking some herbs ...excuse me. You have no need to know this." She turned back to her sons. "What will you be doing today?"

"Sailing our boats in the park," the younger one, Richard, said.

"Having a war with our tin soldiers," black-haired William answered.

"Ah-ah, not before you have practiced your reading with Sarah."

"Why not with you?" William whined.

"I must take Miss Barton shopping, and your grandmama and grandfather Longleigh are arriving today.

"Grandpa Bear is coming!" In his excitement, Richard upset his milk, but Sarah had prepared with nearby rags to sop it up.

"He will want to see how your reading and writing has progressed, also."

"No, he'll want to play Indians with us! Reading is boring."

Betsy found herself saying, "Never if you have the right books. I have some in my trunk you might like, tales of adventurous boys and knights, giants, and wicked witches. I will read some of them to you, but you must help me by pointing out words you know."

"But not today," Katherine said. "I've ordered the carriage to take us to the shops as soon as they open. Clement informs me you are in need of a corset and some proper gowns to meet the duchess, not that Lady Flora stands on ceremony. She'd greet any interesting stranger with kindness, but the duke often won't allow it as he fears for her safety."

Is that what she'd become, an interesting stranger in need of clothing? "Papa left me a bit of coin, but I am not sure how much it will purchase in London."

"Don't worry about that for now. We discussed it last evening before you came down and all will be taken care of by the last of Justin's quarterly remittance. He is due for more at the start of April and rarely spends it on anything but books."

"He has done so much for me already. I shouldn't take advantage."

"Yes, saved you from a fire, he said. The Chinese say that makes a person responsible for that life forever, according to what he's read."

"How terribly unfair."

"I don't think so. My life was saved, and the people responsible want me to thrive. It seems very natural. Regardless, we are going shopping. I will see you later today, my loves. We have enough time for Clement to arrange your hair." Lady Katherine kissed each small cheek and led Betsy from the nursery, which seemed to be such a warm and nurturing space she could have stayed there all day without having her hair done.

~ * ~

Clement removed her to Lady Katherine's room and positioned her on the small stool before the dressing table with a mirror that caught the early morning sun and caused her to squint.

"None of that, now. Young men will presume you need spectacles and lines will form by your eyes," Clement chided.

"But I do use spectacles to read."

"Never be seen in public wearing them. Weak eyes imply poor health or a woman who reads far too much. Suitors want neither. So glad you left the ribbons in. Now we shall have more to work with."

Clement ripped the ribbons from the braid, leaving the hair crimped behind. Carefully, she took a comb and brush to the newly formed curls, parting and extending them on either of Betsy's face. Out came a sharp scissors and snip, snip, most of their length fell to the rug before she could protest. More of her hair was combed over her forehead across her face, and with more snipping, left a few short ringlets behind. After that, Betsy could see no more as the maid gathered and twisted the rest of her locks to rest atop her head in a tall heap. Shock kept her quiet.

"No need for much more than a bonnet if you are shopping. Lady Katherine has given me free rein with her wardrobe, not that it amounts to much." Clement opened the despised wardrobe and took a few hat boxes from the top shelf. She swept through them, rejecting most until a high-crowned straw bonnet with blue ribbons and tiny white silk blossoms around the crown met her standards. "Here, this will be perfect for your bucolic appearance. Keep your shawl. It will add some interest."

Betsy did not lack vocabulary. She knew full well that bucolic meant countrified, and the maid meant it as an insult. At least, she'd found no fault with Mama's shawl. Clement placed the hat on her head, fussed with the side curls and ringlets, then showed her how to properly tie the ribbons beneath her chin, not tightly but dangling and forming a becoming bow closer to her chest.

"There now, some gloves and your reticule and you are as good as I can make you for now. On your way."

Betsy fled before Clement thought of anything else. Lady Katherine stood waiting for her and outside, a small coach that seated four pulled by two black horses that made 'Arry seem like a plow animal. The driver helped them inside and mounted the box. They were off with one quick snap of the whip to Bond Street.

"What are the men doing this morning?" Betsy asked, for want of anything else to say.

"Riding in the park. We keep two coach horses and two more for exercise-good animals but nothing flashy. Joshua has no need to show off for young ladies anymore, and Justin usually likes to ride when he visits."

"Does he show off for the ladies?"

"Justin? Good lord, no. You'd think he was a virgin protecting his honor."

"Is he, do you think?" Perhaps an unseemly question, but she really wanted to know.

Lady Katherine could not suppress her mirth. Once she stopped laughing, she replied, "I admire your forthright curiosity, but I am sure he is not. All the Longleigh men are indoctrinated in the art of lovemaking at an early age by experts in the trade. Believe me, you don't want a fumbling boy to be your first. However, I gather Justin lives a rather monastic life at Oxford, to his mother's dismay. She'd rather he marry for love and give her more grandchildren, though they have an abundance of those already. No, no, our men have gone early to avoid scheming females and their mamas on the prowl for suitors. Our stable will soon be filled, every space with the Bellevue coach and four plus the duke's massive stallion. Of course, he does require a large mount. Do you ride, Miss Barton?"

"Oh, no. I've rarely left the university. We walk everywhere. I'm a very good walker."

Lady Katherine gave her a small nod of approval. "I am sure you are. We must take some strolls through the parks and squares of London very soon. Ah, here we are at Lady Flora's favorite dressmaker."

They waited for the step to be put down and accepted the hand of the driver safely over the curb. "Meet us at the Piccadilly entrance to the Burlington Arcade in three hours, Peterson."

"As you wish, Lady Katherine."

Her hostess took a deep breath. "Here we go. Brace for the onslaught."

No sooner were they inside than the shop owner herself greeted them with a deep curtsy and a pleasant, "So wonderful to see you again, Lady Katherine. Do you have any word of the arrival of the duchess?"

"Shortly, Madam Violette."

"I must say the morning gown I designed for you suits you well, milady. Do you need something more for the start of the season?"

Madam, though somewhat up in years, did wear a corset and her black skirt flared out beneath it. Her bodice was high, beaded and embellished, and well-matched by jet earrings in her lobes. With upswept hair, dark and possessing two distinguished white wings on either side of her brow, both her style and her strong features commanded respect for a woman who'd made her way in the world very well. Betsy hid herself behind Lady Katherine, who drew her forward regardless.

"Nothing for me, but this young lady requires four day dresses, nothing too fancy, two for evening wear and one for special occasions. Again, all should be serviceable but stylish. Have you anything on hand that can be altered for her in a few hours? The rest of the day dresses will be needed tomorrow, and the other items by the end of the week."

"Certainly. Should they be charged to Lady Flora's account?"

"No, to mine, delivery to Bellevue House."

"But I thought Jus..." Betsy began.

"We will discuss that later. Now, what have you, Madam Violette?"

Madam inclined her head in assent. "I keep several white muslin gowns on hand for just such emergencies. They are easily and quickly embellished, but first, she wears no corset. I also have some in stock. You needn't go elsewhere for it. Come into the fitting room while I send Giselle for what you require."

Betsy had barely taken notice of a younger woman standing behind a counter displaying trims and other furbelows. Not saying a word, she scurried off with a rustle of fashionable skirts far better than most shop girls wore, perhaps advertising what Violette designed.

In the privacy of the small, mirrored space, she was commanded to stand on a low pedestal and awaited further orders.

"Take off your bonnet, child, your gown, and petticoat. We can hardly do a fitting with them on." Lady Katherine put the bonnet on one peg and the dress and petticoat on another. There she stood in nothing but her unadorned shift and cotton stockings, thankful that both were clean, and a pair of slippers someone had polished for her in the night. Never having been seen in so little before strangers, she resisted the urge to fold her arms over her breasts and allowed them to dangle.

"Ah, here we are."

Giselle offered several corsets draped over her arms. Madam Violette eyed them and chose one, the smallest. After looping the straps over the shoulders and settling it in place below the bosom, the assistant began lacing the garment up the back. Not so bad, thought Betsy, until her waist was reached and the woman pulled tighter and tighter. She gasped.

Lady Katherine intervened, saying in a sharp tone, "That is not necessary. Loosen it."

"Dear lady, we must now define the waist. Women no longer want to resemble a sack of potatoes."

"But they do want to breathe rather than faint."

The lacing slackened until finally finished. Madam's assistant took her measurements, up, down, and around, noting each one with pencil on paper. The pencil paused. "Your name, miss."

"Elizabeth Barton."

"A relative of yours or Lady Flora's?" inquired the madam of Lady Katherine.

"An acquaintance from Oxford who came unprepared for the start of the season."

How easily she managed this imposing woman. Despite the lacing, Betsy's chest swelled with admiration. But now the assistant returned with several gowns of white. Each was held up against her until Katherine said, "That one. We shall add a few embellishments, and it will do."

The dress, with a flounce on the hem and a bit of lace on the modest neckline, also had puffed sleeves with room for longer white sleeves to be worn beneath them. A few pins were set in place before they removed it and allowed Betsy to dress again. Off to the counter to pick out some small artificial pink rosebuds to edge the neckline and set in the flounce, and a sash printed in a small floral pattern to tie around her waist. Madam suggested a second petticoat as a necessity for a fuller skirt and a bustle pad to enhance the girl's hips.

Lady Katherine approved the petticoat but not the bustle. "Allow her to be natural for a while longer. Let the other day dresses be in pastels or printed cotton, not overly embellished, silk for the dinner dresses and evening gown. When can we expect the white gown to be finished today?"

"I will put my best seamstress to work at once. Give us two hours. I will send along the rest of the garments as they are finished for your approval."

"I am sure they will be satisfactory. Good day, Madam Violette."

Lady Katherine steered Betsy out the door. She'd remained silent during the selections, overwhelmed by the variety, letting Katherine choose. Now, she brimmed with questions.

"Are all women involved with fashion so intimidating like Madam Violette and Clement?"

"Well, they certainly are opinionated, and most dressmakers will try to run the bill up with extra ornamentation and accessories. One must be firm with them. However, Lady Flora prefers Violette because the woman does not fawn over her or affect a French accent as many do. She is aware of the latest styles and can be trusted in that. No one intimidates the duchess."

Betsy nodded. She lowered her voice to ask as they moved along the now busy sidewalk, "I thought Lord Justinian planned to pay for the dresses."

"He will reimburse us. A young man buying clothes for a woman might be taken wrong. Some would assume that woman to be his mistress. Do you know what that is?"

"Oh, yes, a woman kept for pleasure, I've overheard. Men like to brag about them even in Oxford. I am a good listener. But why cannot a wife also give pleasure?"

"They can, but so many marry for wealth or status that they don't feel they must. Let's change the subject. We have more shopping to do and have only a short way to walk to the Burlington Arcade, but it does appear the weather is turning on us."

Before long, they turned into a corridor between two shop windows. A beadle dressed in a black cape and top hat gave the women a bow as they entered what appeared to be a lane roofed with glass to let in the light. Small, two-story shops displaying luxury goods—laces and leather goods, feathers and fans, shawls and shoes, silver and jewels—lined both sides. Pairs of fashionable women strolled the aisle, some trailed by servants carrying their purchases. Awed, Betsy stood still and gazed upward toward where raindrops began to patter.

"Yes, God bless Lord Burlington. He grew tired of lowlifes throwing oyster shells and other rubbish into his lane and gardens, the smell and nuisance, you know, and so he built this arcade. His house is right next door. Others say he did it for his wife so she could shop without fear of being robbed or jostled in the dirty streets. In the arcade, the beadles make sure there is no whistling, singing, humming, running, or boisterous behavior, which cannot be said of other places. I do thank him from the bottom of my heart as I dislike shopping, but here it all is in one place and well-guarded by the beadles who are retired members of his old regiment, the Tenth Royal Hussars with him at Waterloo. Forty-seven shops in all—and half a dozen industrious women running six of them. Lady Flora patronizes their shops. Turn here into this milliner's establishment."

Besides those on display in the windows, they entered a world of hats, bonnets, turbans, and caps. feathered and lined, bedecked with artificial flowers and an occasional stuffed bird. There seemed to be no end to what could be piled on top of a hat. Again, no ordinary clerk waited upon them but the proprietress herself, a plump and cheerful woman who wore only a lace cap on her fading red hair. Her blue eyes sparkled when they lit upon Lady Katherine.

"Is the duchess in town, then, Lady Katherine? You rarely visit us when she is not."

"Expected imminently, though this rain might slow her journey."

"How well you look in that chapeau since we lined it to match your gown. And I see your young friend has borrowed the spring bonnet."

"Yes, Mrs. Cherry, but I do feel the spring bonnet is too youthful for me and suits her so nicely, I plan to let her have it. This is Miss Elizabeth Barton, a friend of the family. She will need several more to extend her wardrobe, if she is to stay in London."

"So happy to assist both of you. Please browse and select what you will, or we would be happy to design something new." Mrs. Cherry opened her arms wide to include all of her stock.

"Do you see anything you fancy, Miss Barton?"

"I hardly know what to pick."

"High crowns are definitely the style now. Will the young lady be wearing her hair up as she does today?"

"Truly, I do not know. Let's choose one that will accommodate other styles as well. Here, try this one." Lady Katherine whisked a straw bonnet with pink ribbons, a single white plume laying along the brim, and a cluster of cherry blossoms to one side. It seemed to fit Betsy perfectly. She nodded as she peered into a mirror. "I like it."

"How about this bicorn with an upturned brim and this charming cockade of red, white and blue?"

"It shows all of my face and seems very bold. Shouldn't I be worried about my complexion?"

"You are very pale, but that is what parasols are for, after all.

And then there was another with a ruching of blue silk inside the bonnet that framed the face. and more and more, with Mrs. Cherry bringing others from the back of the shop. Finally, the number was narrowed to three that were placed in a round box and tied with a ribbon. After that, the purchase of a pelisse, a parasol sturdy enough to keep off a light rain, one pair of silk stockings, a pair of black slippers similar to the ones she wore that her feet would shape as she walked, and an order placed for half boots measured to her size, plus gloves both long and short.

Overhead, the rain had ceased, but the sky remained a sullen gray. Burdened with packages, they had reached the end of the arcade.

Lady Katherine sighed. "This is just the time when dragging a man along to carry for us would have come in handy, but they dislike coming here unless they need boots or swords or exotic tobacco. Once the duchess arrives, we will have footmen at our disposal, but Joshua and I do not keep any. Far too pretentious for a barrister, even a prosperous one. I am both exhausted and famished. I recall a tea shop just outside these doors."

She peered into a store selling watches, ormolu clocks, and tall case clocks to the rear, all showing the current time. "We can enjoy some refreshments before Peterson meets us."

A beadle held the door for them as they exited. They secured a table made pleasant with a small bouquet of posies in the tea shop and ordered a pot of Darjeeling along with a tray of sandwiches and cakes. Their packages cluttered the other two chairs.

"So, we've made a good start today," said Lady Katherine as she poured for both of them.

"A start? I can never repay you for what we have here."

"As I said, a certain person is footing the bill." Her hostess did peer around for listening ears.

"I do want to thank you for saving me from the tight lacing at least."

"Let me tell you a brief story. At the age of twelve, my mama decided my posture was poor and had me laced so tight that when I ran outside trying to follow the Longleigh boys, I fainted. My dear Joshua cut my stays with his pen knife, which involved also opening my gown. My mother found us thus and demanded he propose to me immediately. At the age of fifteen, he hardly wanted a twelve-year-old bride. Fortunately, Lady Flora prevailed with her usual good sense. She assured mama that when I came out at the age of eighteen, he would offer for me. He became my hero."

"How romantic." Betsy selected a cucumber sandwich before revealing her own experience. "After Lord Justinian saved me from the fire and took me to his lodging to help me dry out, my papa arrived and insisted he offer for me at once. I confess I was wearing only blankets and my shift, but your brother-in-law did not lay an improper hand upon me. I told my father that after saving my life, Professor Longleigh should not be punished by losing his freedom to be an academic. Yet, he still insisted on bringing me to London when I had nowhere else to go. He is *my* hero."

"I can believe it of Justin, but Joshua reneged on his promise to me, which set off on a competition between us that we could each marry the catches of the season. I came to great harm because of this foolish wager. The people of the ton can be vicious, and we rarely socialize with them because of what they did to me, but the invitations still come. All believe that Joshua will be the next duke of Bellevue, but he prefers his practice of law. Being noble, he attracts clients from his class—the lord who shot his wife's lover in the bedroom rather than proposing a duel, the lady who was wrongly accused of infidelity because her husband wanted a divorce, the way in which he punished those who harmed me without causing a scandal. Somehow, that last story came out when it was meant to be private, but it did bolster his clientele."

"You are so happily married I would have thought he loved you always."

"It took him some time to realize that. But I was on the verge of winning that bet and could have married a man I liked but did not love."

The sandwiches disappeared one by one along with the cakes and the tea down to the last drop. Outside, their carriage arrived, and they gathered their packages and spilled into the coach with Peterson's aid.

"Back to Madam Violette's, if you please. We have a gown to receive."

As the driver closed the door and mounted the box again, Lady Katherine pondered. "What have I forgotten? Oh, yes. Have you any jewelry, necklaces, earbobs? You may borrow freely from me, but no, I see your ears are not pierced. We must remedy that."

Betsy hands flew to her lobes as if feeling the pain already. "No need to go to all that trouble. I do have a gold locket with miniatures of my mother and father inside, Papa's wedding gift to Mama and painted by an art professor for them. I rarely wear it for fear of its being stolen from my neck, but it is very nice."

"I am sure that it is. At your age, a colorful ribbon can set off your neck just as nicely."

"Lord Justinian gave me a handful of those, and Clement said she would iron them. We needn't do more shopping."

Lady Katherine gave her such a sweet glance it warmed her insides. "You are a person after my own heart. We are done with shopping today. However, you should see more of what London has to offer. We might take the boys with us to see some of the sights. They always beg me to buy a monkey, but I say I already have two. Or a parrot, but they can become quite attached to only one person. The duchess has a tortoise keeper with a parrot named Miss Rosita who will attack any woman that shows an interest in him, one-eyed and one-legged as he is."

There was so much to the world beyond the gates of the university where one only learned of it from books, Betsy marveled. "I've never heard of a tortoise keeper."

"Oh, you must see the giant tortoises kept at Bellevue Hall one day. In the summer, they rove about grazing like sheep. They reside in Lady Flora's conservatory in the winter and sometimes they mate with great gusto to produce many eggs. The young are much coveted by members of the ton but the duchess will only give them into good care. The tortoise keeper, a very battered naval veteran, watches over them, quite a plum job when one can rest under a tree for most of the day and still keep them in sight."

"How wonderful."

The carriage paused in front of Madam Violette's shop. No need to get down as the assistant immediately carried out the garment, beautifully wrapped and delivered into their hands. They continued on toward the townhouse.

"It is largely believed that Giselle is Madam's daughter, but one doesn't ask. No one knows of a husband, but perhaps he perished in the Terror. For a dressmaker, she does have a regal air and probably has a right to a French accent but has suppressed it. I am sure the Longleigh twins could write a romance of it."

"There are authors in the family?"

"Yes, and female ones at that, Clio and Calliope. Of course, they use a *nom de plume*. Most believe one of their heroes is based on James Longleigh. I am sure some copies are in our library, but I am not certain I should recommend them to you. They can be quite racy."

"I have studied anatomy texts."

"Believe me, it is not the same. Ah, here we are, home at last. Still no sign of the duke and duchess or footmen would besiege us immediately to help with the packages. Peterson, would you mind?"

The coachman assisted cheerfully enough in getting them and all their baggage to the front door, where Mrs. Crump and the maid of all work assisted in getting the packages upstairs and into the blue room where Betsy had been transferred in their absence.

Mrs. Crump gave them a report of the whereabouts of everyone else. "Lord Joshua has gone to his law practice. Sarah took the boys to the park to sail their boats, but the rain brought them back to the nursery. A rider arrived bearing a message that the duke and duchess will arrive for dinner, but in the meantime, Cook has set out a cold lunch of lamb and ham in the breakfast room. She is frazzled now that word has finally come and is preparing a more elaborate meal for the evening."

"And Lord Justinian?" Betsy blurted out, drawing the eyes of all the women in her direction. She should not have asked.

"Why, he had his meal and then rode out to meet his parents' coach, ma'am."

She quelled her disappointment. Perhaps after all the purchases were stowed away, she could find the library and search for scandalous novels written by the Longleigh twins, but she'd been hoping for a long conversation with Justin.

"I for one plan to rest this afternoon. I suggest that you do, too, Miss Barton," said Lady Katherine, already headed toward her bedchamber.

"I thought I'd choose a book from the library to make me drowsy, if you would point the way."

"Nan will take you. The offerings are not nearly as great as the library of Bellevue Hall, but I am sure you can find some dry tome to bore you into slumber."

"I find very little boring. Show me the way, Nan."

As they passed down the stairs again, her mind worked on only one problem. What pseudonym might the Longleigh twins use for their racy tales?

Six

The mystery wasn't hard to solve as six volumes bound in red with tempting titles sat in a row within easy reach, each one written by C.C. Leigh. The first, *Castle Blackpool*, seemed the place to begin. Betsy, having retrieved her spectacles from her chamber, settled into a very large armchair smelling slightly of pipe tobacco, which reminded her of the one in Justin's lodging and began to read the tale in which the hero, Lord Jasper Leithmore, saved not one but four virgins from being despoiled. Nothing like this in the Christ Church library. Not boring at all, but still the fatigue of shopping overcame her. The next she knew, the rather rough hands of Nan shook her awake.

"I've been sent to find you, miss. The duke and duchess have entered the city and will arrive shortly. Clement says you must come upstairs and be made presentable for them at once."

Had she not been presentable all day? Regardless, she did hasten to the blue room where Clement awaited, full of orders as usual. "Off with the spectacles and into your new gown at once."

She complied, even though that meant being laced tightly. While Clement fussed with her hair, stripping out the blue ribbons and pinning several spare silk rosebuds Madam Violette had included with the gown into place, she schooled her in the proper forms of address. "You must always address the duke and duchess as Your Grace since you are nowhere near their rank unless they tell you otherwise. It is Lord Joshua, Lord Justinian, and Lady Katherine to you. All proceed you into the dining room. Do you understand?"

"Yes, ma'am," she answered rather breathlessly due to her corset.

"Have you any jewelry? I found none among your belongings."

"Wait a moment." She stood very straight because she had no other choice and went to a drawer in the bottom of the wardrobe that held her cotton stockings and undergarments. Searching a little for the one with a lumpy toe, she spilled out her locket and presented it.

"Very nice, but did you think anyone in this household would steal from you?"

"My, no. But it contains the only likeness I have of my mother, and I would be loath to lose it."

For once, Clement said nothing, merely fastened the necklace around her neck. "Now go and stand with Lady Katherine and the rest of the servants."

They seemed to be lined up in some kind of order behind Lady Katherine, who had changed into a silk gown of a bronze color very becoming to her. The autumn leaves still adorned her hair. Behind her, Mrs. Crump stood just before the cook, then Nan, the scullery maid, and Peterson, who preceded the stable hand with his boots scraped clean and his hair combed and slicked back for a neater appearance. Clement arrived and pushed in front of Cook and just behind the housekeeper. Betsy had no idea where to stand until Lady Katherine took her hand, eyed

Clement and the rest of them. And declared, "Miss Barton is our guest, one the duchess will be pleased to meet," and drew her to her side not a moment too soon.

With a clatter of hooves and the grinding of wheels against the cobblestones, the ducal coach arrived. They processed outside and arranged themselves on both sides of the staircase while Lady Katherine stood at the top with Betsy by her side. Footmen in blue and silver livery jumped from the coach and lowered the step. One added a small stepstool and opened the door of a vehicle as large and black as the four horses who drew it. The impressive Bellevue crest adorned one side. With a gloved hand, a footman handed down a petite lady with blonde hair as light as Betsy's own and in possession of discerning large gray eyes and a pleasant demeanor as she made her way through the tunnel of servants who bowed and nodded as she passed. She greeted each one by name. However did she keep track of so many?

Upon gaining the top step, she embraced Lady Katherine and said, "My dear daughter, so good to see you again, and this must be Miss Elizabeth Barton, about whom I have heard so much in the last few hours."

A sharp glance from Clement standing near the top of the chain sent Betsy into a deep curtsy. "Yes, Your Grace."

When she dared to raise her eyes, she noticed the coach had disgorged several others: a lady's maid, a butler, a valet, another man whose rank wasn't immediately obvious by his dress but who did sport a thin mustache she associated with the French, and Justin at last.

Had he really spent hours telling his mother about her as there was so little to tell? She had no time to ponder that as a huge man on a dark horse the size of a knight's charger swung from the saddle and declared, "Glad to be here at last. I am famished."

All the servants arrayed on the stairs did their bows and curtsies, murmuring, "Your Grace." Betsy did the same.

"Peterson, the other coaches have gone directly to the stables and await you. Cook, I know you have prepared a fine meal for us, so off with you to the kitchen. Monsieur Pepin is here to assist you this evening. The rest of you to your posts," the duke said in his booming voice. He waved them away, and they fled. Indeed, the duke seemed very intimidating until a commotion coming from the house made his burnished face beam.

William and Richard, clad in their small nightshirts, rocketed out the open front door and shouted, "Grandpa Bear is here!"

A frantic Sarah followed them. "So sorry, Your Grace. I allowed them to watch your arrival. They became overly excited and were gone just like that. There is only one of me and the two of them. They are so very good at escaping."

The duke scooped up both boys, one on each brawny arm. "Yes, aren't they," he said as if very proud of his grandsons. "Willy and Richie, you must tell me all you have been learning since last I saw you, but tomorrow."

"They have learned very little since driving off their tutor, I am afraid," Lady Katherine told him.

"Ah, I see they take after the rest of the family, all except Justinian, of course, but how goes their riding skills? Have they learned to swim yet?"

"In my parents' pond and took to it like ducklings, but we don't get to the country often enough for them to practice their riding. Joshua is so caught up in his practice, he rarely has time to take them out to the park, and Peterson has enough to do."

"Never fear, their Grandpa Bear will remedy that."

"Tomorrow, please," both boys begged.

"Certainly tomorrow, if we all get enough rest tonight. Now off with Sarah and to bed."

"Mama, are you coming to tuck us in?"

"I will be right along. Do everyone come inside. We are lingering here on the doorstep when all of you must be tired and hungry."

As the duke set his grandsons down, his eyes like dark caves turned on Betsy. She automatically dropped another low curtsy and a Your Grace.

"I believe we have already concluded the formalities. I am pleased to meet you, Miss Barton, the only lass who has gotten Justin's nose out of a book. May I escort you inside?"

"I am honored." She did another curtsy.

"You will wear out your knees doing that. Come along."

She hoped he could not feel the trembling of her arm beneath his dusty riding coat. Justin offered his arm to his mother, who seemed vastly amused by the proceedings, and Lady Katherine led the way to the drawing room, but their group parted at the staircase to allow the travelers time to repair to their chambers and freshen themselves for dinner. Lord Joshua appeared in the doorway.

"Did I miss their arrival? A rather engrossing case and a client who would not leave."

"You will see them shortly at dinner. They know how you are."

Word must have been sent from above because the dinner gong sounded a short time later. It appeared to Betsy that the duchess had made a swift change of clothes, but the duke had settled for a brush down and a wash up. He escorted his wife to the table and Lord Joshua his. She dithered. Did she follow Justin like a stray pup hoping for scraps? He took her arm before she could decide where she fit in this world. They moved to a new place Betsy had not yet discovered, a dining room with seats enough for twelve and two chandeliers overhead to illuminate a table bedecked with fresh spring flowers, fine china, possibly the fabled Sevres, crystal she suspected of being the famed Irish Waterford, and heavy silver flatware embossed with the Bellevue crest having enough pieces to rattle her nerves.

The clear soup arrived, and its spoon was obvious enough. Betsy waited until the duchess applied a small fork to a salad of early greens to begin hers and watched the duke guide his fish onto yet another fork with a piece of bread. And so, it continued. She ate little and spoke less, thanks to her tight lacing and fear of making another gaffe by going on about scientific experiments. The duchess did try to bring her out by asking polite questions. How did she find London as compared to Oxford? She did not say out loud, crowded, dirty, and smelling of horse dung, but rather large and full of wonderful and extraordinary goods as opposed to the quiet of Oxford and its lack of luxury. How had she passed the afternoon? Reading a delightful book by C.C. Leigh—for light entertainment.

The last brought a sly look to the duchess's face. "You have found us out already. My twin daughters wrote that book, but we are to keep the secret from society. I know we can trust you to do the same."

"Oh, yes, Your Grace."

"Please, simply Duchess to you."

"Oh, Mama, everyone knows who writes them and that they are based on James' adventures," Justin said with perhaps just the slightest tinge of envy in his voice.

"Nearly all of us have had stories written about us, often inaccurate, all amusing," the duchess countered.

"I should like to read them," Betsy replied with enthusiasm.

"Most are housed at Bellevue Hall, but perhaps one day."

The duke cracked a few walnuts with his bare hands and popped the meat into his mouth as the dinner came to a close. "I propose we have our port, sons, and call it an evening after our long journey. Will you be coming right along, my dearest?"

"I do believe I will have tea in the drawing room with Kate and Miss Barton."

The big man seemed rather disappointed. "Very well, but don't tarry."

The men stood as the ladies left for their tea. Betsy soon discovered that she was the final dish as the duchess poured each a cup and immediately began an analysis of her situation.

"I understand you have been put out of the university because of your sex, but are very well-educated even if not acknowledged with a degree of any kind."

"Yes, Your …I mean Duchess—and you must call me Elizabeth or Betsy or whatever you wish. Women cannot attend classes or attain a degree, but might sit in on all but anatomy and life drawing if given permission by the professor. Your son's lectures are brilliant."

"I would expect so and that he would allow women to attend as he has many strong-minded sisters, not to mention his mother." The duchess regarded her thoughtfully. "I believe I should like to call you Bess after the great, good queen. We have so many servants named Betsy, and I think you deserve something more in tune with your knowledge. What does that span?"

"Oh, mathematics, chemistry, a bit of physics, English literature, foreign languages—French and German being my best, some understanding of Spanish and Italian, Latin, but not very much Greek—history and geography."

The duchess offered her a gentle smile. "I, too, have a gift for languages but would have so loved to be schooled in all the rest. Life is very unfair to women of all ranks."

"Yes, I was tolerated until I reached my fifteenth year and my monthlies began. I had no idea what those were until the housekeeper explained to me at my father's bidding that I was not dying of a hemorrhage but becoming a woman belatedly and would have the curse every month until I became too old to bear children. It seemed a terrible thing, but she helped me prepare rags to take care of the matter. I've brought them with me so as not to be a bother." She lowered her eyes to stare into the teacup as if it held her future.

"You are no bother, but a guest until we can see you safely settled. When I lived among the Shawnee, the women did not take to their beds but gathered in a special hut with others having their courses where we chatted and sewed moccasins and were brought our meals, making a very cozy time of it. They were up and about soon after childbirth, too, a practice I continued after each of mine. It makes for a faster recovery, I believe."

"That is very fascinating. You should write it down and encourage others."

"Sadly, the Christian world considers something very natural to be Eve's curse and so we are supposed to suffer. Ridiculous."

"Nor do anatomy texts have much to say about monthlies and the cramps they cause," the newly renamed Bess concurred.

"Precisely. Such knowledge only travels verbally from woman to woman. Now on to our original topic. What other accomplishments do you have? Music, drawing, needlework?"

"None of those, I am afraid. I began my first sampler, but when my grandmother died, I did not complete it. My aunt, a retired governess, felt those skills should be taught by mothers or experts. She had no use for the first two and went to a seamstress if she required any sewing done, but she was a superior teacher. I could read, write, and do simple maths by the age of six, thanks to her, but then she too passed. My dowry of six hundred pounds comes from the sale of her house and belongings and the interest it earned. I know that is a very modest amount."

"Some would be glad to accept it. Many poor girls have none. I have from time to time supplied them with enough for them to make a better marriage. You are very bright and presumably know your choices are limited to marriage, becoming a governess or a companion to an older woman. You are far too educated to be a maid, though some prefer pretty ones such as you."

The duchess poured a second cup of tea as if she needed more fortification to tackle the problem and turned to her daughter-in-law. "What say you, Kate? There are gaps in her learning that must be closed. I could teach her needlework and singing. With Iris back among us, she might instruct her in watercolors. We can work on these during our stay here."

"Her knowledge is of a masculine nature, yet members of the ton will not want their daughters learning anything more than French and basic literacy before they send them off to be finished in fine deportment, which is a shame."

"It certainly is," said Justin who had entered the room quietly and now stood by the fireplace as if he had materialized out of thin air.

Bess blurted without any consideration of his rank or the fact that he lived there, "How long have you been here? What have you heard?" She felt her face grow hot with embarrassment that he might have learned about her monthlies.

"Do not bother about that. Justin has six older sisters. Nothing about women is a mystery to him. Tea, my son?"

He shook his head. "I was sent to remind you that you need your rest by Papa, but aren't you overlooking the possibility that Miss Barton might profit by being introduced at Almack's. Even Miss Stilwell, now the Countess of Edgemont, had her year there."

The duchess demurred. "While I'd like to think I can make any match, and Lucia Stilwell was one of my greatest triumphs, from homely spinster to countess, the patronesses of Almack's would never give her a voucher. Lucia is the daughter of a country squire with a thousand acres and granddaughter of an impoverished baron. Besides which, she had Lady Mayberry, her aunt, as a sponsor. Without some nobility in Bess's line, she is ineligible for entry and my status cannot make her so. However, you will accompany me to the marriage mart and dance with the young ladies. There is always a shortage of partners and with all my daughters married, your father is more reluctant to attend than ever."

Justin shifted his position to cross his arms across his chest. "As am I. Why should I dance with these maidens with nothing but air between their two ears when no good can come of it? I cannot marry in my profession, and they are not looking for a younger son so far from the succession that he will never be Duke of Bellevue."

Bess, finding she liked the change of name, spoke before she thought once more. "That is untrue. Young women flock to his lectures and leave him apples tied with pretty bows acknowledging Newton's laws, and also their calling cards. Each hopes he will leave his profession and consider them for marriage. A connection to the Duke of Bellevue's family is no small thing, even if it does not come with a title or a fortune."

The duchess's finely arched brows rose. "Very perceptive of you and true, but that is not why I want him to attend. The two of us can keep our ears open for possible positions for you, women complaining of not being able to keep a governess or with a difficult elderly relative who needs someone to read to them and pour their tea. We might also snuffle among the younger sons who might consider six-hundred pounds and a connection to Bellevue an enticement. While they cannot meet her at Almack's, we could certainly invite the best of the bunch to dinner or our own soirees."

"She is too good for any of those types. Once married, they would not allow her to be herself and continue her studies," Justin asserted with great vehemence.

"Well, then, perhaps we can lure James home. He prefers women of intellect and as Bellevue's heir can marry as he wishes with no consideration of rank or fortune."

"James! His is likely to be a benedict, only marrying in his old age. He's practically there already. Betsy is far too innocent for a man of his experience."

"I can attest he is sixteen years your elder, but not yet forty, and a man of the world. Such matches are not unusual. Men often prefer an innocent they can mold to their ways," the duchess said, suppressing the mirth that tugged at her lightly rouged lips.

Bess added, "I am a very quick learner and enjoy new experiences."

"Oh my, I am sure you do, but first we shall try Almack's. And dress like a gentleman, not a cleric, Justin. Do see a barber between now and then. Remember not to wear boots or you will be turned back at the door as Lord Wellington once was."

Bess noticed for the first time that he'd added only riding boots to his *sub fusc* wear and did resemble a traveling minister except for his youth, handsome, gray-eyed face, and unruly hair. She'd miss those curls. They looked so soft and touchable, untamed by any hair oil.

"Enough for tonight. We have several good ideas for Bess's future. Do go upstairs and tell your papa that I am on my way." With that, she dismissed her son who had no choice but to go.

As soon as the door closed behind him, the duchess said, "We had very little privacy on the long drive, and the duke's needs must be attended to, not that I have any objections. Go, dear child, and sleep well. Your future is in good hands."

"Believe me, you will miss nothing at Almack's. Very proper and boring. I was exiled for my antics there and did not regret it one bit," Kate added.

Bess left, feeling she did have a future of some kind for the first time in several years and found Justin waiting to light her way up the stairs to the blue room.

~ * ~

Lady Flora lay with her head on the warmth of her husband's broad chest, cheek pressed against one of his thunderbird tattoos, and listened to the booming of his great heart. As it turned out, neither had been all that fatigued, and the bed sport had been gratifying after several days of abstinence. Soon, he would fall asleep, but she had an important issue to discuss with him. Gently, she prodded him with her elbow.

"What? Do you want more, my little yellow flower?"

"Not me. You were entirely satisfying. It's about Justin. He has found his perfect match but will not acknowledge it because of his profession, and Bess is already more than half in love with him."

"They have my blessing." Her duke rolled over on his side and burrowed more deeply beneath the covers.

She rolled him back to her side again. "The problem is how to part Justin from his career so that they might wed and be happy."

"Nothing is beyond your abilities, my dear. Given time, you will find a solution. Poor child, that girl has a world of knowledge and no knowledge of the world or anyone to protect her from it. We had best keep her until you figure it out." Her husband sank into sleep the moment his mouth closed, not knowing he had provided an answer.

Keep Bess close. Perhaps add a soupcon of jealousy to open her youngest son's heart to his emotions. Surely, her eldest son would want to assist in seeing him happy, though the two had little in common. She'd write in the morning and pray her letter found James sooner rather than later.

Seven

Rechristened, Bess awoke in a new world—again. The townhouse seemed to bustle with energy outside her door, footsteps passing, breakfast trays rattling as some decided to dine in their beds. She would not have the courage to ask for such service, and so arose, put on the silken dressing gown purchased for her and went to the little gold and white vanity with the curlicue legs to brush her hair. The task proved difficult with all the concoctions Clement had used to sculpt it into place. Too tired to attempt a braid last evening, she'd simply taken out the pins and let the tower fall.

Think of the devil and here she came. Clement entered, seized a comb, and began yanking out the knots until her scalp burned. "I had to attend to Lady Katherine, now you. If you'd taken the time to braid it last evening, half my work would have been done and you'd have some curl. What will you wear today?"

"The same as yesterday or my blue sprigged muslin, as they are all I have."

"Never the same gown twice in a day's time. The sprigged muslin has been washed and ironed and will have to do. As the duchess will be organizing the household today, she will not be receiving guests. The young lords have breakfasted and gone for an early ride. The duke and duchess are still abed, but Lady Katherine is up and ready for the day, as you should be."

Clement parted her hair into many segments, braided each, and reconstructed the tower from yesterday, not bothering with ribbons or other adornments. "I do hope the rest of your wardrobe appears soon or everyone will know you as a poor relation."

"I am no relation at all. A guest, the duchess says."

In the mirror, she saw the maid's lips tighten but remain closed. Finished with her task, Clement withdrew the simple muslin dress from the armoire and let it drift over Besty's shoulders. "No corset needed for this one it is so out of style, but perhaps a blue ribbon about the neck. Never let it be said I send my ladies out unfinished."

With the ribbon tied in a fetching bow to one side, the maid at last released her to find her breakfast, most fortunately served in the same place as always. On the way, she passed a number of maids with Nan among them, dusting various rooms, preparing the fireplaces by scraping out the ashes and laying wood or coal as desired, ready to be lit by spills placed nearby. If only her experiment with self-lighting spills had worked, she and her father might have been rich someday, but now she dwelt in a great house and was less than a poor relation.

Footmen appeared to be everywhere in their blue and silver livery and short, white wigs that made them look as alike as a herd of sheep, but very elegant sheep to be sure. One opened the door to the breakfast room for her as if she hadn't the strength or knowledge to do it herself. Inside, she breathed freely unhindered by a corset for today and took in the familiar sight of eggs on the sideboard, but now both scrambled and boiled, bacon and sausages, kippers and kidneys, coffee and tea, double everything and twice as much toast in twice as many racks.

Lady Katherine sat sipping tea and eating marmalade on toast in a dress the color of bitter oranges with a flounce of ecru lace adorning the neckline and another surrounding her waist, probably more at the hem hidden by the table. Her coiffure was the "same old thing" Clement had moaned about but thick and a beautiful shade of brown. Bess thought she looked lovely and not overdressed as so many ladies in the arcade had been. Kate welcomed her as she filled a plate with bacon and eggs and toast and took a seat opposite her hostess who poured a cup of tea for her.

"I thought we might take the boys to the Tower of London today and keep out of Lady Flora's way as she makes assignments for the household staff and double-checks the linens and such. All is in perfect order, of course, but she will have to count the pillowcases herself to be sure. Better yet, we shall insist Justin come along to provide an escort to ward off unwanted attentions and run after the boys as necessary. Ah, here he comes from the stables. I see he has taken the duchess's order and wears the garb of a gentleman again. How handsome he looks, don't you agree?"

Naturally, she agreed. He wore top boots with buckskin trousers, a bottle green frock coat covering a pale yellow waistcoat topped by a simply tied neckcloth. His hair had not been shorn yet. He'd been handsome in his black gown and would also be if naked. The thought heated her cheeks. She fanned her tea as if it had been to blame for the flush, but it only grew deeper when he entered the breakfast room, poured a cup of coffee, added a dollop of cream, and joined them at the table.

"Justin, if you have no specials plans for the day, why not accompany us and the boys to the Tower of London to show Bess some sights. With the barracks there occupied by Wellington's soldiers, we could use your protection. I loved going there as a child to see the menagerie and listen to tales of beheadings," Lady Katherine wheedled.

"Since Josh has gone off to practice law and Papa has not commanded my presence at Gentleman Jackson's to spar with him or cross swords at Angelo's fencing academy next door, I do believe I am if we move quickly enough. Is there a decent barber nearby where I can carry out Mama's orders?" He raked one hand through his rowdy curls and with the other snagged a piece of toast to spread with strawberry jam. "Might I say you are both very attractive this morning?"

Another layer of blush suffused her cheeks. "It's only my old gown, Lord Justinian."

"It's the person inside that makes it so, Miss Barton."

"Come now, we all know you call her Betsy with her permission, though I think she prefers Bess now, and I do believe you can drop the lord and know him as Justin like the rest of the family," Lady Katherine prompted. "By the way, I am Kate to you now. If we are finished here, let me call for the carriage and collect the boys. You can wash the odor of horse off of you while we do so. Bess, with me to the nursery."

They found William and Richard fed, washed, dressed in fawn trousers buttoned to their black jackets covering a white shirt with a frilled collar, and raring to go. Bess wandered the nursery, opening their primers and examining their neglected schoolwork. The books were similar to the ones she'd learned her reading from at an even earlier age with the alphabet on the first page, a pronunciation guide second, and pictures to illustrate each letter—A is for Ass, B is for Bell, C is for Cat. Simple sentences followed along with vocabulary lists to be memorized. By the end, whole paragraphs using simple words. She wondered how far the boys had gotten and how the primers might be made more interesting for restless youngsters such as these.

Lady Katherine inquired of Sarah if her sons had given any trouble in getting dressed that morning. "Oh, no, ma'am. When I told them their reward for good behavior would be a ride in the carriage to the Tower, they could not get their clothes on fast enough."

"Good then, no more nonsense about Indian children going about naked or with only a breechcloth to cover them. They do love their grandfather's tales of life among the Shawnee overly much. No telling when we shall return."

"Do you not need me to go along?" Sarah asked.

Bess caught the longing in the question, but Kate answered, "Not this time. We will have Miss Barton and Lord Justinian with us to keep them in line. Off we go then. No running on the stairs."

But of course, being little boys, they did. All survived to meet again in the foyer where Justin waited in dark pantaloons and a fresh jacket of deep blue. The carriage arrived, now with footmen to put down the step and help the ladies inside, no more need for Peterson to get down to do so. The boys began to scramble inside but halted when their uncle placed hands of their shoulders and proclaimed, "Ladies first."

Kate was handed up, followed by Bess. Justin released his nephews and followed them. The lads claimed a window each, and he let Kate and Bess have the others, taking a middle seat like a true gentleman, Bess thought, thoroughly enchanted by his new appearance and fine manners. They set off for the center of the city of London, its oldest core since Roman times. In fact, from her reading she knew the tower had been built over a Roman graveyard. To be in the presence of so much English history delighted her no end, even though the shallow moat they passed over to gain access stank rather badly.

Peterson left them in the safe hands of one of the Yeoman Warders, resplendently dressed in his antique red uniform. Justin paid their admittance fee, and the tour began with the tale of the tower being built in 1066 by William the Conqueror to keep an eye on the vanquished from its famous white tower. The boys delighted in the collection of armor and weapons, but even they noted the knights must have been much shorter than their Uncle Justin. Yes, he would have required a custom-made suit of metal plates to clothe his tall form and perhaps ridden a black charger much like the horse his father favored today. Bess let her imagination wander shamelessly to mental scenes of Justin carrying her blue ribbon tied to his lance in a joust.

In the Martin tower, they viewed the crown jewels not as lavish as they had once been since Cromwell had most of the metal melted down and the gems broken up after his victory in the Civil War. Only a twelfth-century spoon and three swords remained once the leader of the Roundheads prevailed. The collection had been slowly rebuilt with returns, purchases, and loans, but had not yet regained its former glory. What was there dazzled Bess, but the young lads fidgeted.

Upon their release, they ran at a clump of six ravens pecking in the grass, trying to shoo them as they did crows at their grandfather's estate. To Kate's embarrassment, the stern Raven Master reprimanded them as the birds flew awkwardly to a nearby perch.

"Here now, can't you see their wings are clipped to keep them in the Tower? Don't you know if the ravens ever leave, the British empire will fall—and it might be your fault?"

William's eyes went round. "So sorry, sir. We thought they were just big crows eating your grass." Richard nodded in agreement.

"Go on then, but leave my birds alone."

"Come along. I know what will interest you more," their guide said. "We are at the Bloody Tower. Do you know what happened here?"

Bess wanted to raise her hand and say, "Yes!" but she restrained herself.

"In this tower, two young boys not much older than you, but heirs to the English crown, Prince Edward the Fifth and his brother Richard, were kept captive by their evil uncle who became King Richard the Third. They were never seen again, probably buried here."

"My name is Richard." Bess watched the boy take a deep swallow.

Their Warder did give some reassurance. "Not likely anything will happen to you, unless you are heir to the throne. Are you?"

"Oh, no! But some people say I am the Bellevue line's spare."

"That so? I don't imagine your grandpa will let anything happen to you. His reputation is very fierce. But other famous people have met their end here, beheaded as that was considered an honor reserved only for nobility like Lady Jane Grey and Queen Anne Boleyn. It's said the last still wanders here with her head tucked beneath her arm. Others were hung."

"Could we move along to the Royal Menagerie by the Lion Tower? I have such fond memories of going there as a child," Kate plead.

"Certainly, but that will cost an extra nine pence. Used to be three half-pence or a cat or dog to feed the lions, but I am not sure it is entirely worth the price anymore."

"We'll pay." As an aside walking with Bess, she whispered, "Now that a connection has been made to Bellevue, we'll have to give more as a gratuity."

"Oh, I think this tour is worth every penny. To think we are treading the very ground where Anne Boleyn met her fate."

The warder's advice proved true. Kate gazed at the skimpy exhibit of one lone elephant and a grizzly bear so old it barely raised a tired eyelid to see who disturbed its slumber.

"But where are the lions? I know there was a tiger and a leopard, too. So many monkeys and baboons, a hyena, and wolves, and many birds."

"Gone, ma'am, But I hear the new Keeper is planning to rebuild the collection. You must visit again."

Bess gazed on the elephant who gazed back, its eyes filled with a gentle intelligence, not at all frightening despite its size. "Just think, boys, we have seen a real elephant. Did you know they only live in the wilds in Africa and India? The Indian elephants have smaller ears. Which do you believe this is?"

"I think Indian," said William. "But where are the monkeys?"

"I think you are right. Monkeys are very interesting and clever, but rather nasty. Did you know they throw their feces at people who annoy them?"

"Feces?" questioned Richard.

"Um, manure, dung, horse apples."

One step ahead of Bess, Kate said, "You are my monkeys, but don't ever, ever try that."

"Oh, I didn't mean to encourage bad behavior," Bess stammered. "I only wanted to share my knowledge."

Kate patted her arm. "No harm done, I think. My sons were totally engaged by your information. I do believe we should go elsewhere now for some refreshment. Justin, will you show our gratitude for our tour?"

He fished a pound note from a pocket and slipped it to the warder who beamed. "Hope you enjoyed it."

"Very much," Bess told him as she had no funds of her own and could only dole out compliments.

The ever-faithful Peterson awaited them with the carriage not far from the gate. "Where to?"

"The tea shop by the arcade where you met us yesterday. Also, is there a good barber nearby?" Kate questioned.

"I know where Lord Joshua has his hair cut."

"That should be conservative enough," Justin grumbled about his brother's short cut locks. "Grooming me for Almack's tomorrow night, I suppose."

"Wonderful. I've done my duty by the duchess in reminding you. How about a cup of chocolate, young men, and a tray of sandwiches and sweets. Do not worry, we'll save you a scone, Justin."

The boys cheered and forgetting their manners again, clambered aboard. Justin handed in Kate and Bess. She couldn't help but feel his unhappiness about the plans for the next evening. She felt that way herself. How plain and gauche she would appear compared with those fine ladies.

Eight

The duchess did indeed count the pillowcases and check the condition of the linens, though she knew Kate kept things in good order. After assigning the servants she had brought along to their tasks, she sat down at a small escritoire tucked under a window with good light, withdrew a sheet of paper, and after some thought, wetted her pen in the inkwell.

My dearest eldest son, James,

We have not heard from you in some time and hope you are well. I will send this to your last address in Cairo and pray that it reaches you. I fear that like our disgraced and exiled Lord Byron, you might embroil yourself in the rebellion of the Greeks against the Turks. It is said he plans to give a fleet to the Greeks, a better use of his money than some, but a dangerous endeavor.

I write to you now about a smaller personal matter. We have taken on the care of a young woman of intellect and quite attractive but of no connections. She was brought to the townhouse as we are now in London for the Season by your brother, Justinian. It is clear that they are smitten with each other, but he is most stubborn about continuing to live like a monk in the arms of academia. I request that you return home and provide some competition for her affection in order to steer him toward the marital bliss he deserves. No, no, no, this is not a scheme to lead you into the same. You need only return home for a short time. I swear I will not importune you to attend at Almack's, but I do hope you will remain for their wedding.

Please let me know that you are on your way. I do not ask much of you as a mother and our heir. Help me now.

Yr. loving mother, Flora

Content with her brief but effective letter, she sprinkled sand to dry the ink, shook it off, and folded it carefully. After adding her son's last known location, she turned the missive over and melted a blob of sealing wax using the flame of her candle. She found the Bellevue seal rather carelessly tossed in a drawer by her husband, who had no patience with correspondence, being a man of action, and applied the crest to the fold of the paper. Now to get it on its way. Perhaps the duke could prevail on the military to transport it as their ships constantly trolled the Mediterranean delivering orders to the most distant of places rather than trying to find a trustworthy person headed to Egypt to deliver the missive.

She prayed her request would arrive before Justin's term recess ended in mid-April and took him back to Oxford. If not, and James still answered her summons, she would delight in one of his rare visits for as long as she could keep him.

With her husband gone to take exercise of one kind of another and probably now dining at his club, she ordered a light repast for herself in the breakfast room where she enjoyed the quiet and the view of her garden welcoming spring. No secret when the family returned, as her grandsons sought her out as she sipped a second cup of tea. They regaled her with the details of their outing.

"We saw a ele-phant," Richard exclaimed. "They are found wild in Africa and India."

"There is a ghost of a queen who walks around with her head tucked under her arm, and two princes were killed there. One was named Richard," William said just to tease his brother.

"Enough for now. Go to Sarah and lie down for a nap," their mother directed.

"We aren't tired.

"We do not need naps."

Their guest intervened. "Perhaps you could ask for some paper and draw a picture of what you liked best before lying down," Bess suggested.

"Yes!" Off they went, scampering up the stairs to the nursery.

"A fine idea to quiet them down, Bess," the duchess commended her.

"I was often alone with my studies and copied pictures from the books I read. I'm not greatly talented, but it is a pleasing pastime."

Ah, yes, Bess Barton was proving useful already. She turned her eyes on her son. "A vast improvement in appearance. You will make the young ladies at Almack's swoon tonight," she commented as she took in the closely cut sides of his hair and the remaining topknot of curls, a few artfully allowed to fall across his forehead.

"Heaven forbid that I make any maiden faint over me. Perhaps I should not go."

"Recall we are doing reconnaissance for Bess, trying to find her a good position."

"If I must, then."

"I rather liked your curls. To think you sacrificed them for me," Bess murmured as if he'd been wounded in a duel.

So smitten with Justin, almost painful, the duchess thought. But she'd put her plans into motion to resolve this happily.

~ * ~

Almack's on a Wednesday evening crowded with the mothers of the ton offering up their marriageable daughters like promising fillies on the auction block. Donned in his formalwear always kept available by his mother—stockings, breeches, both a waistcoat and evening jacket plus gloves—and dancing shoes, he was escorted by the duchess from one prospect to another. Justin ran a finger around his high neckcloth trying to alleviate the choking tightness that his father's valet had insisted upon to sustain a complicated knot. The duke never wore such styles, and the man had gone mad with power in designing it. He'd passed the inspection of the lady patronesses with ease but disappointed one mama after another when introduced as Lady Flora's youngest son, an academic at Oxford, which meant no fortune, no title, and no wife allowed. Still, he dutifully signed dance cards that had not been filled like that of Lady Mayberry's latest offering, a grandniece pretty enough in an ordinary sort of way but dressed in so many frills, puffs, and ruffles that her body was largely obscured. Something simpler like Bess's gowns would have become her more.

The some of the dresses he had bought for Bess had arrived that afternoon. She'd been whisked off to her bedchamber to try on each garment, which seemed to fill all her time until dinner where she'd appeared in a pale blue frock with a minimum of lace and furbelows that suited her exactly. Kate had told him there was more to come, three in silk for special occasions. The dent in his quarterly allowance would be substantial but for a good cause. How could she attract a decent husband without them? Such a shame that women had to be judged on their looks and apparel rather than on their wits and character.

As his mother took her place among the gossiping matrons lining the dance floor, he dutifully sought out the first of his partners, a girl so unfavored that he'd been the first to sign her card at nine p.m., long after the ball commenced. She must lack both fortune and connections, and so, grateful not to be a woman, he greeted her kindly and led her out for a country dance. When they were close enough to converse briefly, he tried to do his assignment by asking the girl if she knew of anyone who needed a governess or companion for an elderly relation

He received a bitter laugh. "I am close enough to becoming either if I do not wed and would not tell you if I did." That concluded their conversation. He returned her to her grandmama with a bow.

Intermission came and he felt no need to compete for the scanty refreshments as he pushed past the dusty palms lining the rooms and the clumps of men his age arrayed around the most popular misses and plying them with cups of lemonade, plates of brown bread with butter, and thin slices of pound cakes baked days ago and gotten cheap. He did indulge in the weak tea to whet a throat dry from trying to get information out of vapid girls who would comment only on the weather, still a bit brisk, and ask him about his horses and hounds. Since he had none of his own, they soon lost interest. He joined the quadrille that opened the second half of the evening, then country dances, and the more daring waltzes learning nothing that would help Bess. He did not want to have her end up as embittered as his first partner, but none of the young ladies seemed in the least interested in helping another of their sex in need.

His mother flitted from acquaintance to acquaintance. He prayed she'd have more luck. At last, she tired and called the coach near three a.m. He'd never been more grateful to escape from a social situation. That did not mean the duchess failed to query him about his success.

"None. I've rarely been in a room full of people with less compassion or kindness toward others excepting a meeting of professors with opposing views."

"Not a single young lady stood out or caught your eye?"

In answer, he rolled his.

"Well, I've had some success but none that I like. Lady Tartt seeks a companion to fetch and carry for her, but she won't hire anyone who can compete with her in looks, not to mention her dubious morals. A few want governesses but prefer to go through agencies. We must polish Bess a bit before considering that. Also, they rarely want a girl who will tempt their husbands or sons as she would. We will keep trying."

"It is criminal that a decent girl with a wonderful intellect like Bess must fear such treatment. Perhaps you would like an interesting companion."

"Do I seem to be in my dotage, lack friends, or enough people to do my biding?" she replied rather sharply.

"Not at all, but I do know you would treat her well and not give up on her prospects."

"I've taken her on and will not give up until she is happily settled. I promise you that."

He believed her yet did not sleep well for what remained of the evening.

Nine

Morning came far too soon when the duke rousted Justin from his slumber to go for an early ride with Willy and Richie. His mother still lay abed and would no doubt take her breakfast there, but he did not dine alone. Kate and Bess sat at the breakfast room table, both looking like people who had not been up all night doing something they despised. Bess seemed especially fresh in a gown of pale yellow the color of the daffodils in the garden. Perhaps the seamstress thought the same, because she had outlined the bodice, sleeves, and hem in a spring green resembling new leaves with a sash of the same. How lovely she appeared to his bleary eyes. He started his meal with coffee, two cups in rapid succession, followed by soft-boiled eggs and toast in hopes of recuperation from last night's ordeal.

"We did not expect to see you so early after your late night, Justin," Kate remarked. "But I have to ask if you had any success in finding a position for Bess?"

"I did not, and Mama found none she wanted for her. In case you did not know, the duke is taking your boys riding in the park shortly, and I am to go along to help with any emergencies."

Kate nodded. "That is always a possibility with them. Thank you. I know you would rather be asleep."

"As if I had any choice when Papa banged on my door as if he meant to break it down. I was expected to don my riding clothes and snatch some breakfast as fast as possible before the park becomes crowded. So, I am snatching. Where is the duke, by the way?"

"He's come and gone," Bess answered, cocking her dear blonde head toward the offerings on the sideboard which showed large inroads into the food. "He went to the stables to arrange for the horses, the calmest ones for the boys. He figured you could handle a mount with more spirit, even if out of practice."

"Maybe when I am not nodding off."

"But do tell us about Almack's. How many ladies did you dance with? What did they wear? Were any very beautiful?" Bess chattered as if this had been a magnificent gala instead of a dreadful bore.

He answered. "Too many dances. Overdressed, and none more beautiful than you." Her cheeks pinked with pleasure. Kate shot him a warning glance that he should not be saying such things.

A commotion sounded from the hallway, and the boys burst in, waving sheets of paper and pursued by an exasperated Sarah. "So sorry, Lady Katherine. I really do need more help in the nursery to contain them."

"I understand entirely, but what have we here?"

Her sons had clustered about Bess, offering her a view of their art. She studied each very carefully. "I see an elephant with its long nose and floppy ears."

She showed the picture to Justin, who marveled at her ability to decipher a large blob with two fat legs, yes, a long nose, and a single pencil point eye. He waited for her analysis of the second page, which bore a smear of red in the middle and a stick figure garbed in a triangular dress and holding a ball with markings on it.

"Anne Boleyn, carrying her head. Well done, William. But where did you find red paint? Did your aunts leave some behind for your use?"

"Oh, no, Miss Barton. I made it myself by stabbing Sarah's sewing needle into my thumb just this morning so it would be fresh." The child held up a thumb still oozing.

Sarah covered her face, all but her mouth, with her hands. "Again sorry. I should have locked it away, ma'am."

"No need to worry. He would have found a way to get at it regardless," Kate sighed.

"Very inventive," Bess complimented, not at all upset. "But we must get you some paints so you needn't go to such extremes. Let's hang these in the nursery after everyone has seen them."

Justin marveled at how well she handled his nephews, who seemed to have inherited all the rebellious Longleigh spirit and none of Kate's good sense. He could picture her surrounded by children as a teacher or with some of her own—fathered by a man who could not possibly appreciate her as much as he did.

The display of art took second place when the duke appeared in the doorway and announced, "Ready to ride?"

"Yes, Grandpa Bear," the boys shouted, but Willy added, "See my picture of Queen Mary with her head. That's real blood, my blood."

"Hmmm, brave of you," the duke managed, indicating he was no patron of the arts but admired audacity. "I will put you on your father's mount, since he took the small carriage to visit a client today, and Richie on the horse Justin usually rides in the city. They are docile and used to traffic. We walk them to the park. No racing until we are out in the open."

"No racing at all," Kate declared.

"Only at a gentle trot or canter, I promise," the duke swore. "Come along, Justin. Are you going to dawdle over that egg all morning?"

"No, Papa. What am I riding?"

"One of the best carriage horses also trained to saddle. You'll enjoy Black Lightning. He loves being in the lead."

"Pray for me," he muttered to Bess as they left the room.

~ * ~

Bess wondered how she would spend her day, but it seemed the duchess, once she arose, had plotted out every hour. She was summoned from the library where she glutted herself on the C.C. Leigh novels, finding them very educational about relations between men and women in a sensational sort of way. Her father would say she rotted her mind, but he was nowhere to be seen.

After a light meal, she sat with the duchess and Kate for a sewing lesson by a sunny window. They started her on a sampler to learn all the various stitches and knots. While she admired the fine work of the duchess's embroidery and Kate's more practical handiwork making shirts for her boys, she did find it tedious compared to mixing chemicals. After two hours of finger pricks and ripping out mistakes, they moved to the drawing room where a large pianoforte stood.

A new arrival joined them there—the eldest Longleigh daughter, Thalia, Countess Danelagh, so tall and regal Bess did not question why they called her Queenie. She was in the city for the Season, of course, and greeted by her mother and Kate with hugs and kisses as they seldom traveled the distance to her estate of Battle Hill near York.

"I received your summons, Mama. I am at your service to assist you with Miss Barton. Everyone should have music in their life and be prepared to share it with others."

She commanded the piano, despite a rather bad scar on one hand, and sang a popular Irish song called "Robin Adair" with an easy melody and a sad story as it seemed to be a young woman pining for a man who was all the world to her. Bess understood the sentiment.

"Now, sing with me, Bess."

"I've only sung in church among many other people and hardly know the sound of my own voice."

"Come, the words are easy and the chorus repetitive."

She did her best and guessed that Lady Thalia suppressed her talent to lead her along. In the end, she received an assessment that she did not have a strong voice, but one that was light and pleasant. The countess moved over on the bench and showed her the relationship between the piano keys to a page of music. The scales came next. Her tutor arose and left her to practice these over and over. They made sense like mathematical formulas, and she thought she might come to enjoy playing, but never singing in front of others unless they joined in. As she learned, the other women called for tea and caught up with many tales of grandchildren, various travels, books read, and the gossip of the ton.

The boys had come home and stayed downstairs only long enough to see their aunt briefly, with their best manners on display. No sign of Justin, though. She managed to ask very casually, she thought, what they'd done with their uncle.

"Nothing, Miss Barton. After Richie slid off his horse, Uncle got him back on, and he also stopped mine from running away with me. After that, we came home, but he and Grandpapa decided to go practice fencing. I wish I could go with them."

"Oh, we forgot to tell you," Richie said, lowering his voice and puffing out chest in imitation of the duke. "We shall be taking the afternoon meal at my club." He addressed the duchess who rewarded his acting with a laugh, rather than a rebuke for mocking his elders.

A long morning of fresh air and exercise had at last tired them out and gotten them to nap directly after eating their meal. They were not seen again until yet another Longleigh aunt who had also been requested to aid in polishing Bess arrived with a case of watercolors and a portfolio of paper cut to size. This one was revealed to be Iris, Viscountess Valls, an artist of some renown. Though all of the Longleigh offspring were tinted in various degrees by their Shawnee heritage, Iris was darker than Thalia and wore her glossy black hair shorter and in a less complicated way. Both had those nearly black, beguiling eyes they owed to the duke. Only her Justin and the heir, James, had inherited their gray orbs from Lady Flora, she'd been told. Not her Justin, she had to remind herself.

"Pleased to meet you, Miss Barton. I live in the city much of the year and suppose we will be seeing a lot of each other. Shall we set up in the breakfast room? Mama, have you covered the table with an old cloth and requested bowls of water?"

"Of course."

They walked as they talked and found the room as Iris wanted it. She called for two smocks to cover their dresses. "Watercolors seldom stain permanently, but it would be a shame to damage your pretty frock. At least, that is the excuse used to prevent women from painting in oils. But watercolors are a good beginning for you."

Iris laid down two thin boards from her portfolio and mounted squares of heavy paper upon them. "Now what to paint?" Spying a bowl of apples on the sideboard, she examined a few before choosing one she thought more interesting than the others because it still bore a shriveled leaf and had some minor defects and set it in the center of the table. "Now, we paint flat to do watercolors so that the paint doesn't run. Wet your paper with this wide brush so that it will take the color, but not too much. Use a wet, fine-tipped brush to outline the apple as it is, not as you think it should be."

Good, they were starting with an apple. She'd often copied botanical pictures from books in the university library and wouldn't make an entire fool of herself. Following orders, Bess didn't seek to perfect the apple. It listed to one side and wasn't perfectly round. She picked up some red from the box of watercolors and made her outline.

"Good start. Now observe how the light shines on the apple. It is darker on the sides and paler towards the middle. This will give a semblance of roundness. Where the stem joins the fruit at the top, there is a dark dip. Try brown for that. Nice. Well done. Lift a bit of color with another wet brush to give it some shine. There you go. We'll let it dry a little then add details like those three brown dots."

On the loose again, the boys rampaged into the room calling out, "Auntie Iris, can we paint, too?"

"May we paint?" their mother corrected.

"Yes, may we?"

She gathered they knew this aunt better than the countess since she lived nearby most of year as they did and were less intimidated by her. Iris turned over the sheet she had prepared for herself and let them gouge out gobs of red to make circles with a chimney of a stem and a slash of a bright green leaf, though the one on the table had turned dull.

An idea crossed Bess's mind. "Young men, do you know your ABCs?"

They dutifully recited the alphabet as they splashed more paint on the paper. Bess drew a capital A under her apple. "What does A stand for?"

"Ass," they both said, because their primer showed a donkey.

"And apple. Can you make an A like this under yours?"

They managed fairly well.

"Now let's spell the whole word."

They struggled more with the lower case letters she printed out for them, but she assured them it would be easier using pencils. The duchess and Kate exchanged glances across the table where they'd continued with their needlework. Had she made a misstep again? She had no time to consider what she'd done wrong because masculine voices sounded in the house at last, the basso of the duke and the baritones of his sons. They crowded into the small room, taking it over with their size and height from the ladies.

Kate greeted her husband who kissed her cheek. "Home early for a change."

"Yes. I see you are teaching my lads the girlish art of watercolors, Iris," he teased after giving this sister a lighter kiss.

"No, I am instructing Miss Barton, but there is no reason why men shouldn't paint," she replied a little defensively.

"Not if they are as talented as Valls and yourself, but I do not think my sons are precocious in art at the moment."

"But look, we spelled apple." Willy held up the sheet of wet paper and red ran to the bottom.

"Excellent," Joshua said, ruffling his hair.

The duke selected an apple from the bowl and asked before biting into it, "Any chance of a decent tea, my dear? We've had quite a lot of exercise today. Ran into Valls at Angelo's. He might be an artist, but he has kept up his skills with an epee, which is more than I can say of Justin. I invited him to dinner, since he said Iris would be here today. And Queenie, we encountered Danelagh at Gentleman Jackson's and made the same offer. That man was created to be a warrior."

"Heaven forbid that should ever be. His being shot by Pandora was quite enough for me."

"A case of mistaken identity. You must forgive your sister."

"Certainly, though she almost made me a widow."

Amidst all this conversation, Justin remained silent until he viewed her apple and whispered beneath the noise, "As tempting as the one in Eden, I am sure."

Could one blush the same color as an apple, because she was certain she did. So many Longleigh stories she did not know, so much bantering affection, so much family all in one place. And she had no one but a father glad to be rid of her.

Ten

Bess's days fell into a pattern of practicing her lessons in the accomplishments of sewing, playing the piano, and doing watercolors. In the last, Iris often left her assignments to complete if she could not be there. She made the most progress in music, catching on quickly and learning simpler songs, some appropriate for dancing, which the ladies, if all four were present, paired off to show her the steps. At times, they managed to put the duke and Justin to use in doing the same. Queenie took over the keyboard to allow her to try a reel or two, often with Justin as a partner. On occasion, the duke engulfed her in a waltz which he danced energetically if not gracefully. They merely laughed at small mistakes and bigger blunders as none of this mattered within the family when pairs bumped into each other or took their turns too soon. After all, this wasn't Almack's, where every misstep would be judged.

Some days, she took her watercolors into the garden and painted the flowers which turned out recognizable with the shading nicely done. She knew she wouldn't reach Iris' level of accomplishment when shown a quarto volume of Lady Valls' paintings of the red Indians of America that she'd done from life, as she and her husband had spent several years among the various tribes recording them for posterity.

Iris had chosen to concentrate on the women, some in their best finery, featuring elk teeth and beadwork exquisitely done with ornaments of feathers and shiny objects in their black braids. Others featured them at work tanning hides and working in the gardens of maize, beans, and squash or nursing their babies. One Iris pointed out as a self-portrait in native garb with her son, Logan, born among them and carried in a cradle board during his early months. How scandalized the priest had been on their return to England when asked to baptize the boy as Logan Tecumseh Longleigh with no saint's name. Iris, laughing, said they'd been required to insert Luke after Logan to satisfy the church. All the Longleighs had Shawnee sobriquets in their names, and Bess longed for one, too.

Iris' husband had created a folio volume of the chiefs and braves in all their stoic dignity. Both his work and his wife's had been sent back to England to be etched on copper plates and hand-colored. Iris always sent two, one sketched out and the other which she painted to show those who would copy them how to do it well. Valls followed her example. Though nobility were not to stoop to trade, the expense led them to selling subscriptions, as the costly works were produced page by page and finally bound. To be sure, all in Lady Flora's sphere ordered copies, since she'd often told tales of her captivity by the Shawnee when she'd also hoed maize and tanned hides. Bess could listen to these stories all day and sometimes begged for them to make the more tedious needlework time pass.

"You have captured a dying way of life, which makes your art important," she'd said one day.

"Very perceptive of you, Bess," the duchess told her. "With the death of our friend Tecumseh—which means Shooting Star—who fought to keep their lands, the tribes of the woodlands are being pushed further west out onto the plains. Their lives will never be the same."

Sunday provided some relief from instruction of the domestic kind. They went to church at Westminster Abbey and stayed after the often long-winded services to let her view the ornate tomb of Queen Elizabeth, which made her proud that the duchess had renamed her Bess, and the famous Poet's Corner where Shakespeare was represented only by a plaque, as he'd chosen to be buried in his hometown of Stratford. Chaucer was there in name, if not perhaps body, but he lay elsewhere in the great cathedral. She'd read the *Canterbury Tales,* delighting in the bawdy ones as well as the more pious, but kept that to herself. Afterward, a hot Sunday dinner and later a cold evening meal in order to give the servants a half day off to worship, though she thought most of them did not. She was content with a quiet afternoon of strolling in one of the nearby shady squares or being taught the card games played by the ton: vingt et un, loo, and whist, in front of a small fire on inclement days. Always having had a retentive memory, she proved very good at these. If Justin were there, like Robin Adair, her entire day brightened.

Then the seasonal routine started again. The duchess began receiving guests one afternoon a week when Bess was requested to sit quietly after being introduced as Miss Barton, daughter of an academic who was visiting, and take note of the conversation. That squelched any interest of hers in the matchmaking game, though the duchess did mention her modest dowry once or twice. Wearing one of her three nice dresses, today the spring green gown whose remnants had lined the yellow gown, she sat and avoided the conversational arrows that crisscrossed the room dispensing poisonous gossip or obsequious compliments aimed at the duchess.

Justin managed to evade these gatherings, but he was not dismissed from going to Almack's on Wednesdays. Invitations to various balls, soirees, and musicales came in by the dozens. Most were declined politely as the duchess had no more children to marry off except the absent James, and the duke disliked most of the events unless he could vanish into the card room for most of the duration. She did not attend those crushes but went along to some musicales to enhance her knowledge. She was given the assignment of elbowing the duke if he dozed off and snored too loudly when the duchess got tired of doing so and went to sit elsewhere.

~ * ~

Three weeks after her arrival, while the time dwindled before Justin had to return to Oxford and his lecturing duties, an authoritative knock sounded on the door while the duchess held court in the drawing room on the day she was receiving. Not unusual, except for the vigor of the knock. A footman dashed to answer it while Busby stood nearby to announce the visitor. The unflappable butler appeared stunned but nevertheless managed to announce, "James Longleigh, Viscount Laughlin."

All eyes turned toward the man towering behind him. From her corner, Bess observed his form, not quite as massive as his father's build but threatening enough, his complexion dark from his heritage and darker still from an outdoors life, a small scar high on one cheek, and those gray eyes peering as if hunting for prey, both intimidating and thrilling all at once. Then, he walked past Busby to hold his arms out to the duchess. "Mama, as beautiful as ever."

The duchess deserted her throne-like chair and went to his embrace. "James, at last you are home."

"Actually, I was on my way when I received your letter in Gibraltar where I awaited proper transport for my latest treasures. I intended to take them to Bellevue Hall, but you reminded me that you and much of the family would be in

London for the Season. When I am rambling, I tend to forget about English social life." He bowed and said, "Ladies," acknowledging the other women gathered around the tea table, some with small cakes raised halfway to their lips.

Bess swore several of them had to blot their mouths to keep from drooling over the rarely seen but often talked about Bellevue heir. He appeared somewhat up in years, nearing forty, and a few strands of silver stood out in his black mane of hair, but nonetheless, a very handsome man with no softness about him. She startled when those gray eyes gazed upon her and shrank back in her chair even more when he said, "Who is this lovely flower, Mama?"

"Our guest, Miss Elizabeth Barton, a very well-educated daughter of an Oxford don who is seeking a position as a governess, and a friend of Justinian's from the university."

He crossed the room to bow over her shaking hand. "A pleasure to meet you, Miss Barton. Justin has exceptional taste in women, I can see."

"Alas, because the dons cannot marry, they must remain only friends," the duchess said in a dramatic way not usual for her.

"Where is my baby brother if not by her side?"

"Your father felt he'd gone soft at the university. I believe today it is boxing at Gentleman Jackson's."

"The last time I saw Justin, he was reedy and not yet filled out, but I have heard he is quick on his feet and likely to see openings others don't. Papa won't be too hard on him, I am sure."

Why she felt she had to defend Justin she did not know, but Bess spoke up. "There is a story that Justin fought off five upperclassmen who sought to dunk him in the Mercury fountain, and he went on to defend others weaker than himself."

A smile, startling white against his dark visage, spread across his face, worldly wise rather than rakish but every bit as beguiling. "I see my brother has an admirer in you. Papa was so proud of that action he wrote to me about it as a sign that Justin followed in his footsteps protecting others."

She could not stop herself. "He also saved my life when my skirts caught fire." She omitted that he'd dumped her in another Oxford fountain.

"In the orient that might mean he is now responsible for your life."

"He appears to believe that, because here I am, but he should not feel that way."

"Sadly, I spent most of my time rescuing my sisters before I left for the continent."

"I must have read that somewhere." She put her hand to her lips as if concealing a secret but as she had not mentioned C.C. Leigh, took it away again.

"Been reading in the family library, Miss Barton?"

"Reading is my chief pleasure."

"Then we shall have much to discuss later. Mama, I keep you from your guests. I shall need a safe, dry room for the mummy case, its occupant, and other articles I have brought from Egypt. A guest bedroom, perhaps?"

As the duchess pondered this odd request, Bess could feel the arrows of the ton sailing her way. Who was she to gain the attention of the most eligible and elusive bachelor in all of England when they had superior daughters, filled to their bonnet brims with accomplishments, to marry off?

"Her?" "Not a drop of noble blood." "Pretty but a very ordinary young lady." All true. However, neither Lady Flora nor the viscount took any note of it as they settled on a chamber with a proper Egyptian theme where the mummy should rest comfortably.

"Very well, then. I sent the cart around back and will have the stable hands help me bring it in." James turned toward their audience, bowed again, and said, "Wishing you a pleasant day, ladies." With that, he left their presence, taking much of the air in the room with him gauging by the sighs that followed.

Eleven

Why did James have to return now? Justin had so little time to spend with Bess as it were, and still did not have her safely settled in a good household free of lecherous husbands and sons and filled with lovely, well-behaved children. None of the forays to Almack's amounted to anything but a waste of time. Those of his mother's friends who were mildly interested and came to observe Bess when the duchess was receiving declared her too young and too attractive to set a good example for their granddaughters. Not that he wanted to deny his mother the pleasure she took in her eldest son's rare visits, but when James arrived, all attention focused on him. He feared her interest would stray from Bess and her predicament.

He'd spent much of the day feinting off low blows, ducking right jabs, and landing a few of his own in endless matches with sparring partners where no one came to much harm, but he would be sore tomorrow. Grateful now that they'd washed at the gymnasium as James held him in a manly embrace and said,

"Baby brother, all grown up. But perhaps I should call you Professor Longleigh now."

His brother smelled of sea air and foreign places rather than ordinary soap and water, earthy patchouli from the Near East rather than the sandalwood most of the Longleigh men favored. Justin could not help but see Bess watching their reunion with interest. Though they owned the same height, she'd easily notice his shoulders were several inches not as broad, his arms less muscular. How much time had his brother to influence her while his father had insisted on wasting a couple of hours at his club reading newspapers and sipping coffee? James drew glances wherever he went, partly because of his strong physical presence and more so the knowledge that this man might be the next Duke of Bellevue, which he would never be.

"I'd prefer if you simply dropped the baby part. Good to have you home again for whatever reason, brother." Ordinarily, he'd mean that. He delighted in James' tales of foreign places and adventures as much as anyone.

"I came with a special guest exactly like you." James shifted his glance to Bess, who pinked up a little.

Please let it be a foreign woman he'd brought home to marry or had already wed.

"Come upstairs all of you and I will make an introduction."

By all of you, he encompassed Thalia and her husband, Godric, Earl of Danelagh, imposing and pale, Iris with her Lord Valls, and one of his twin sisters, hard to tell which as they traded off coming for the Season, both claiming to be the Marchioness of Blackwater. As their husbands were identical twins, even that couldn't be used to differentiate them. One of them stood behind either Clio or Callie, tall, auburn-haired, and silent. Most of the year, the twins kept to their castle on the edge of the sea, churning out novels based on James, in their turret writing lair. He supposed they'd have new material now. Joshua had been summoned from his practice and stood by Kate, giving off an air of propriety rather than derring-do.

"We should wait until Pandora is finished with her Abolitionist meeting. She won't want to miss this. Her husband is on his way from the shipyard," the duchess suggested. "Let me call for more tea and sandwiches to tide us over. With so many added, dinner will be late this evening."

Yes, his strident sister, Pandora, had married a commoner and an American at that. He'd given up his single slave and his inheritance for her, but now practiced naval law and was deeply embedded in building a ship for trade financed by the duke. The man could sail a sloop single-handed and, to his father's approval, was able with a sword and other weapons. He earned his keep, did Daniel Clary of the sea-green eyes and sandy hair so unlike the Longleighs. He called Pandora his Raven or by her Shawnee name of Black Wing, which she adored.

His mother must have been busy sending out footmen all over the city to gather them so quickly. He suspected she'd already sent letters to Phemie and her laird in Scotland and Jason, wedded to Daniel's heiress sister in the American state of Georgia with the news of James' return. So occupied, the duchess hadn't thought to summon them from the club as he and his father would be home sooner or later. He should have known when they found the mews crammed with carriages and riding horses as if his mother were hosting a party. How fast his unusually long stay with his parents had fallen into second place.

Swiftly, the tea table was reset and bedecked with sandwiches, slices of cake and plates of biscuits on a larger scale than that provided for ladies, since so many men were present. Extra chairs appeared without being called for, Busby at work. He managed to claim one closest to Bess, who sat on the settee with James in the middle and his mother on the other side. Oh, how her blue eyes glimmered with excitement and her hands trembled as James offered her the plate holding the seed cake. He'd already infected her with his charm.

By the time Pandora arrived, her husband coming before her, great inroads had been made into the food and both of his nephews had escaped the nursery to beg to stay and partake of their tea in the drawing room where treats abounded on the table, rather than have their usual bread and butter upstairs. They'd been allowed and sat cross-legged on the floor with napkins draped over their knees and a careful selection of foods—two sandwiches and two biscuits each chosen by their mother. Their cups of milk sat on the table's edge threatening to spill at any moment.

"So sorry, the meeting ran late. We are making such good progress that I believe we shall see emancipation in our lifetime. Papa, Valls, Danelagh, I urge you to take your seats in the House of Lords and support the cause." Her dark eyes gleamed with the furor of the fanatic. As ever, she wore her sleek, black hair simply and her gown uncorseted, but still a handsome woman to be sure, despite having given birth twice, a son and a daughter she already trained in women's equity.

"Allow me a cup of tea and a bite to eat, then on to see James' latest treasures."

She didn't stand for any lady-like hesitance but poured her own cup and filled a plate with all she wanted. She finished with alacrity rather than nibble. Justin thought he detected Bess watching her with admiration as he did, too. He'd shared the nursery with her and gentle Phemie, listening in on their lessons and absorbing the knowledge. Out of six sisters, she was perhaps his favorite.

All finished, they processed up the staircase to the Egyptian room where a brilliantly painted mummy case rested on the bed with a turquoise spread and gold-tasseled pillows. Hand-painted hieroglyphs formed a frieze at the tops of the walls. Various jars and artifacts cluttered the dresser, a dressing table with an uraeus diadem topped by a serpent framing the mirror, plus windowsills and floor space between the bed and night tables.

"A shame I couldn't bring the sarcophagus as well, but far too heavy. I believe this specimen to be a priest of Ptah, from his proximity to the temple near Memphis where I found him. A man of high status, though not a pharaoh. We also discovered a mummy of a sacred Apis bull, but again too unwieldy to bring home. While many mummies are for sale in Egypt, I prefer to find my own in an undisturbed site. There are fakes, and so many have been ravaged and ground up for medicines. At least, I have spared him that indignity. I wish I could give him a name, but alas, hieroglyphs have not yet been deciphered. Now that we've liberated the Rosetta Stone from the French, I believe translation will go faster. The British Museum has sent plaster casts of it to various scholars."

Justin felt moved to interrupt this long-winded lecture. "Yes, Oxford has received a copy, but we can see the original right here in London. Would you like to go there, Bess?"

"Oh, yes."

James reclaimed the attention. "I am corresponding with two scholars, Thomas Young and a Frenchman named Champollion and believe they are close to deciphering the symbols. I only wish I had their knowledge of ancient Greek and could participate, but must wait on the experts. Now, I have opened the case just once before and will now give you a quick glance. My plan is to have an unrolling for some scientific organization here in London in the near future."

Making a show of it, he slowly raised the lid and revealed the figure wrapped in bandages but topped by a thin gold mask with features similar to the effigy on the case. Rather than the smell of decay, an aromatic scent lifted from the coffin. The women who were allowed in front vowed that it smelled similar to some expensive perfumes.

"The corpse was thoroughly dried in the mummification process and fragrant herbs added, not disgusting at all," James assured them.

Perhaps that was James' mystery scent—mummies. Justin wondered if Bess would find that revolting or intriguing. She'd put her head very close to the case and inhaled deeply as James lectured.

Willy and Richie had wormed their way closer. "Is that really a dead person?"

"Yes, dead for a thousand years and still well preserved. Nothing to fear."

"Did he play with dollies?" Richie asked, holding out a small figure in painted garments grasped in his hand.

"That is a ushabti intended to serve this man in the afterlife, servants for the dead. Now put it back carefully where you found it."

Rather in awe of this uncle, Richie obeyed, but immediately reached out a hand for one of the colorful containers topped by a falcon head.

"No, no, Willy, Richie, whichever you are. Do not touch the canopic jars. They contain the internal organs of the mummy: the liver, lungs, stomach, and intestines which are also embalmed."

Kate muttered, "I hope this doesn't give them nightmares. Bess, would you take the boys upstairs and keep them occupied until their dinner? As for myself, it is very close in here with so many people, and I feel a bit ill. I will rest for a while." She made her way from the room.

Justin, who had been standing directly behind Bess, turned sideways to allow her to go with the two children in hand. She'd already begun a lesson. "What letter do you think mummy begins with. Mmm," she said, giving them a hint.

"M," shouted Willy.

"Yes, not just one but three. Let's go write that down." They went with her so eagerly that Justin wanted to tag along and watch her teach.

"She is so good with the boys, but I know she'd rather be here learning more. Bess is very inquisitive," the duchess remarked.

"Then let's not disappoint her. We'll save more lectures for later. I've hardly had time to wash off the travel dust," James answered. He carefully closed the lid and left for his chamber.

"True enough," said his father. "Why don't all of you amuse yourselves until dinner. I wouldn't be averse to a game of whist if we can put together a table. Read in the library, stroll in the garden, whatever you like. When is dinner, my love?"

"Eight at the earliest, in the dining room. We'll sound the gong. So wonderful to have so many of my children and their spouses gathered around, and it is not even Christmas," the duchess replied. "I for one might lie down."

The duke rapidly lost his interest in whist. "I will join you. Make yourselves at home. No need to dress for dinner, but do not be tardy." He offered his arm to Lady Flora and led her to their bedchamber.

Joshua deemed it necessary to take over as host. "Anyone for whist, playing for points, not money?"

"What is the fun of that?" the marchioness complained.

Justin laughed. "Ha, you've given yourself away, Clio, Callie would not object to playing for points. Then this must be your husband, Tristan, and not Gareth, the true marquess."

"That and the ruby jewelry she insists upon wearing as red is her color," Pandora remarked.

"Please do not reveal our secret. I so love to keep the ton guessing."

"Not I. I loathe the Season and such frivolous wastes of time when they could be working for good causes with all their wealth. I believe I shall go to the library to read the latest tracts on slavery I've brought along. Cards are just another unprofitable way to fritter away the hours." Pandora swept out of the mummy's chamber.

"I'll go with her and write a report reviewing the progress on the ship for the duke." Daniel followed his wife.

"Justin, if you will partner with me, we can play Clio and Tristan," Joshua proposed. "What about Iris and Luke, Thalia and Godric?"

"I think we shall go sketch in the garden while we still have some light left. Don't worry about us." Off they went as if they were setting out for America again. Thalia merely said she and her husband needed some exercise.

Joshua led the way back to the drawing room and called for a deck of cards and a table to be set up. Justin endured several hours doing yet another thing he excelled at but did not enjoy. His mind calculated the odds, but his heart yearned toward the nursery and Bess.

~ * ~

The duchess might as well have been hosting a dinner party, considering all the people gathered around the vast dining room table. The chandeliers above with their crystal drops glittered and silver candelabra spaced out among small floral arrangements added more light. James had cleaned up well, freshly shaven, thick black hair swept back from his forehead and tucked behind his ears where it fell below his collar. Although not formally dressed, he'd changed into fresh clothes and exuded that strange scent even more strongly. He looked every inch the hero of the C.C. Leigh books—and was seated right next to Bess. Justin fumed farther down the table and beside Clio, who still pouted about losing to him at cards, though she hadn't lost a penny.

His mother sat to his father's right as always, freshly coifed and dressed, but he suspected she hadn't been sleeping. As he'd gone to wash before dinner, he's heard lots of bed sport noises in unassigned bed chambers, his being at the far end of hall from Bess. Iris and Valls, Thalia and Godric? Used as he was to such activities among the Longleighs, all of whom had married for love, they grated on his nerves. Why, he couldn't say.

The duchess appeared to be facilitating a conversation between James and Bess. Drat, he was too far away to hear what was being said. Across the table, Tristan said little since he bore the blame for the defeat at whist. He liked the man, but Tris was better at physical play than at games of the mind, and he feared Clio was often too hard on him. She seemed to think he was responsible for her bearing twin girls rather than twin boys like Callie, though the common opinion always blamed the sex of a child on the mother.

On his other side sat Kate, looking better, hair newly styled after sleeping upon it, but eating lightly of the soup and bread and accepting small portions of all else. He had a fondness for Kate and hoped she suffered from no long-term illness. Joshua headed up his end of the table and the duke the other, both carving whatever was set before them, whether it be chicken, duck, or pheasant to be passed around. Josh did coax his wife to eat more. As the whole family knew, he'd almost lost her once and fretted about losing her again.

Thalia and Godric, Pandora and Daniel, Iris and Luke filled out the center of the table and often blocked his view of Bess, who appeared entranced by James' every word. How could long rows of formulae and simple examples of Newton's laws compete with world travel and mummy unrollings? At last, the pudding came to the table, a light lemon mousse served with the usual cheese and nuts, which proved Chef Pepin had taken control of the kitchen as Cook usually served heavier fare. He noted Kate ate all of hers, a good sign. He tried to hurry things along by scraping up his portion as if starving after that exceeding long meal. Still, his father insisted on port with the men while the women floated off to the drawing room for tea and whatever women discussed in private.

When they finally mingled again, Bess sat at the piano working her way through a book of music entitled *Five Easy Pieces* as Thalia turned the pages for her and gave a prompt now and then. The rest of the women possessed coy expressions as if they'd been exchanging secrets. Before he could say a word to compliment Bess on her progress, James spoke up as he made his way to the instrument.

"The way you play is utterly charming, Miss Barton."

"You should say not bad for a beginner, Lord Laughlin," she countered. Good for her. She knew flattery when she heard it.

"Better than I could do, but as we are all family here, please address me as James, if I may call you Bess."

"Certainly, James. I would rather hear more about your experiences. I spent a night in your bedchamber before you arrived and was intrigued by all it contained. I mean the housekeeper put me in the wrong place. I am in the blue room next to yours now, but it is not as interesting."

"Really? Let us remedy that. Come upstairs, and I will give you a tour of my belongings."

Why wasn't his mother stepping in to stop such a bold advance? He'd been placed far from Bess's room for propriety, he supposed, but James could get away with this. Was Mama plotting to trap his brother into a match? It wasn't usually her way. She often said love should progress naturally without traps being set for unwary men, though he thought she might have ensnared Danelagh for Thalia. No one talked about that.

Justin found his voice. "I'll accompany you. Anyone else?"

"We've heard it all before," said Pandora. "But you should go along."

"Bring a candle, brother. Light our way."

Only the three of them mounted the stairs and approached James' bedchamber. His brother threw open the door and allowed Bess to enter first into the darkness. He hastened to light candles set in reflecting sconces along the wall. James took a small lump of something from a box on the mantle and placed it into one of the incense burners. He borrowed the candle to set it alight. A pleasant but heavy aroma filled the room. So that was his secret scent.

"I find frankincense relaxing before bedtime, which is fast approaching."

"Then we had better get on with the tour," Justin said with impatience.

Bess's eyes flicked toward the dragon bed, but she asked, "If we are keeping you from your rest, please tell us about the screen first."

"A four panel Coromandel screen, Ming dynasty, of carved rosewood lacquered over thirty times. Each figure is brought to life by being painted in rich colors. We see not only the progress of pilgrims to the top of a mountain but all that goes on along their way, a whole microcosm of ancient Chinese life. Splendid, isn't it?"

"My, yes," she breathed, her eyes on James.

"I can see you are interested in the bed but are too modest to say so. It is my own design. The dragon is a symbol of good luck, health, strength, and masculinity. What more could a man ask for?"

"Humility," Justin suggested.

His brother slapped him on the back. "I leave that to you. You must have humility when no one understands what you are talking about."

Bess to the rescue. "He is excellent at explaining abstract concepts to his students. I've sat in on his classes and learned so much."

"Have you, now? I do like a woman with intellect who is not afraid to show it."

Now, the duchess chose to arrive and intervene. "Come downstairs. Your sisters are leaving. Bid them goodbye."

"Of course. Would you allow me to place the incense in your chamber, Bess, for sweet dreams? I can light another."

"I would adore that."

That task accomplished, they started out for the foyer, where the many Longleigh women were retrieving their wraps and bonnets. "Any plans for tomorrow?" James asked.

"An early two-hour ride in the park, then practice of swordsmanship in the afternoon," the duke declared. "Join us, James."

"Do not wear Justin out. Tomorrow evening is an Almack's night," the duchess said.

"Sorry. I plan to take Bess to British Museum in the afternoon and defer to James in going to Almack's. I am of little interest there, and he will be the center of attention."

His brother laughed heartily. "Exactly. You would have to take me there in shackles, and even then I'd escape through a window. I would welcome a ride, however. In the afternoon, I must seek a new resting place for the mummy and the other treasures. After, I might join Justin and Bess at the museum."

Who had invited him? He'd make sure they left early before James could arrive and show off his knowledge at every display.

Twelve

James had gone off on horseback to find storage for the mummy, as if he hadn't already spent two hours riding the rougher sections of Hyde Park far from Rotten Row where the suitors showed off their fine mounts and prowess, and proud mamas displayed their marriageable daughters decked out to attract attention. Justin had immediately ordered the small carriage to be brought around for the excursion to the British Museum located in Montagu House after eating a cold collation.

While he had been contending with James and the contrary Black Lightning, Bess had gravitated to the nursery, where she continued to school the boys in reading and writing and simple maths. They had also produced enthusiastic, rather hard to decipher drawings of the mummy but had printed out the word beneath their strange figures covered in crisscross lines to be sure viewers would know. When she came down to take her own meal, she suggested Willy and Richie might profit from seeing the Rosetta Stone as well.

Kate, appearing wan again, had laughed. "Oh my, no. The stone is unprotected. They'd have their sticky hands all over it before the guardians could stop them. I am sure the Elgin Marbles, which you must see, would meet the same fate. Some of them even lay upon the floor, and my sons are sure to point out all the naked figures loud and clear. But you should have a chaperone. It will not do to have some of the duchess's acquaintances see you there with Justin alone. Your reputation would be damaged. Only give me some time to rest a bit before going."

"Nonsense. You need your rest. I have no commitments today, only Almack's tonight. I shall go with them. If I see anyone I know, I can tout Bess's interest in ancient history," Lady Flora offered as she sliced into a piece of cold glazed ham accompanied by pickled beet root and a hardboiled egg half cut to resemble a flower. Kate had taken only the eggs and bread again while the duke created large sandwiches from all that was offered. He'd done the same on a smaller scale, eager to be gone. Now, he would have to wait for Mama to finish and primp before leaving. James might catch up with them.

But they made their escape in less time than he'd thought and soon stood in front of the famed stone displayed in a metal cradle especially made for it. The massive, dark stone lay at an angle as if being offered for reading. Its top, part of a larger stele, had broken off and been lost. Bess leaned near to it.

"I can see how people are tempted to touch it. Here are the hieroglyphs, and I recognize the Greek lettering, but what is the third language?"

"It's called demotic script and is not well understood either," Justin answered, reading from an explanation to the side of the stone.

They stood back to allow two gentlemen to peer at the rock. He recognized them as friends of the duke, a father and son pair from the club, and had already been introduced to them. When they finished their perusal, they begged for an introduction to his charming companion. The duchess intervened with the usual information, Miss Elizabeth Barton, daughter of an Oxford don, and staying with the Longleighs while seeking employment as a governess. Their polite interest immediately changed to one much more lascivious. Why, the first was his father's age and the other close to that of James, but not as in good condition. He had a paunch and his father the red nose of a tippler. "We might have a place for her in our household," said the younger.

"Then do have your wife contact me with the understanding that she is under the protection of the Duke of Bellevue." His mother stared them down with her best cold-eyed gray glare.

"Yes, understood, Lady Flora. Let's be off to see the other curiosities, son."

"I do pity that man's wife. He is a despoiler of young women, and her father-in-law lives with them. She can barely keep a staff they are so free with their hands. Off to see the Elgin Marbles, as they are going the other way."

The famed marbles were housed in their own room, some of friezes mounted on the walls and larger pieces of statuary sitting on pedestals. One very fine head of a horse lay on the floor. Nudes, especially of men, did abound, many of them missing legs and arms but not their private parts. Bess appeared completely unembarrassed. Instead, she gazed upon the dynamic scenes of warriors on horseback fighting centaurs and other enemies. She loved studying each object with appreciation.

"I know some say Lord Elgin stole the Parthenon marbles from Greece, but I am so glad they are here for me to see."

"Oh, no. Eglin paid the Turks seventy-four thousand pounds for these pieces. The temples had already been destroyed by earthquakes and an explosion. Now war threatens them again. Elgin saved them. I am sure he would have kept them for himself, but a nasty divorce left him short of funds. To give him credit, he sold all of this to the British government for far less than he could have gotten elsewhere. Now everyone can enjoy them."

Justin glanced over his shoulder, expecting James to overtake them at any moment and regale Bess with tales of his visits to Greece. So intent on his studies, he had never left England, and she knew Oxford as well as he did.

"If you have seen your fill, might I suggest we move along to view the treasures acquired during Captain Cook's voyages."

After viewing a collection of carved images, fishhooks, war clubs, and a fine cloak made of feathers, he steered them toward the many primitive wooden instruments brought from Africa and the museum's own resident mummies. Still no sign of James, but they did find him at home having tea with the duke and Kate, fuming over his offer of a mummy unrolling being snubbed by the Royal College of Surgeons because he was neither a member nor a surgeon. Besides which, Thomas Pettigrew had done this the year before, and they felt no need to repeat it.

"Kept me waiting for quite a while as well. Evidently, I am an adventurer, not a man of science." James stirred cream into his tea almost violently.

James would agree with that but noticed Bess's sympathetic expression and held back his opinion. His mother spoke consoling words. "I am sure you will find another more appreciative venue."

"I for one would love to see you unwrap a mummy," Bess declared as she took a seat and accepted a cup of tea poured by Kate. "What would you expect to find?"

"Jewelry, amulets, perhaps a hint as to how the subject died from examination of the desiccated body."

"Please," Kate said, pressing her fingers to her lips. "No more talk of bodies, desiccated or otherwise."

"I've never known you to be so squeamish, Kate," James said as he heaped small sandwiches on a plate.

"Enough of mummies," the duchess declared. She turned the conversation toward what they had seen at the museum, encouraging Bess to give her opinions freely. James rolled out his many anecdotes about Greece and Egypt, stealing all of her attention. She had stars in her eyes as she gazed on his brother. Justin crumbled a biscuit on his plate in frustration.

"It would be better to eat that," his mother prompted. "We do have Almack's tonight and you know how poor the refreshments tend to be."

"I cannot see any sense in going anymore. The young ladies know I am ineligible to marry, and none of them wants to speak about hiring governesses. That is their mothers' problem, and you have had no success with them either."

"We do this for Bess. Make the sacrifice," his mother reminded him.

Put that way, he knew he'd don his formal clothes and dance with the wallflowers, all the while envisioning James turning the pages of Bess's music as he leaned close to her or lauding her skill at cards with Bess as his chosen partner in a friendly family game. Another biscuit crumbled onto his plate.

Thirteen

Justinian's time was running out. Shortly, he'd have to leave for Oxford to begin Trinity term with little chance of having any time to return to London until it ended in June. James showed no sign of departing, odd for him, as he usually grew restless after a month in the city. For him, a scalding desert or moldering ruins held more interest. Now, his brother spoke of staying until the Season ended in early August and taking his mummy to Bellevue Hall for safekeeping. Months and months of time for James to spend time with Bess.

Of course, he did note that Bess usually stayed in the nursery while his mother went about her visits or entertained. She taught the boys things they delighted in, such as making a catapult using a lever that could launch balls of paper across the room. The fun came after their lessons of learning their spelling words and improving their handwriting skills. She'd even translated those words into French while they were at it and taught them short phrases, which seemed to make the grind more interesting. Even she had trouble making mathematics exciting, but he believed eventually she could.

Just yesterday, he had caught James and Bess exiting the mummy's bedroom where the priest of Ptah still lay in state. The door was open, but surely they should not be in there alone as James impressed her with his Egyptian lore. He had to act and act soon.

First, he would make himself clear to his eldest brother. They were of a height, but James would always excel his breadth of shoulders and a striking visage despite their both having gray eyes. Still, thanks to his father, his own physical condition had peaked to perfection after so much riding, boxing, and fencing. He believed he might be able to beat James at fisticuffs if he ducked and struck fast, always his best strategy. He doubted it would come to that or a duel between brothers, once he made his thoughts clear in a rational manner.

Two nights before his departure, with his mother off at some fete to which she'd dragged his father and James had wiggled out of attending, they'd passed a quiet evening listening to music played by Kate and the steadily improving Bess and followed by a friendly game of whist, in which he'd secured Bess as his partner and beaten Joshua and James rather badly. Kate had gone to bed earlier claiming fatigue. When the time came for slumber, James beat him to a candle and an offer to show Bess to her chamber, the one right next to his. Justin trailed behind them, not peeling off to the left of the stairwell where he stayed. He noted the warm gaze Bess bestowed for this simple service as she closed the bedroom door—and all rationality fled.

Before James could enter his own abode, he spun his brother around and seized him by the lapels. Staring with serious gray eyes into a startled pair of the same, he declared, "Do not toy with Bess. Either offer for her or be on your way."

The candle James held wobbled in its holder. "No need to set the house afire over a lovely lass with an intriguing mind. I have no designs on her in any way, but have enjoyed the freshness of her company. Anything else is merely harmless flirting."

Justin shook his brother again. "She is an innocent with no idea of how to flirt. You will break her heart. Stop at once."

"And if I don't, what will you do about it?"

"I'll challenge you to a duel."

James threw his head back so hard it hit the door as he broke into laughter. "You might be in fine condition after all of Papa's efforts, but I doubt you've handled a pistol in years, while I have had occasion to do so on a regular basis. I might be a crack shot but I could not promise only to wound you, and Mama would kill me herself if I hurt a hair on her baby's head."

"Don't call me a baby. We could use swords or our fists to settle this." Why did his brother have to be so, so—everything— handsome, dashing, and in this case, logical. A hand clamped on his shoulder. Joshua had come up the stairs last with his own candle in hand and intervened.

"Here, here. What's this? You will awaken Kate, and in her delicate condition, she needs her rest."

Justin dropped his clutch on his brother's lapels and turned. "Oh, so sorry. I didn't realize."

"Naturally, because neither of you have married or have plans to do so. You've had no occasion to be around women in the family way. They require respite, bland foods, and some coddling. Bess has been wonderful in keeping the boys occupied during these early months. Kate will rebound soon as the babe is due in October and these early symptoms will pass, but until then, do not add any burden to her days by squabbling in the hallway like two adolescents. There will be no duels of any kind. Justin, you will return to Oxford the day after tomorrow and forget all this. Perhaps you might wish to remove the mummy from our house sooner rather than later, James, and take it north to Bellevue Hall at this time. Its gruesome presence might affect the child-to-be. We will continue to care for Bess until she can be settled somewhere." He pronounced all of this in his most judicial voice, giving a hint that he would make a fine judge someday.

"I greatly admire Kate and am relieved to find she is not seriously ill," James claimed.

Justin could only nod in agreement. This settled nothing in his mind, but as James had just been invited to leave Bellevue House, too, he did feel a bit easier about Bess's safety from his wiles.

"Now both of you to bed. If I hear anyone moving about tonight, it might be me who proposes a duel."

Chastened by their middle brother, both did as he directed. None of them took note of the sliver of a crack in Bess's door that closed quietly afterward.

Justin slept restlessly until near dawn when the duke and duchess returned from the soiree and sought their own chamber. The perfect solution occurred to him. However, he would not have the chance to announce his decision with his parents sleeping in late, and Bess probably spending time in the nursery again. A farewell family dinner had been planned to see him off with Iris and Luke, Pandora and Daniel, Thalia and Rick, Clio and Tristan summoned to attend. He would make his big announcement in front of all of them after the meal and in the drawing room when the men and women reunited. Why had he not reached this obvious conclusion sooner?

Fourteen

Daylight extended at this time of year, keeping people active later and allowing them to linger in the park. As if to irk Justin, James had taken Bess out in the small carriage to parade her up and down Rotten Row in order, he said, to increase her knowledge of British society. Justin had immediately saddled up and followed them, forcing him to tip his hat to the many ladies he'd danced with at Almack's but he did not dismount to chat with any of them.

Pulling alongside the carriage, he watched James whisper in Bess's lovely, shell-like ears as he pointed out this and that and made wry comments, some of which made her blush. Black Lightning put on a good show, tossing his head and prancing, which drew Bess's attention and earned him some notice before James commanded her attention again, this time drawing her attention to some ridiculously dressed dandies with their waists so nipped in they had to be wearing corsets. She laughed and told him she disliked corsets herself. James lauded her good sense. He wished that laugh had been earned by him. James had not heeded his warning at all. His only comfort came in knowing that his alluring brother would be leaving shortly, too, yet still he led her on.

Upon their return, the coach stopped at the front entrance to let Bess and James down while Justin rode his horse to the stable and entered by the rear door, giving off as much steam as his mount after the ride. He should change his clothes and join the gathering for tea, but instead, sought out his father's handy stash of weapons: knives, pistols, sabers, sword canes, and a fine set of epees for fencing. The duke could possibly arm his entire family, including the women, in minutes if Bellevue House should come under attack, unlikely as that would be. He chose the epees and set the case on a hall table before opening the drawing room door to summon James away from his place beside Bess on the settee.

"A word, brother."

James excused himself to the duchess and the gathering of his sisters who had come to visit both of them before their departures, and with one brow cocked in inquiry went to see what Justin wanted. With the door safely closed, Justin hissed, "Now, in the mews. We are going to settle this disagreement between us while Joshua is not around to stop us, and Kate cannot see." He jerked his head toward the sword case.

James held up his hands. "I have no quarrel with you. As I told you, I have no intentions toward Bess, but merely enjoy her company and like widening her knowledge."

"Yet you flirted with her in the carriage and exposed her to the view of all society who will now wonder if she is your mistress or your intended."

"I am sure they thought neither, not with you breathing down our necks the whole time."

"Now, in the mews." He picked up the case, and with a shrug, James followed him.

Once in the lane behind the house, James called to one of the stable boys to assist him out of his jacket and charged him with keeping it clean while they fenced. The lad, all eyes and open mouth at having been given such a duty, nodded and stepped back. Justin piled the sword case on top of the coat and struggled out of his. He should have thought of it first. Draping his jacket over the boy's shoulder, he opened the case and allowed his brother to choose a sword.

James whipped it through the air. "Papa's weapons are always in good order. You do know we cannot kill each other. A fight until first blood is drawn. Will that satisfy you?"

"If it will protect Bess from your further advances. She is not right for a man as sophisticated as you."

James rolled his eyes. "As I have said in so many words. Very well, *en garde*."

Both assumed the proper stance, one foot forward, the other at a ninety-degree angle, free arm kept behind the body and sword arm extended.

"*Allez!*," Justin shouted and went on the attack, hoping a fierce opening lunge might slip beneath his brother's guard and end this quickly. Instead, he drew a strong parry and a counterattack. He was forced back. Parry, reposte, parry, reposte. He soon realized that fencing on the smooth surface at Angelo's differed from fighting on uneven cobblestones that threw off the balance. James appeared unbothered by it, but did not seem serious about wounding him. He tried for a high shoulder strike and was repelled, but fought on in a fury—another mistake.

Forced backward another step, he felt his rear foot slip and went down. Quick as a viper, his brother struck, a quick swipe high on his cheekbone. He felt the sting and knew first blood had been drawn. He'd failed to defend Bess's honor, only made worse when he realized he'd slid in a pile of manure the stable hand had been sweeping up, probably deposited there by Black Lightning.

As he sat there panting, James accepted a rag from Peterson, who had gathered round with the other stable denizens to watch the match, wiped the blade of his sword clean, and replaced it in the still open box. He retrieved his jacket and accepted Peterson's aid in shrugging into it.

"Not a word of this to the duke and duchess or Lady Katherine and Lord Joshua. Do all of you hear?"

The audience of drivers, grooms, and stable hands nodded. "Yes, Lord Laughlin."

James loomed over him. "I'd offer you a hand up, Justinian, but it is resting in *merde*. I don't believe that mark will scar, but if it does, the ladies do find mine fascinating. Perhaps Bess will too. And once and for all, I have no designs on her." He left the scene as coolly as he'd come.

Peterson came to the rescue, using the same rag that had wiped the sword to raise him up. He surrendered the sword to the man to put back in the box, removed his coat from the boy's shoulder, and slung it over his own, using his cleaner hand. He tucked the sword box under his arm and whispered, "Not a word to anyone." Humiliated, he retreated to his bedchamber and called upon his father's valet to set him to rights, if that could ever be done again.

Fifteen

Had any dinner ever lasted longer? The ladies, joined by their spouses, filled the vast dining room table to capacity. Monsieur Pepin had sauced everything that could be sauced except the soup and the nuts. The month of April brought fresh greens and new peas, but the greens were served in a heavy dressing and the peas in a mint sauce. They worked through the fish course (sole), the game course (rabbit), both a good, rare beef roast with Cook's traditional Yorkshire pudding, a mutton roast with small new potatoes, other side dishes, and at last the jellies and puddings, the cheeses, and nuts. Because of the number of to be served, the meal lasted several hours. Then, port for the men and the usual male blather concerning sports and politics before they joined the ladies in the drawing room, interrupting a discussion of whether Kate would carry high or low, indicating a boy or a girl, which terminated quickly on their entry.

Having missed tea to repair himself, Justin did have an appetite, but Bess sitting opposite him and beside James distracted him from his food. She'd appeared for the first time wearing one of the silk dinner dresses he'd purchased for her. Midnight blue in color, it made her skin seem even more like alabaster in contrast to the gown, and clung to her in a way that muslin did not. Clement must have styled her pale hair as it towered atop her head in a most attractive way. Pins topped with black pearls were dotted through it, borrowed no doubt from Kate. She'd filled the space between her neck and a décolleté he thought far too low for her age with the simple locket she so often wore. The tops of her small, round breasts presented a constant challenge to keep his eyes raised higher. James appeared to have no trouble with this, but leaned in to tell her amusing anecdotes throughout the meal. He'd earned that privilege by defeating him in the duel. He could do nothing but swallow his bile and wait for the meal to end.

His own appearance had caused a stir when he went downstairs to join the dinner procession. He'd rather they admired how well he wore his evening dress rather than all the exclamations over the scratch on his face. As his mother fussed over him and Bess looked on with concern, he swore that on the way back from the park, Black Lightning had taken him under a low hanging branch and caused the mark. James smirked but stayed silent. His father backed up his lie by saying that sounded exactly like the horse's known antics. He'd washed the wound and put to use the scented astringent he normally used on shaving cuts. No, most likely it would not scar, and remind him constantly of his defeat, but he would remember regardless.

Now the time had come for him to announce his solution to the problem of Bess before his father tried to organize a card game or one of the women asked her to continue playing the piano as she had been when the men entered.

"Ahem." He posed before the fireplace in what he hoped was an attention-getting manner. Just to be sure, he repeated the ahem.

"Are you ill, dear?" his mother asked. "Have you caught a chill? If so, you should postpone your return to Oxford."

"No, no, I am fine." All eyes were on him now, searching for traces of illness and wondering if it was contagious, especially Kate, who seemed alarmed.

"It's not that at all. I've deliberated long and hard about Bess's predicament and have arrived at a conclusion."

His mother steepled her hands as if in prayer. The other ladies adopted expressions of hopefulness, all except Pandora, who murmured, "At last."

"As you all know, Bess has been doing wonders tutoring William and Richard, but no family other than the Longleighs would hire such a young woman to be a tutor, only a governess, and expose her to the possibility of molestation by the men of the household. None of us wants that for her. So, I propose..."

Bess gasped and was echoed by several of the others.

"That Joshua and Kate hire her as a tutor, paying the same wages as a man would get and holding the same place of respect a male tutor would demand, staying in her current room and taking meals with the family rather than sleeping in the nursery with the boys. As the boys grow older and leave for boarding school, she might continue in residence to teach their expected child, giving her a permanent place in the household. There, what do you think? Perfect, right?"

James glanced toward the duchess and mouthed something that made no sense. "I am sorry, Mama. I did my best."

Pandora, who could rarely stay silent, said, "Not what I expected, but I laud your commitment to treating men and women with equity."

Clio sniffed. "Justin, you will not make a romantic hero for any of our books."

The person he really wanted to respond had lowered her eyes toward the piano keys where her hands lay still. After a moment, she mustered a pleasant expression and turned her gaze upon him.

"Of course, that is a brilliant solution, Justin. Now, I, too, can live a life of the intellect among people I have come to care for as my family. That is, if they want me as their tutor."

Kate spoke before her husband could open his mouth. "We certainly do want you as our tutor, don't we, darling?'

"I suppose so. Bess does seem to know how to engage the boys in their studies, which no one else has been able to do. She has been a great help to you in your current condition and will be in the future, I am sure. Justin seems to have set the terms, and we will discuss wages tomorrow. But tonight, we are seeing your brother off, and James right behind him. Let's continue to enjoy our time together as a family. Bess, some joyful music and perhaps some dancing, if we roll up the rugs."

"An excellent suggestion," the duke said as he squeezed his wife's small shoulders. "You cannot match them all, my dear, but this is still an occasion to celebrate. I will look after Bess as one of my own daughters regardless."

Ah, so his mother had been trying to match Bess and James and failed. He thanked God for that. What a life she would have led following him hither and yon into dangerous places or being left behind to twiddle her thumbs at his country estate. Not a life for one with an active and inquiring mind.

Satisfied he'd done his best, Justin asked, "Will someone else play so I might have one last dance with Bess before I leave?"

As the servants rolled the rugs and moved the furniture, Thalia, who actually enjoyed playing, took her seat at the piano. The duke and duchess led off a reel, and he and Bess followed close behind with all the married couples pairing off and James awaiting a turn.

Such a perfect solution, yet why wasn't he thrilled to be leaving tomorrow for his academic pursuits as usual after spending time with his family?

Sixteen

Clement removed the pearl hairpins rather roughly from her coiffure as Bess sat before the mirror in her now permanent blue room. She fumed as she worked.

"I will brush out your hair one last time. You'd best braid it tonight and prepare to put it in a bun tomorrow as you are no longer a guest but the family tutor. Nor will you have much use for silk gowns and pastel dresses in the nursery. Best dye the muslin ones more practical colors, gray or dark blue, if you are to work with little boys and ink. I shall fold the finery and put it in your trunk."

My, how fast news spread among the servants. She'd barely adjusted to the idea herself. As a tutor, she would outrank Clement, part of her peeve, to be sure. Tutors did not have maids to wait upon them, and frankly, she would not miss Clement's ministrations and hostility. Bess gazed in the mirror and did not see Clement tearing out her creation and combing through the snarls. She saw only what might have been, two different versions.

In the first, James offered for her, which would have caused both delight and fear in her heart. He'd spoken and flirted with her endlessly, laughed when she made frank but indelicate remarks such as the one about wearing corsets. The very idea of escaping the confines of Oxford and sailing off to exotic places with such a man enticed. However, he had never hinted at marriage nor touched her in any way inappropriate. She suspected he carried on in this way with many women and was practiced at it, way beyond her experience. How uncomfortable to be wed to a man who overawed one.

When Justin had uttered the word "proposal," her heart skipped a beat as it often did in the heroines of Clio and Callie's novels. Such things did happen when one was in love, she guessed. She had only the novels she'd been devouring to rely upon. When he'd gone on to spell out his perfectly sensible solution to her problem, her heart sank, a sure symptom of severe disappointment, but she'd gathered herself and given him thanks. In romantic fiction, men made sacrifices for the women they loved—giving up a title to run away with a gypsy lass or live among the Shawnee with an Indian wife, or in her family's case, ceasing to be a don in order to marry. That last had not turned out well, considering her mother's early death in childbirth and her father's swift return to academia. Evidently, Justin was not prepared to take that step because he did not care for her enough to do so.

She could have suffered worse fates than being a tutor to two little boys she enjoyed teaching, all the while residing with a loving, lecher-free family and able to pursue her intellectual longings in their library and bookstores around London. Possibly, she might travel with them to new places as well. She'd avoided being a governess or a companion to a sour and demanding elderly woman or marrying a man who found her six-hundred pounds tempting and being confined to running a household and bearing children.

As soon as Clement finished with her, she went to bed and slept fitfully because she intended to be up and dressed in her most becoming day gown to see Justin off to Oxford, her excuse being to give him a letter for her father that she'd composed earlier in the week and added a postscript to before Clement arrived to tend to her. It contained the news of her new position in the household, certain to cheer him since he'd be absolved to having to care for her in the future.

As soon as the spring sunshine peeped through a crack in the curtains, she arose and scrubbed her face into rosiness with cold water, since the maids had not come around with hot as yet and coiled her braid at her nape. In donning the pale blue dress that enhanced her eyes, she had a bit of trouble tying the sash in the back but succeeded at last. After chaffing her lips to make them redder, she hurried down the stairs clutching her letter. Let his last glimpse of her be one of her at her best.

Hasty as she was, the family already sat at breakfast, all of them nearly done eating but only casually dressed as if they hadn't given their maids and valets time to put on the finishing touches. Justin had resumed his dreary academic garb, no longer a gentleman but a scholar. On a chair beside him sat a huge hamper of provisions for his travels, enough for himself and Peterson, as he'd be taking the small carriage. So different from their trip to London.

He stood as she entered and said, "No need for you to arise so early, Bess, as we danced into the night last evening." More than once with her. "I'll will be gone within minutes."

One of the footmen grasped the hamper at this announcement. All of the family rose and prepared to see him off. She took her chance to hand over the letter. "If you please, would you deliver this to my father? I want him to know of my changed circumstances as quickly as possible."

He took her message, touching fingertips with her only slightly and yet yearning shot through her body. Clio and Callie were correct about that also—the briefest touch from one you loved could have that effect. She doubted he felt the same.

"Will you write to me as well, Bess? I do want to know how you progress, as I am somewhat responsible for your life."

Leave it to James to remark, "Entirely responsible for bringing her here. It was my delight to know Bess. Will you also write to me?"

"Of course, to both of you if I have the time and if my life will be of interest to either."

Except for exchanging murderous glances, both repeated their desire to hear from her. How nice. How meaningless.

The group followed Justin out to the front entry, and they stood on the steps in the chill early morning air as he mounted the coach steps, settled a portfolio of papers he meant to read on the seat, and took charge of the hamper. At the last second, Sarah arrived two paces behind Willy and Richie, still in their night dress. They waved their uncle off enthusiastically before their mother scooted them inside as the coach turned the corner.

"Back to the nursery before you catch your death. Have they had their breakfast, Sarah?"

"No, they escaped as I was setting it out."

Bess volunteered. "I will be happy to escort them back and resume their studies after they eat."

"You haven't eaten a bite yourself and will need nourishment to teach these two. Let Sarah take them. I will sit with you and have a second cup of tea. We'll discuss their lessons."

The others returned to their chambers to fully prepare for the day, James to shave his early morning scruff of beard that made him seem even more an adventurer. Bess enjoyed this small respite before taking on her duties full-time. Kate informed her that she would receive the same wages and time off as their last tutor and would be paid at the end of the month.

Good. She'd begun to take Clement's advice to heart and though she couldn't bear to dye her pretty frocks somber colors, she'd try to find a suitable dress or two she could buy on credit. The Longleighs could not be expected to clothe her after all they'd done already. After she ate her toast and eggs, forcing them down because she had no appetite, she resolved to return to the blue room and put on her old, sprigged muslin. It would have to do for now.

As she stood to leave, Kate waved her back to her seat. "Have another cup to fortify yourself for a day with my sons. Sarah probably only has them half-dressed by now. They are as wiggly as pups. I so hope this one is a daughter." Kate placed a hand on her belly, showing just the slightest curve at this stage.

"I should go help Sarah."

"No, that is her job. Yours is to teach. You hold their attention so well I am amazed. Still, you must be disappointed that Justin did not offer for you last evening. We all thought he might."

"I had no expectations and so suffered no disappointment," she lied.

"The duchess certainly did. She's been trying marry off her two unwed sons for years and thought you perfect for Justinian. By dragging him to Almack's, she allowed him to notice the contrast between those husband hunters and a sincere and intelligent young lady like you."

"Not to find me a position?"

"That, too, if all else failed."

"I am flattered she thought so well of me, but I am not noble."

"Pshaw! The duke's grandmother was an Italian opera singer and his mother a Shawnee Indian. Pandora married a commoner and an American at that. The Bellevues do as they please."

"I did not please Justin enough." She tried to keep a quaver from her voice and tears from her eyes.

"Nonsense, he is simply stubborn and has closed off his mind to marriage."

"He has a life he loves, a life of the mind, and in some ways, he has given me that as well. I can continue to learn as I teach and perhaps someday might retire on a pension as my aunt did and provide help to poor children without an education." She meant those words, she really did.

"Now that is truly noble. If I should have a daughter, I do hope you will stay on and teach her the same as you do my lads."

"I would be glad to do that. Now, really, I must change my dress and go forth to challenge young minds."

Kate laughed. "God speed with that!"

She rushed away to change and climb the stairs to where her students waited fully clothed and seated at a table with their hands on either side of their slates and primers. She'd never seen them so still.

"How to we greet your tutor?" Sarah prompted.

In unison, they replied, "Good morning, Miss Barton" with no joy in their voices.

"Why the sad faces?" she asked.

"Because now you will hit our hands with a ruler if we don't know our lessons," Willy stated.

She countered this with, "I shall do no such thing. If you don't know a lesson, we will repeat it until you do. No outdoor time until it is learned."

Richie had other concerns. "Will you no longer read to us stories with evil queens and brave knights and horrid witches that eat little children?"

"If lessons are learned quickly, we will have time for stories. Any other questions?"

"Say, if one of us brought a little frog inside for a visit, would you take a cane to us?"

"No, we would study it and learn about amphibians, then return it to its pond."

"Amphi..." Willy started to say as he wrapped his tongue around a new word,

Sarah interrupted, "Even if they put that horrid thing in someone's bed?"

"That will not happen again," Bess asserted with a level gaze directed at her students. "Will it?"

"No, Miss Barton," they chorused.

"Good. Let's open our books to the page where we left off. Willy, read the first five words of the spelling list and Richie the next five aloud. Remember the sounds of each letter in the alphabet, if you find yourself stuck."

That chore competed , she pronounced the French equivalents she'd written in their books and had them repeat after her. Primers closed, she asked them to print each word on their slates. If one was missed, she required them to write it five times over, ten if missed again. They went back to their books to read the short paragraph that contained all the words.

"Very good. Now on to our sums."

She suppressed any mirth at their joint groans and led them in repeating one plus one is two, one plus two is three, and so on until they'd run through all the basic tables. Their former tutors must have drilled them well as they had no trouble with these. She picked up a handful of toy soldiers and lined them up. "We have ten soldiers ready to do battle. Three are killed." She knocked them over. "How many are left?"

They both replied seven though she caught Richie counting on his fingers. "None of that. You will soon run out of fingers and toes, of which you have only twenty. You must memorize your tables as you won't always have soldiers in front of you." They returned to the tables by rote.

"That's a good morning's work. Story time." She picked up her copy of *Kinder und Hausmarchen* by the Brothers Grimm, which she'd joyfully translated on rainy days in Oxford when she could not get out to the lectures. "Once upon a time," she began to their rapt attention, Sarah's as well. Noting this and once finished with a happily ever after, she asked the nursery maid if she had read to the boys in the past.

"Oh, no, Miss Barton. I cannot read a word, but have much familiarity with raising children as I am the eldest of ten and had the care of my younger brothers and sisters until old enough to apply for this position. Before, Nanny told them tales she knew by heart, but she was pensioned off when they became of an age to require a tutor."

"Would you like to learn to read and write?"

"How wonderful that would be. I do know the alphabet from hearing the lads repeat it so many times."

"A good start. You shall join us tomorrow."

A noon meal followed and a rest period which she needed as much as her charges. Afterward, they stalked a nearby wooded square with a small net but caught neither frog nor toad. With one butterfly captured and a caterpillar found on a leaf, she explained the concept of metamorphosis. After releasing the butterfly, she allowed them to bring the caterpillar home with their pockets stuffed with the same leaves it had been eating in order to raise it in a glass jar with a paper top punched with holes. At last, the day came to an end as the boys had their tea and playtime supervised by Sarah, who had accompanied them to the park, partly to run after them if they scattered and partly because Bess felt servants needed fresh air as well.

She did dine informally with the family after changing into one of her other gowns, but not the deep blue silk. That one would forever be associated with Justin and his failure to propose. James paid her some attention but not as much as when Justin sat across from them. His own departure loomed ahead. He planned to take one of the lesser coaches to transport himself and his mummy to Bellevue Hall far in the north and from there go on to his property in Scotland and visit with his sister, Phemie, and the physician/laird she'd married. Both served as stewards of Castle Laughlin, he explained to Bess, extolling the heathery beauty of the area, the salmon streams and fine hunting, the quarries that generated income, and the small railroad his brother-in-law had devised to haul the stone. Perhaps she would have a chance to visit there one day if Joshua could be persuaded to leave his practice for any length of time.

She doubted that would have any chance of occurring. Her life now revolved around tutoring the boys with little time for anything else. Momentarily, she felt a bleakness take over her heart, but soon banished it as the duchess urged her to discuss her first day as a tutor and seemed absolutely charmed by a butterfly being raised in her home.

Seventeen

Ah, yes, so wonderful to be back in Oxford starting a new term with both eager and not so eager students, striding the campus in a long, black robe garnering respect, and dining in the hall with fellow professors on less saucy meals. Apples began appearing on his desk again and filled the wooden bowl which now sat among jam pots and packets of biscuits that had been inside the travel hamper. He saved the ribbons for Bess, though he did not know when he would see her again, and eagerly awaited the post with her first letter, simply to hear how she fared in her life as a tutor, or so he told himself. He needed other news such as when James departed Bellevue House, keeping his promise not to linger.

Professor Barton had received his letter happily and his smile only broadened as he read to the very end as Justin stood by watching. "My greatest thanks, Professor Longleigh, for placing my daughter in such fine circumstances. Truth be told, I cannot see her as a wife, though I will continue to protect her dowry if it should ever be needed. However, men do not care for women who know more than them. She is best off as a tutor—a female tutor. Whoever thought of that?"

"I did, and I must disagree. Some men are attracted to women with intellect."

Barton threw his head back, laughing and unseating his mortarboard. "Show me one."

One stands right here, but he answered, "My brother, James, for instance. He spent much time with her—properly chaperoned, of course—but he is determined not to marry."

"Really? Fancy that. But her future is assured now. Shall we go to dine?"

He nodded and followed, unable to utter any polite words to this man who did not value his daughter enough.

In his lecture hall, he patiently and clearly explained that Newtonian physics had been built upon the work of Galileo, who died on the same day as Sir Isaac Newton had been born. He went on to explain Newton's First Law of Motion, that of inertia, easy enough to demonstrate with a small ball resting on the floor, inert, lacking motion. When he kicked the ball, it ran in a straight line until his foot stopped it, acceleration. He glanced at his audience to see if they understood and missed that pair of bright blue eyes that had once peered at him from the very last row. Perhaps he'd receive a letter from Bess soon.

He did not. One arrived from his mother who claimed Bess was doing well as a tutor and told of her and his nephews raising and releasing a butterfly into her garden. Finally, after three weeks, a note appeared in his post in Bess's handwriting, the plain and inelegant script of a young woman who had not been sent to a ladies academy and taught to write invitations with a flourish. She apologized for not writing sooner but teaching the boys filled her days and left her tired at night. She repeated the tale of hatching out a butterfly from its cocoon and how the family had gathered to watch it fly off into his mother's love-lies-bleeding plants.

James had indeed left Bellevue House riding in a carriage with his encased mummy. His brother had written immediately upon arrival in the north and explained that he'd removed a statue of a Greek goddess from her niche inside the Hall and replaced it with the colorful case. He'd spent only a short time there before moving on to Castle Laughlin. She had not heard from him since, but also needed to take the time to write him and so had to close now. She'd addressed him as "My Dear Patron," and ended with the formal "Sincerely, Elizabeth Barton."

If he'd written first, he might have gotten a faster reply and did not delay in answering her. He wanted to explain a new formula he was working on, knowing that she would understand the mathematics, and filled his letter with that. He also added that his father had been correct in his needing more exercise, and he'd joined both a fencing and a rowing club to stay in better condition. He added that he could never tell when he'd need the strength to rescue another maiden, hoping to bring a smile to her lips, so pink and perfect. At least, he need not fear that James remained to tamper with her affections any longer. His venturesome brother would soon be bored with life at Castle Laughlin and Phemie's many children and hare off to foreign parts again. He posted it the next day and began waiting again.

She wrote more promptly in two weeks' time and praised his mathematics. The rest of her words were given over to what she taught the boys and their antics. She'd enclosed two short notes from them full of ink blots and errors. "Today we caught a frog and learned about amphibons, animals that live on both land and in water. We had to let it go."

He could imagine their reluctance. Bess explained that writing their uncle would be good training in penmanship, and he should encourage them by writing back. They had also written James inquiring, "How is your mummy doing? We do not mean grandmama, as she lives here with us." She'd made him smile, but now he had to pen brief letters to them as well. Her opening and closing salutations remained formal.

This time, he would begin his with My Dear Bess, not My Dear Miss Barton as he had the last time and remind her that they were on first name terms. He'd sign it Ever your Admirer, Justin. Or was that going too far and raising false hopes? He lived his dream life as an academic and would not give it up, though lately his way of life did not seem as satisfactory as it once had. Daily he faced blank minds excited to fill them with knowledge. Only a few received it gladly. Many, including some professors, still resented his youth. He'd gained some new acquaintances in the fencing and rowing clubs and was more often invited to go to the pub for a pint afterwards once he assured them the outcome of various matches would not affect their grades. Now and again, he rented a horse for a ride in the country. This left him less time to work on his latest formula as his new companions and surely the horse had no interest in hearing about it.

He took the chance and wrote, "My Dear Bess, do you not recall we agreed to use our first names?"

He included more information about his current project but did not make that the sole subject of his letter. Instead, he told of his success in many fencing matches and his sore muscles in getting used to rowing. On one of his riding excursions, he'd seen a charming cottage up for sale on the edge of town and wondered if he might prefer more room and space for a laboratory than his university dwelling provided.

Again, he had to wait for a reply. The mail coach passed directly through Oxford from London and communications with the city were more rapid than elsewhere. If his family resided at Bellevue Hall far north, letters might take weeks to arrive. No, he couldn't blame the mail coaches for her lack of response.

When it did come, she addressed him as Professor Lord Justinian Longleigh, Sir, making him laugh at her mimicry of one of his students. But still, she did not refer to him as Justin. Again, she lauded his formula and filled the pages with stories of tutoring two lively boys and one nursery maid who yearned to read and write more than they did. How kind-hearted of her to teach Sarah as well. He desired to learn more of her personally, not how Richie had fallen into the pond sailing his boat and had to be promptly fished out just as he had once lifted her from the fountain. A fond memory of her nearly transparent gown that day came to his mind.

Another missive briefly mentioned that she did dine with the family in the evenings and at times they added an interesting guest or two of the lower but respectable classes, a banker or a ship captain who had recently delivered goods on a craft owned by the duke. The banker, a widower, had been stuffy, but the captain had tales to tell of foreign places and often brought letters from his brother, Jason, and his wife, Miranda. They had added a third daughter to their family in case he had not gotten the news as yet, and named her Nerissa, thus using all the female names from *The Merchant of Venice*. His mother had quipped that now they might move on to the male names, though in America females could inherit and the need for a son was not as urgent. She'd signed this one "Yours, Bess Barton, Female Tutor Extraordinaire," which brought him joy.

The joy faded quickly when it occurred to him that his mother might still be trying to match Bess with an appropriate husband. She'd shown no interest in the banker, but he recalled how James' tales of travel had enthralled her. Didn't his mother know that sea captains rarely brought their wives along? These ladies spent their days ashore waiting for the return of such a man only to lose their spouse again to the sea for another voyage or in a shipwreck. How lonely Bess would be in a match like that.

He made a decision to return to London when the term ended in mid-June, which he often failed to do. This time he had a plausible excuse. He'd been informed of a lecture that Bess would enjoy attending, though she'd need to be accompanied by a member to sit in on the talk to be given by Charles Babbage on his difference engine, a new type of calculator, early in July at the Royal Astronomical Society which the man had founded. As he was a fellow of the group, she would be welcome as his guest. He envisioned a perfect evening without James or any other family member intruding. This became the theme of his next letter which he ended with, "I shall be seeing you soon. Justin."

Eighteen

"What did Justin have to say?" Kate inquired as she shared a quiet moment with Bess, putting her feet up in an unlady-like way on a hassock while she had the chance. The duchess had gone on afternoon visits, and Kate told Bess she was delighted to have the excuse of increasing as a way of avoiding society. "He neglected to write the rest of us."

"He is coming here at the end of the term and wishes to take me to a lecture about the difference engine Charles Babbage has invented." Bess held the pages close in order to hide the informal way he addressed her.

Kate looked up from her sewing. It seemed to Bess that babies needed endless supplies of hemmed nappies and little shirts. "Babbage? Another don?"

"Yes, from Cambridge. He founded the Astronomical Society where the talk will be held and has revised some of Newton's mathematics, which Justin has begun to teach."

"Rather you than me. I have enough mathematics in my life seeing to the household accounts."

"But just imagine if you could set up those accounts inside a machine that would keep track of them and could be added to at any time, if you simply put in the numbers."

"Yes, that I could get excited about, but not until it is built and ready to be used." Kate sipped tea half diluted with cream. Good for the baby, she claimed.

"Oh, it would have so many uses for far grander things like astronomical tables. With your permission, I would like to attend."

"You don't need mine. It will probably be held in the evening this time of year, and the boys will be tucked away by then. Go, of course. What is more curious is that Justin is returning to London for the end of the Season. He usually holds out until we have all deserted this steaming, dirty city for the fresh air of Bellevue Hall and joins us there in August for a month or so."

"His intellectual curiosity knows no bounds," Bess suggested. She sipped her own tea, hoping to regain some of the energy that tutoring little boys required.

"Did you by any chance mention that the duchess had invited several single men to dine lately?"

"Why yes, but that cannot account for his desire to visit his family."

"I do believe Justin is jealous, as he was of James."

Bess felt a blush spread across her chest and cheeks. "He only wished to protect me from a man of the world." She had to believe that now as he had not spoken for her either. No sense in harboring false hopes.

"I think there is more to his visit. I shall consult Fair Annet if she is about. At her last appearance, she assured me I carry a daughter."

"Fair Annet?" A great many of the women who visited thought they could predict the sex of a child, but none by that name.

"Yes, you see she is the spirit of a young woman who was starved to death for refusing to wed as her father wished. She came to me as I suffered the same fate, nearly dying in the tower where she was held. She kept my hopes alive and hounded one of the servants to bring me food. Later she entered Josh's dreams, trying to convey what I truly wanted from him."

Kate paused in her sewing which Bess now observed bore a ring of tiny poesies around the neckline. She'd heard that those in the family way often had strange cravings, but delusions? Or perhaps being with child was not the fault. Kate's ordeal in the tower, which she was fairly sure had been used in the plot of *Hidden Treasure* by the Longleigh twins, might have unsettled her mind, though to date, Bess had considered Kate supremely sensible.

"Do you mean Bellevue House is haunted?"

"Not exactly. Fair Annet attached herself to me, ever so glad to haunt other places than that dreadful tower. She appears to me when she wishes. Even Joshua has seen her in his dreams and at our wedding, but he will not speak of it to anyone. She continues to watch over me and has been present when I gave birth. When I am in a quandary, she might offer help. She realized my wish to have a girl child and eased my mind on that account. I could ask her to enter Justin's dreams and see what is really on his mind."

"That would be a great intrusion of his privacy." Bess stared into her teacup as if she wanted to read her future in a few stray leaves as some gypsies did, taking advantage of gullible young girls for a few coins. Yet, she wanted to know.

Kate smiled with understanding. "You are tempted. I am not sure when Annet will come again, but if she does, I will ask it of her. I am not certain she can travel to Oxford if I am not there also, but when he visits, I shall do my best to persuade her to help."

"Very well, but know that I am person who trusts science over spirits."

"Of course, my dear, of course."

~ * ~

Trinity term ended in mid-June, and Justin had asked for a carriage to carry him to London immediately, even though the lecture he wanted to attend had been scheduled for the first week in July. He resumed dressing as a young gentleman. When Bess remarked that he looked well, he attributed that to all the rowing and fencing he had been doing. In fact, he thought his jackets fit more tightly across his shoulders and his calf muscles filled out his stockings even more so.

Although he returned the same compliment to Bess, he truly thought she appeared diminished somehow. Perhaps because her hair was bound in braids coiled at her nape, or the dresses she wore were not the ones he'd purchased but drab affairs in gray and dark blue. He changed the subject and asked her how she enjoyed living the life of the mind with a steady income, housing, and food as he did at Oxford.

"I do enjoy coming up with new ideas to teach the boys, but keeping them constantly engaged is a challenge. I make sure they have physical exercise each day and threaten them only with losing our reading time if they do not learn their lessons. I spare the rod. But that does mean I must always be alert and sometimes that tires me."

"Yes, I can see that. I shall speak to Kate about shortening your teaching hours."

"Please, no! My position here is enviable. Well, we have talked enough. I am due to take them for an outing in the park to see what we can learn from nature today. You may come along if you are not too spent from your journey."

"I would enjoy that."

"Sarah shall accompany us, as usual. All proprieties will be observed." Somehow, that disappointed him.

They set out with the boys running a bit ahead like small dogs tugging at the leash and Sarah constantly cautioning them not to run into the road or other people. Inside a gated square,

Bess set them loose to explore and report back if they found anything of interest. That did not take long. They gathered around a small pile of turds.

"Tell me what you observe," Bess challenged.

'Well, miss, they are small and round," Richie offered.

"Yes, and I suspect if we smashed one you would find them grassy." Willy raised his foot.

"No, no, spare your shoes. Animals that expel round, grassy turds are herbivores who eat plants. Look around and tell me what this creature has been eating."

"Grass! It's a hervore," Richie shouted.

"Right, an herbivore, a small one. Horses are large herbivores. Rhinoceroses, which are African beasts with horns on their noses, are also herbivores but very dangerous as are hippopotamuses. I shall find you some pictures of those when we are back at home. Some animals are carnivores and eat only meat—like lions. But the bear we saw at the Tower is actually an omnivore, which eats both plants and meat. Can you name another omnivore?"

Her students pondered that for a while until she hinted, "You are looking at one right now."

"Ladies?"

"Yes, and gentlemen and you. Now, what animal made these turds?"

Willy shot his hand up as if in the classroom. "I bet it's a rabbit."

"You are correct. Now, I see more excrement over by the pathway. It is long and smells bad. What kind of animal dropped that?"

The boys shot off to observe with Bess right behind. Justin turned toward Sarah and commented. "She really is amazing. How I wish I'd had a tutor who studied excrement when I was small. I might have turned to the natural sciences rather than the mathematical."

"Pardon me for saying, she would have made a shocking governess, but the boys do love her and want to please her."

"Still, they are a handful. She seems somewhat tired."

"Since she has her own chamber, I cannot say exactly, but I believe she does not sleep well."

"Why? Does the family not treat her fairly? If so, I will..."

"It's not that, milord." Sarah lowered her eyes toward the grass. "I think she pines for you."

"For me?"

"Yes, you are far off in Oxford where young ladies leave you apples tied with ribbons in abundance, I have heard, while she is here living upon your letters."

"Which reminds me, I have brought her more ribbons, not an improper gift since I pay nothing for them. Could you take the time to iron them?"

"Certainly. She is as kind to me as she is to the boys. I am learning to read and write along with them because she allows it. I've long been trying to speak like my betters, and she helps me with that, too, never making fun of me. All of this could mean I will not always be a nursery maid but can reach higher."

"As I said, she is extraordinary."

One of the boys shouted, "It is a dog turd. It looks like ours. Dogs are omnivores."

"Excellent deduction, Willy. Sadly, we cannot take such specimens home, but I am sure your grandfather would be delighted to show you the droppings of fallow and roe deer, and foxes when we decamp for Bellevue Hall in August, not to mention the famous Bellevue tortoises. Come, we must be home in time for your tea."

Their small group reassembled and returned with no mishaps except for the launching of a horse apple that had fallen on the curb into the street by the tip of Willy's toe as the boy proclaimed, "Herbivore!" while watching it smash.

Sarah prompted him to use the boot scraper to clean his shoe before entering the house. She marched them up the stairs to the nursery, leaving Bess and the young lord behind in an awkward silence.

Justin cleared his throat. "I, ah, brought you more ribbons. Sarah will iron them for you."

"Are there a great many?" she questioned, not meeting his gaze.

"A fair amount, in many colors."

"None of the donors have tempted you to give up academia for wedded bliss, then?"

"None, none at all. I think we are missing our own tea. Shall we go in—but I would not mention your science lesson today while we are eating." He added a grin to show her he teased rather than criticized and offered his arm.

She pines for me. Could it be she pines for me?

Nineteen

His days at Bellevue House fell into a pattern in the few weeks before Professor Babbage's lecture. His father, always an early riser, persuaded his youngest son into morning rides, large breakfasts, then a bout of sword training and sometimes fisticuffs. Younger members of Gentleman Jackson's might refer to the duke as the old man, but few wanted to be on the receiving end of any of his jabs, which often set them on their backsides. After so much exercise, the duke dined at his club, taking Justin along.

Bess always ate lightly and went directly to the nursery afterward to tutor the boys. They rarely saw each other in the morning, but he insisted on being home in time to accompany her and his nephews on their nature walks. One never knew what Bess would find to teach a lesson, an empty bird's nest or an interesting feather.

She'd discovered a book of etchings of hand-colored African animals in their library and showed the boys a rhino and a hippo among others. In fact, they'd gone through the entire volume, classifying them by eating habits. He'd sat in on that and enjoyed it immensely. While Bess returned the valuable volume to the library in its place next to Iris's prints of American Indian women, and her husband's of chiefs and warriors and medicine men, he watched his nephews complete their assignment of painfully writing out rhinos and hippos are herbivores, then making their own messy drawings of the animals beneath their words. By the time she returned, face glowing with success, she'd asked him to move the globe in the library up to the nursery so she might show her students where Africa was—with the duchess's permission. He'd stayed on for story time and found himself equally enthralled.

Bess seemed to be blooming again, her eyes bright enough to offset her somber garb and from time to time wearing ribbons woven into her braids while he saw a man in his shaving mirror who lacked sleep. He dreamt night after night of kissing Bess deeply, stroking her fair breasts, lifting her skirts, none of which must happen in his family's home. All he could ask of her was that she wear one of her finer gowns to the lecture and put her hair up. He wanted to show her at her best, though he would be wearing academic garb with a black tie around his neck rather than a neckcloth intricately tied.

On the night of the event, he handed her down from their carriage like a fine lady and introduced her as Miss Elizabeth Barton, daughter of an Oxford don who had achieved the rank of tutor. The audience, nearly all male, consisted mainly of academics, but also contained gentlemen who fancied themselves to be scientists and members of the government who held the purse strings for projects of this nature. Looking her best in that fetching gown of dark blue silk, her hair dressed by the duchess's maid, she aroused entirely too much interest for his comfort. However, the men flocking around them soon settled into their seats to learn about the difference engine for calculating logarithms and trigonometric functions, or as Babbage called it a "Note on the Application of Machinery to the Computation of Astronomical and Mathematical Tables". He could tell she followed every word, intelligence shining in her blue eyes as Babbage described columns of number wheels and section gears hand-cranked into place to give forth a complex result.

After the lecture, they partook of light refreshments and managed to gain a word with Babbage. He was grateful the man did not disdain a question from Bess, who asked how many moving pieces the machine would require. "I estimate twenty-five thousand, which is why having the support of the British government is so essential."

Glancing around, he noticed men who were not sworn to stay single by their profession closing in on them, and not to speak to Babbage. The first to breach the crowd asked if he might have Miss Barton's address in order to call upon her. Bess flushed, perhaps embarrassed to say that her work as a tutor did not allow for male visitors. He let them know she resided with the family of the Duke of Bellevue and was under his protection. That deterred the first, but others closed in. He suggested they leave in order to share their new knowledge with the rest of the family. Bess agreed.

On the doorstep of Bellevue House, while they paused awaiting Busby to let them in, he seemed to catch the toe of his shoe on a door mat, that or else someone had given him a small shove in Bess's direction. He had to apologize for nearly landing in her arms and looked around suspiciously for the possibility of a nephew escaped from the nursery hiding behind one of the large, ornamental urns on either side of the entry, but saw no one.

"So sorry. How very clumsy of me," he said and meant not a word of it. He stepped away from the warmth of her body, the closeness of her lips, and so stood there very properly when Busby opened the door.

The family had not gone out that evening and were assembled as always in the drawing room enjoying a friendly game of loo. They gave Justin and Bess their attention, but the duke soon fell asleep in his throne-like chair. Joshua and Kate gave the excuse of Kate needing her rest to depart, though Kate paused by Justin's chair before leaving.

"Are you having trouble sleeping, brother? I hear you sometimes in the night tossing and muttering as our chamber is nearby."

"I apologize if I have wakened you, Kate. But, yes, I have been struggling to sleep. Bad dreams brought on by too much rich food, I am sure. I must watch my diet." Why did his sister-in-law send a pleased glance in Bess's direction? How odd.

The duke snorted awake, hearing only the last of the conversation. "Probably spending too much time in the nursery these days when you should be out and about enjoying your youth as much as an academic can."

The duchess squeezed his shoulder. "I do not think that is the case. How wonderful that Justin enjoys spending time with his nephews. Rest, my love, while I finish hearing about the difference engine."

She remained to listen to it all. Once finished, she roused her husband and accompanied him to bed with Justin and Bess trailing behind, one going left and the other right at the head of the stairs.

Twenty

At his mother's insistence, Justin had been dragged to a ball given by a dear friend who wished to see him before the Season wound to a close with the approach of August. Once again, Kate had claimed her belly as an excuse not to go. Joshua holed up in the library with some of his legal papers, and this left Bess alone with Kate in the drawing room. As she applied her meager sewing abilities to hemming nappies with a stitch she could use for minor repairs to gowns, she was able to broach a subject weighing on her mind. But how to bring up this delicate subject?

"I am glad that Justin is no longer required to attend Almack's. He truly hated that."

Kate nodded. "There is no need for him to go anymore. By now, all the choicest matches have been made, and those who failed are resigned to coming back next year or retiring to a fireside corner if they have passed the age of twenty-one. You have found a good position where you are happy, and I sincerely hope no one finds out what a treasure you are as a tutor. They will try to lure you away. I have never seen my sons so interested in learning. Why, only yesterday Willy asked if I knew the French word for turds was *merde*. I did, of course, but let him teach me the pronunciation." She laughed so heartily the candles flickered in their sticks.

"Oh, I could not be lured away. My loyalty is to the Longleighs."

"Not for money—or love?" Kate questioned as she took a moment from sewing a rosebud on a small shirt to glance at Bess.

That gave her an opening to say, "Certainly not for money. However, I am worried about Justin. He is no longer under any pressure to wed, yet he seems distressed and is not sleeping or eating well. After the lecture by Babbage, he tripped outside our door and nearly took me to the ground. It is not like him to be clumsy. I am concerned about his health."

Kate waved a hand over her sixth month belly. "Nothing that a little self-examination won't cure." She patted her baby to be. "Fair Annet tells me my daughter is thriving and that she is encouraging Justin to follow his heart."

"By sending him nightmares and shoving him around?"

"I doubt he experiences nightmares. Are you having any troubling dreams?"

The flush surged through her body so strongly she reached out to grasp and open one the duchess's stray fans lying on a nearby table to quell the heat. "My dreams are hardly nightmares, but rather of a very carnal and lascivious nature—all involving Justin."

"Ah, Fair Annet at work."

Attempting to apply logic to a ghost, she said, "If she were a maiden doomed to haunt that tower alone until you came along, how does she know of such things?"

"I suppose she has had centuries to learn, but I'm guessing she has observed Josh and myself at our best in the bedchamber. Please don't mention this possibility to my husband. Like you, he wants to pretend ghosts do not exist, though he saw her at our wedding. Despite this, we have agreed to name our daughter Annette. It is so fitting because she brought us together and now wants to do the same for you and Justin."

How hard it is to argue with a true believer. Bess shook her head but said, "Perhaps you could ask her to desist for a bit and let us get some rest."

"I will do so, but she does have a will of her own." They left it at that.

~ * ~

Entertainments ceased as members of the ton packed to leave the heat and stench of a London summer behind in favor of the fresh air of their country estates and rural pleasures. The duchess bustled about, deciding what and who went with the family to Bellevue Hall. The best coach bore the duke and duchess, her maid and his valet, along with Busby and Chef Pepin, though the duke preferred to ride most of the time, leaving more room for the women and the men across from them. Kate, Joshua, Justin, Bess, and the boys took the small carriage with Peterson handling the reins and the fractious Black Lightning leading the team. The more docile mounts remained behind as the Hall did not lack for horses and Joshua would return before the rest of his family as his profession demanded it. Household maids occupied an older carriage and filled it with their giggles while the extra stable hands rode on top with the drivers. Behind them came the baggage train of boxes filled with fine clothes and clean bedding to be used at the inns along the way. Mrs. Crump and Cook waved them off, along with the rest of the staff who would see to the townhouse in their absence. The Longleighs were on the march north as well organized as a Napoleonic army, it seemed to Bess.

She'd never traveled so far and had no experience with inns. While Josh brought along legal briefs to study and Justin caught up with scientific papers, Kate enjoyed lighter reading. Bess had hidden one of the C.C. Leigh novels inside of her Brothers Grimm collection of tales which she'd brought along to entertain her charges. She would hate to have her employers think she'd grown frivolous, but the twins' novels were educational in their way and probably explained her vivid dreams more logically than the work of a ghost. But truly, she enjoyed watching the countryside change as they left London on roads rimmed with tall hawthorn hedges allowing only fleeting glimpses of the country estates of the wealthy.

The larger cities of England clung to the seashore, but the Great North Road passed through many prosperous market towns, which offered lodging and meals for the entourage as well as lines of hovels where the poor resided and eked out a living. The excursion was an education in itself. She pointed out interesting sights to the boys to keep them from getting restless on the long journey—Roman ruins and the remains of great castles where knights once flourished. They'd seated Willy between her and Kate, while Richie had been sandwiched between the men. At times, kicking spats broke out, and the seating would shift, but somehow, she remained at her window across from Justin and avoided his direct gaze as much as she could, especially when engrossed in the novel.

The Longleigh caravan easily filled the smaller coaching inns, even with the stable hands and drivers staying in the barns with the horses and keeping watch over the carriages. If only she did not have to share a space with Clement, who complained of being relegated to the coach full of lesser maids. A male tutor might have lodged with Justin, but that was not to be. She could dream—but was afraid to lest she utter something unseemly in her sleep. Clement took every chance to remind her that she also served the family and offered no help with her hair or clothes. Not that it mattered. The way was dusty and hot this time of year, though the road was one of the best kept in England. She wore her practical gray dress, an old bonnet, and braids bedecked with ribbons that Clement criticized as unbecoming in a person no better than a governess.

"You know that men will give you ribbons for favors of the flesh, then leave you with child and without references."

"I am not so naïve as that," she claimed.

With a sly grin, the lady's maid added, "Though some who play their cards right might be kept as pampered mistresses. I've heard you play cards very well. Too bad you did not win your hand with Lord James, as you hung on his every word."

"Because he had much to say that was of interest—which you do not. Goodnight." She turned her back in the bed they shared that first night in Stamford at the venerable George. She dreamt of only pleasant things, wide vistas and seeing the Galapagos tortoises, while Clement tossed and kicked and awoke in a sweat more than once. The ghost at work? Of course not.

Three days later, their entourage turned off the road before it crossed the Scottish border going on to Edinburgh and took a lesser path that brought them to Bellevue Hall, as fine and vast an estate as any they'd passed along the way, with its many arched windows and imposing wings. While the servants who had remained there lined up to greet their return, the boys, totally familiar with the setting from past visits, shot ahead, ignoring the magnificence of the black and white tiled vestibule, the many niches filled with Greek statues and old armor, pausing only to shout, "The mummy is here!" and onward past the entry to the conservatory with its jungle of plants and outward to the rear of the mansion where they immediately drenched themselves in the spray from the Triton fountain by stomping on its hidden valve. Sarah and Bess followed as fast as they could, with Kate moving sedately behind them.

The duchess caught up with them before they descended the steps into the formal garden. "Let them play. I recall very well how little boys dislike being confined to coaches for days. Sarah, keep an eye on them and when they tire, take them to the nursery to change. Meanwhile, we have hot water in our chambers, beds to stretch out upon for a rest, and dinner in the making."

Bess, escorted to a room near the staircase to the nursery, as nice as she'd had in London and offering a view of the garden where her charges chased each other along the gravel paths, had no desire to lie down. She wanted to explore. Washing and changing into the gown of sunny yellow and her most becoming straw bonnet, she set out on her own, hoping to come across the tortoises. She passed Sarah herding the sopping boys back to the house and offered her help.

"No need. They've run themselves down and want their tea. Enjoy this fine weather. Once autumn sets in, there will be fogs and rain and snow."

She took that advice and strolled to the end of the formal garden, tempted by side paths that led into wooded areas. Another led straight up a steep hill topped by what seemed to be ancient ruins. No sign of the tortoises. She might catch sight of them if she scaled this mound and started forward. How she missed his approach, she did not know, but Justin came up beside her.

"I spied you from my window. Until you get to know your way around, don't wander off alone. The grounds are vast and not all of it is tame."

"Yes, foolish of me. I so wanted to see the tortoises."

"They are kept on the far side of the rise in fair weather and in the conservatory during the cold months. My mother soon learned they can gnaw through the tender trunks of small trees with their beaks. She prefers that they graze with the sheep on the pasture beyond the rise. We can go up there this way, but there are kinder ascents on either side. And to be honest, they will only appear as large rocks from this distance. Let's save them for tomorrow's nature lesson."

"Then where should I go?"

They had been confined together for days, their toes practically touching, their conversation most proper. The highlight had been passing through Grantham, the birthplace of Isaac Newton. He had discussed some of his readings with her, and she read aloud from her Grimm tales for the entertainment of all—Snow White, Hansel and Gretel, Tom Thumb, and the Golden Goose— until the boys slept leaning against their parents' shoulders. So hard being so near and unable to say more.

"Your choice of a temple with a statue of Diana off to the left or a Shawnee dwelling down the right-hand path."

"Oh, I think the Shawnee dwelling."

He offered his arm and off they went for a pleasant walk in the woods. Coming around a curve in the rustic path, the scene opened on a cleared area with a dome-shaped hut having a garden by its side. The maize plants grew tall and were covered with plump cobs beginning to brown. The beans that climbed them had also gone yellow, ready for harvest. Pumpkin vines twined around the base, some orange globes showing among the broad leaves.

"We are a little late to celebrate the green corn ceremony as my parents once did and so scandalized Queenie's governess into quitting. I understand she considered the dance quite lascivious."

"I would have liked to see it. This is not at all like the tall tents of hides and poles the western Indians use."

"No, this is a wigwam, not a teepee. It's made from bent saplings and covered in bark that is lashed on to keep out the weather. Would you like to go inside?"

"Very much."

He raised the deer hide that served as a door and allowed her to go first as if they were entering a grand home. She stepped inside and tripped over something in the dimness. Justin's arms moved around her preventing a fall and remained there until she got her balance again. His breath warmed her nape. Her heart pounded wildly. She took a deep breath. As her eyes adjusted to the dim interior, she observed piles of furs for bedding and a circular pit for a fire, but nothing on the floor that might have made her trip. Perhaps, she'd stumbled over her own feet. Perhaps Fair Annet had pushed her. Ridiculous. Justin's arms released her as if reluctant to let her go.

She tried to make conversation to get over the awkward moment. Various items hung on the walls: a turkey feather fan, a cradleboard, a... "Is that a human scalp?"

"Yes, taken from an enemy who threatened my mother during their days among the Shawnee. Papa paid a blood price of wampum, strips of shells that had value to the Indians, given to the man's grandmother as well as some horses, but the woman was purported to be a witch who still troubles the family with her curses."

"Do you believe in curses and—and ghosts?

"Of course not. There is no room for them in the study of physics."

"Just as I said to Kate."

Justin shook his head. "Truly, I love her like a sister, but I do think her period of starvation caused her to have delusions. She believes a spirit helped to save her. However, when I underwent my manhood rites, I learned going without food and water for a time brings on strange visions. It's a natural reaction of the body to deprivation."

"Your manhood rites?"

'My father insisted all of his sons at the age of thirteen undergo the Shawnee tradition of living alone in the forest without food or water until we discovered our spirit animal. Very aptly, his is the bear."

"And yours?"

A rueful look passed over his face. "Though part of my name is White Bull as the Shawnee called my grandfather, the best I could envision was an owl. Not that owls aren't venerated by the tribe. They are a link to the spirit world in their beliefs, but of course, James dreamed of a Scottish red deer, as close as we get to American elk and highly regarded. It makes sense since he is viscount of a Scottish estate."

"Was your father as disappointed as you were?"

"Not at all. He said he knew I was not destined to be a warrior and among his people would have been trained to be a shaman."

Bess gave him a consoling pat on the arm. She should not have touched him at all as she tended to feel any contact deep within her heart. "A shaman of science, that is what you are."

The small space of the wigwam seemed even closer. Her next words came to her tongue from nowhere. "Does anyone sleep here now?"

"I suspect my parents come here at times to relive their youth, but our guests prefer featherbeds. As children we played in the wigwam often, though I was the last and smallest, most likely to be taken captive, as Pandora could be quite fierce. It is more beloved by the family than the other follies."

Bess was tempted to grasp the turkey wing fan to cool herself. Images of throwing herself on the mound of furs and taking Justin with her invaded her mind. Instead, she moved toward the deer hide door and away from him. She needed air. Outside, the sun shone, breaking the spell.

As if afraid he'd be considered a weakling, Justin added as he joined her on the path again, "However, I can take down a roe deer with a bow and arrow, or at least I could. I suspect I am quite rusty now and don't care for hunting in any way. But Papa would storm the nursery and hustle me outdoors several times a week to practice woodcraft. He painted my cheeks with the blood of the first deer I slew and told me to give thanks to the animal for its sacrifice. The duke is very superstitious. He still strews tobacco for the spirits when he goes into the forest."

"No more arcane than believing we drink the blood of Christ and light candles to send our prayers upward. Still, it is good to believe in something."

"I agree."

She wanted to believe in the possibility of the two of them together, a subject not to be touched. "Where else does the path lead?'

"Eventually out to a coach road on the edge of our property. Before that, our gardener's cottage. It's very quaint, if you'd like to see it. Duncan will be out and about on a day like this harrying the shepherd to move the sheep to another pasturage before they eat the turf to the ground, or seeing that his underlings prune every plant perfectly to please my mother."

"She does enjoy her flowers, even in the small plot at the townhouse."

"Yes, but she had her fill of getting her hands dirty when she worked the corn and beans as a Shawnee slave serving the old hag, Snakeroot. Duncan takes care of her plot by the wigwam. As the English are not fond of maize, most of it goes to the livestock along with the pumpkins. Perhaps the beans are put to use. Mama said she ground enough cornmeal to never want to see it on her table in any form. I think Papa might enjoy the cornbread she learned to make, but he gave up a way of life he preferred to return to England for the sake of my mother and James, who was born in the Ohio territory."

So, some men did make sacrifices in the name of love as the twins claimed in their books. They based this belief on their own family.

They ambled along the path until a narrow opening appeared among the trees. "Turn here to see Duncan's cottage." Justin held back a small branch that blocked the way as if discouraging people to visit.

Some way into the woods, they came to a clearing bordered with loose stone walls carpeted in the last of summer's white roses and already rich with hips. Inside the ring, no grass grew, only dirt swept clean of debris. In the center sat a squat home with a low hanging thatched roof.

"Why, it resembles a house from the Brothers Grimm stories!" Bess exclaimed.

"Yes, as children we were afraid to come here. Though Duncan has lived on the estate since his fifteenth year and was born after the Rising and the battle of Culloden that broke the clans, he remains fiercely Scottish and says this is a traditional cottage for his people. He cultivates white roses in memory of the Jacobean cause rather than the yellow flowers my mother prefers."

"She doesn't mind?"

"How can she when Duncan is the granduncle of Phemie's husband, the laird of Laughlin? It's an ill-kept secret Scottish blood runs in our family's veins from a long ago stolen bride and now Phemie's children. Not to mention Shawnee and Italian. I would think your family is more pure-blooded English than the Longleighs."

"I would love to have such a mixture and so much family."

"As they say, be careful what you wish for."

They did not intrude inside the house but turned back as Justin's pocket watch told them it was time for the adults to have tea. On their return, Justin plucked two small pumpkins from the Shawnee garden.

"For our nature walk tomorrow. The tortoises love them."

"I can hardly wait." For that and being with Justin again.

Twenty-one

Released from their studies, the boys ran ahead, scaling the steep path to the castle folly like young chamois in the Swiss alps and gamboling down the other side of the barrier which kept the sheep and deer from the duchess's garden. The sheepdog barked as if wolves assailed its herd and moved the animals off to a safer spot. The giant tortoises raised their heads high but did not stray from the plot of grass where they grazed.

Carrying a pumpkin each by the stem had not slowed the young scholars at all. As Justin helped Bess down the slope, a figure sitting beneath a shade tree rose up and saluted very smartly. The turtle keeper, once of the king's navy, fulfilled every detail of a fictional pirate, having an arm that ended in a hook, a wooden leg, and a sun-browned face encircled by a short, black beard.

"Amos Gantry at your service, Lord Justin and pretty lady."

"Amos, this is Miss Barton. She tutors the boys. She's brought them to see the tortoises."

"Always happy to have the company, though the creatures aren't as fond of it, especially noisy ones." The tortoises had deemed it wise to retreat into their shells, one domed, one flat.

Willy and Richie jumped up and down, thrusting the pumpkins at their uncle. "Smash them, smash them!"

Bess held up her hand for silence. "First, greet Mr. Gantry politely. Then take a seat on the grass and listen to him tell us about these magnificent beasts. They won't come closer if you are loud."

"Good day, Mr. Gantry," they chirped, their eyes still ogling the tortoises.

How immediately they obeyed. She had a knack for teaching that he lacked. Oh, he could make complex subjects understandable but many of the students fell asleep in his lectures. Few were as avid as Bess had been peering from the last row. He missed seeing her blue eyes taking in his every movement.

Amos Gantry also took a seat while Bess spread her gingham skirts over a flat rock she chose as a chair. He sat at her feet as the old tar told what he knew.

"Well now, I be familiar with these tortoises from my time aboard sailing ships which would stop at their islands and catch a few, easy enough, to provide meat for the voyage home. Tastes like the finest beef, they do, and require no food nor water for days on end. They store water in their gullets, ye see."

Willy thrust up a hand. "Like camels in their humps."

"Aye, my lad, though I've not eaten camel. After me many injuries in the king's service, I took employment at the Terrapin Inn in London and minded these two along with many turtles who live in the sea and only come to land when it is time for them to lay their eggs."

Richie shot up a hand. "Do these tortoises lay eggs?"

"When the urge is upon them, they make soft round ones, about a dozen at a time, more or less. The duchess gives the young as presents to those who promise not to eat them. They are most likely to go at it when I herd them to the conservatory for the winter, where they have a warm place, a nice sandy pen, and plenty of cabbages to eat."

During the lecture, the tortoises emerged from hiding and took some interest in their visitors. Slowly, slowly, they plodded toward them.

"They like pumpkins, too, Uncle Justin says," Willy added.

"Indeed they do, shell, pulp, and seeds," Mr. Gantry verified.

"Now?" asked Richie, offering his pumpkin again.

Bess tried to suppress a grin at their eagerness. "I suppose we can observe how they eat. Smash away, Lord Justin."

Happy to be of service to her, he rose, chose a small rock with a sharp peak, and crushed a pumpkin upon it. The second soon followed. Split open, they released a fruity smell and a large number of seeds. The tortoises picked up speed a trifle but were beaten to their treat by a colorful red-headed parrot with a yellow and blue body that swooped from the tree above them and began picking out the seeds.

"There, now, Miss Rosita, leave some for the turtles," Gantry reprimanded. "She's been with me many a year and will most likely outlive me, as will the tortoises. I am told both can reach a hundred years and more."

As if Miss Rosita understood she was the topic of conversation, she cocked her head and said, "Turtles be damned. Turtles be damned." Then went back to plucking seeds. The boys giggled.

"She's a mite jealous and a lot foul-mouthed. Begging your pardon. I never taught her that. Well, maybe the damned part, but she adds in other words she's heard often."

"Do tell us more about your parrot. Is she from Africa, Mr. Gantry?" Bess inquired.

"Nay, from a place the Spanish call the Costa Rica in the central part of the Americas. That's where I won her in a game of chance. A scarlet macaw, she be."

"Boys what do we know about how birds are different from other animals?" Bess quizzed them.

"Um, they got feathers," offered Willy.

"And they can fly." Richie flapped his arms causing the tortoises to slow again.

"Most of them can fly, but not all. They also lay eggs. The tortoises lay eggs, but they are not birds. What are they? Think about the garter snake we found in the park."

"Hmm, reptiles because they have scales. I still think we should have brought it home to study," Willy replied.

"Your mother was not keen on that idea."

"I seen some of them flightless birds in me travels around Cape Horn." Gantry pushed to his feet with the help of his crutch and did a funny sort of waddle. "This is how they walk on land but can swim like the devil is after them. Not as tasty as turtles, however."

The tortoises came near and set about gnawing the rinds with the sides of their beaks.

"Can we pet them?"

"May we?" Bess corrected their grammar.

"They don't seem to mind if ye do, but keep to their side or they will hiss and go into their shells." Gantry tapped the domed top of one of the tortoises with his crutch. Being used to him, it took no notice.

"May we ride on them? This one has a saddle back." Richie stood up in high hopes.

"No, they are not for riding. Sit and learn more," Bess said. But her students grew restless with sitting.

"May we pet your parrot, Mr. Gantry?" Richie did not give up easily.

"Not pet, as she has a very strong beak unlike the tortoises, but here, she likes these and will come to your shoulder to eat." He opened a pouch hanging from his waist and took out a piece of cheese and a couple of crackers. The cheese went back into the pouch. Handing over a cracker to Richie, he called, "Cracker, Rosie, cracker."

The parrot swiveled her red head away from pumpkin seeds. "Rosie wants a cracker."

She fluttered to Richie's shoulder, a rather heavy burden for such a small perch.

"Mind now, stand still and let her take the cracker from your fingers."

While the tortoises continued to gulp pumpkin in large bites, Miss Rosita took dainty nibbles of the cracker, turning it this way and that with a claw. When she finished, she flew to the larger boy's shoulder as he revealed his cracker. At the end of her treat, she returned to the pumpkins, but not before depositing a streak of droppings down Willy's back.

"Oh, my!" Bess took a small handkerchief poorly embroidered from her sleeve to dab at it, but Justin solved the problem with a manly square of white linen from his pocket.

While they dealt with this crisis, Richie examined the deposits made by the turtles. He picked one up. "These tortoises are herbivores. I am not sure about the bird."

"Yes, you are correct, Richie, but do drop that. I think it is time we return to the house, wash, and change clothes. What do we say to Mr. Gantry for sharing his tales with us?"

"Thank you, Mr. Gantry."

"Come visit again. While my job here is perfect for a man missing one arm and one leg, the tortoises aren't much company. Quiet, they are. While the kitchen maids bring my meals to the summer hut, they cannot tarry or raise the wrath of Monsieur Pepin."

"I am sure we will. Come along, boys. Your next assignment will be to write several sentences about what you learned today and a note of thanks to Mr. Gantry. We shall find the places he mentioned on our globe." Bess shooed them in the direction of the house and as usual, they took off running.

Justin again offered his arm to steer her across the meadow pocked by the hooves of sheep and deer. They ascended to the folly again. Her students had already reached the gravel paths of the garden. Standing beneath an archway in the crenellated wall that ended in a short turret complete with arrow slits, Bess remarked upon their boundless energy.

"Yes, but you engage them so well. In fact, you are an amazing teacher. If I had had tutors like you, I might have become a world adventurer like James instead of a stuffy professor who rarely leaves Oxford." He watched her eyes fill with light at his compliment, but then she lowered her lids to stare at the ground.

"You are hardly stuffy, and explain complicated formulae very well. But I thought you were content with your life at Oxford."

"I was, but lately feel as restless as my nephews. I thought spending some time in the country away from academics might help with that, but I am not sure it is working."

"We've only just arrived. Give yourself more space. You are welcome on our nature walks at any time. One never knows when one might need a sturdy handkerchief."

Her humor made him beam. "We both had rather strange childhoods with me outshining my teachers and you haunting the halls of Oxford."

"Yes, let's pretend we are six again without a care in the world and run down this hill hand in hand." Bess offered her hand. It fit so well in his.

"But what if you tumble?"

"Then I shall get up and dust myself off. Come." Bess tugged at his grip and set off.

They ran down the embankment without mishap and ended at the bottom laughing and breathless.

"Feels good to take a chance once in a while, doesn't it?"

"Yes," he agreed, failing to release her hand as they approached the garden and the gravel walks.

"Oh, oh, we are late for tea. I can see Kate standing at the window, cup in hand. We might be in trouble."

He dropped her hand. He was in trouble, and it had nothing to do with Kate's approval.

Twenty-two

Bess cooled her flushed face with water from the basin, tidied her hair, and changed to another day dress that had not been wrinkled from sitting on a rock. She'd been informed that the family did not don formal wear for the evening meal unless company was expected and so went off to tea feeling ready for any interrogation from Kate. She discovered a drawing room occupied only by Kate and the duchess.

"Where are all the men?" she asked as she took the tea poured by the duchess and helped herself to a few biscuits and small sandwiches of which many remained, a sign that the duke had not yet joined them.

"While I make sure all is well in the household, my husband is riding about with Joshua checking on the tenants, making lists of repairs to be made and houses that need to be rethatched. Since we have little hope that James will marry, he wants to make sure Josh learns how to run an estate. I do think James enjoyed your company while he was in town and liked nettling Justin."

"I have a feeling you encouraged that," Bess took a chance by saying.

The duchess inclined her head. "Perhaps, but not the result I wanted. The boys, after reporting that they'd studied the tortoises and a parrot who have very different *merde,* were sent to the nursery to wash and have their tea. Justin has not yet shown himself."

Bess felt she had to apologize. "I am so sorry about their obsession with *merde,* both the word and the real thing. Justin went with us on our nature walk and might have splattered pumpkin on his jacket. He certainly needs a clean handkerchief after wiping parrot droppings off of Willy."

The duchess offered an understanding look. "It is the nature of small boys to get dirty and revel in words they think are bad. I rather enjoy their little essays. Their penmanship and vocabulary are improving vastly."

"Yes, they have never been so engaged with learning," Kate agreed. "Nor has Justin ever said he intends to spend his entire term break with us until half-way through October. Usually, it's a couple of weeks with a short trip to visit Phemie and then back to Oxford, his chalk board and books, while the campus is quiet, and he need not spend time on lectures."

"He did say he felt restless and thought the country air might help," Bess told them.

The duchess voiced a hmm and exchanged a knowing glance with Kate. She hated to broach the subject in front of her but forged on. "Kate, is it possible that Fair Annet traveled with us and now troubles his dreams?"

"Entirely possible."

"Our coach was so crowded I wonder how she could fit in. Even Peterson had a stable hand with him on top."

"I don't believe spirits require space."

"All things do, even the tiniest particle of the universe. It's physics."

"Perhaps spirits have substance in their own plane of existence but not in ours, or where ours intersect with theirs," the duchess suggested.

"An interesting idea," Bess admitted.

"Regardless, she is here for my confinement and might be bored with the long wait," Kate said. "She does love to meddle in people's lives. I have to thank her for that."

The commotion of men entering the house and thudding up the stairs to wash and change ended the discussion of ghostly powers. The duke would voice an opinion while Josh stayed quiet, and Justin insisted spirits did not exist. No use in starting a debate, though Bess became more and more sure that some outside force was at work when it came to her and Justin.

~ * ~

He hadn't slept well and so missed breakfast with Bess. She'd gone to the nursery well before he arrived, and his vigorous family had also deserted the room and gone about their tasks for the day. After helping himself to what was left, he wandered into the hallway with nothing more on his mind than the next nature walk. The faint sound of a piano in the drawing room led him to a surprising sight, not Kate amusing herself, but Bess practicing a new song.

He paused in the doorway to enjoy the way she peered at the sheet music and matched the notes so earnestly with the tip of her pink tongue edged out slightly from her lips—her lips. They'd been on his mind last evening far too often.

"No teaching today? Are your students ill?"

She startled and missed a note. "Not at all, as full of energy as ever. We completed their spelling words and reading, practiced penmanship while writing their description of our nature walk and their thank you notes to Mr. Gantry. Just as we were starting sums, the duke burst in and declared his intention to take the boys riding and teach them how to track deer, much more the popular choice. Off they went, and now I have time on my hands and thought I'd practice on the piano, which I truly enjoy. I will never be accomplished at sewing and use the watercolors only to enhance any drawings of plants I might do. I fear the duchess has failed to make a true lady of me, though I appreciate her efforts."

"Well then, we shall go on our own nature walk when you are ready for some fresh air. Still plenty of the estate to discover."

Bess rose. She wore one of her dreary gray governess dresses and still shone with beauty. "I am ready to go now."

"Fine. Perhaps we should take a picnic hamper along, since the weather remains good. Keep practicing until I return. You improve every day."

She assented with a lovely nod of her head and returned to her music. He was not gone very long before she took his arm, and they entered the gardens where they found the duchess instructing Duncan Gardener about which bushes she wanted primped into form before the cold set in. Kate sat nearby on one of the many benches dotted here and there for guests who became exhausted by gravel paths and merely wanted to view the scene. She read a book propped on her prominent belly.

"Since Papa has stolen her students, I am taking Bess to see more of the grounds. Do not wait for us. We have our provisions." He held up the hamper.

"Ah, yes, I recall the chagrin of our many tutors and governesses when he interrupted lessons. All of you loved that, Thalia not so much, my sons and Pandora a great deal. Very well, I trust you will take good care of our Bess." She emphasized the word trust.

It occurred to him that, except on their walk the first day of their return, he'd not been alone with Bess unless the boys or Sarah or another member of the family went with them. "We'll start with the temple of Diana, then."

He led the way down the side path until they came to the folly, an open circular structure ringed round with slender columns sheltering a small statue of the goddess of the hunt mounted on a plinth. Diana, rather scantily clad, had her bow and arrows at the ready.

"Isn't she lovely, the virgin goddess," Bess remarked.

"No more lovely than you," he found himself saying.

"Hardly." She rejected the compliment.

"You are both lithe, but you are better endowed with womanly traits. Her features may be classic, but yours are the epitome of English maidens. I wish you would wear your hair loose again instead of braided." He stepped closer to where she studied the statue.

Not looking at him, she answered, "I understand that braids and buns are the correct styles for governesses. Besides, I am over eighteen now and should wear my hair up."

"But not so tightly bound." He found himself plucking a single hairpin, light in color, from her bundle of braids. Her golden locks did not become unbound but stayed in perfect place, which showed how much he knew about undoing a woman's coiffure. She didn't seem to notice its loss. Whatever had possessed him to do that? He placed the hairpin in a pocket, a remembrance of this day.

"Shall we move along? I fear some clouds are gathering and might ruin our picnic if we don't hurry." Bess stepped down from the temple and waited for him to follow.

The path rounded the folly and led into the woods tamed back from the path, but pleasantly cool beneath a canopy of leaves.

"It's mostly greenery now, but in spring there are crocuses, primroses, and daffodils along the way."

"I'd like to see it then, but we will be back in London, I am sure."

The wandering path intersected another, this one broader, raised and leading up a hill.

"This is the side road that goes to our faux castle ruins, a perfect place to spread our cloth and dine al fresco."

"I agree."

By the time they scaled the gradual incline, the clouds had thickened. They lost no time unfolding the large tablecloth and spreading it under the archway. In the distance, the tortoises and sheep grazed uncaring, but a sudden commotion from the opposite side of the woods had the sheepdog gathering the flock tightly and the turtles withdrawing into their shells. Several young roe bucks burst forth, followed by the duke astride his massive horse and followed by Willy and Richie on ponies trying to keep up. They crossed the meadow and disappeared.

"Are they hunting?" Bess asked with some concern.

"I think not. We have a forester who provides game for the table, and usually the duke doesn't hunt until autumn. But I remember those days when he took me from class for more than book learning. Most likely they looked for deer signs and then flushed them out for the sport of it. If he wanted a kill, they would have left the horses and stalked them quietly. The boys are too young for that, chattering and snapping twigs that warn the animals away."

He set out the jug of lemonade, the cups, and napkins. Ham sandwiches, boiled eggs, a wedge of cheese, crackers, fresh August peaches, and a packet of biscuits followed. As they ate, the scene in the garden changed. The duke appeared again with his charger slowed to a walk. He leaned down to kiss the duchess when she came to greet him and with one arm lifted her onto his saddle to her delight and continued on to the stables. His grandsons dismounted and went to their mother to exclaim about their adventures. Kate rose and walked sedately toward the house with her sons leading their mounts. At the steps where they parted, they turned and waved to the couple on the hill.

"I love your family, Justin. The duke's actions are so unexpected and the duchess so much in command, yet both make me feel at home."

"I suppose I have never done anything unexpected," he confessed. "I am dull compared to my father and James."

"Oh, hardly. You are full of ideas, if not actions. And the stealing of my hairpin—that was unexpected." She bit into her peach and the juice dribbled down her chin.

He was quick with a napkin and caught it before it soiled her dreary gown. Perhaps she might have changed into one of the dresses he'd bought for her if he'd let it go. He hated seeing her so subdued. His hand lingered on her chin. How he wanted to tilt it upward and taste that peach upon her lips. Nature interrupted. Large drops began to fall from the overburdened clouds. They stood and gathered the remains of the picnic into the hamper.

"Shall we cover ourselves with the cloth and try to run to the house before we are soaked," Bess suggested.

"No, we don't have enough time. In the side of the turret is a door. We can take shelter. These storms are a deluge but soon pass." The rusty hinge resisted, but he put his shoulder to it and hurried her inside the tight, circular space with little light coming through the fake arrow slits. "There, now where were we?"

"I was making a mess of myself with a half-eaten peach."

"Yes, and I caught that dribble right here."

He placed his fingers on her chin, no napkin between them now, and raised her face toward his, hesitated, until a bolt of lightning struck nearby and forced him to jump forward, fold Bess in his arms, and take that long dreamed-of kiss, starting softly, then growing increasingly strong. He expected her to push him away, perhaps slap his face. But no, she folded against him, took his head in her hands, and returned it with ardor. His hands free, roved to her breasts and cupped them. One finger stroked a nipple, and it hardened for him. The other hand strayed to lift her skirts, allowing her to feel his desire pressed against her body. When would she stop him, because he could not stop himself? He was possessed.

Something broke the spell, a strange poking at the door. Plonk, plonk.

"Are you in there, Uncle Justin? Mama sent us with an umbrella. The door is stuck."

"A moment, please." Nothing could be more deflating than being caught by little boys, but Bess, was she in disarray? He hesitated to look now that the moment had passed.

She calmly shook out her skirts, checked her bodice, and primped her hair. "I think I will pass inspection. Thank God, Kate did not send a footman who would know what we were doing."

"Yes, that. You know we must marry and quickly."

"Dear Justin, you must realize babies aren't made by kissing, as well as I do. No one knows but us. Just as I told my father, no real harm was done when I sat half clothed in your lodgings, and none has been done now. I will not force you into marriage."

"Uncle Justin?" Plonk, plonk.

Left with little choice, he forced the door open, almost spilling Willy into the mud, not that it would have mattered. Clearly, the boys had dragged the large parasol made of oiled silk behind them, judging by the grass and soil along one side, and not used it themselves. Both were soaked, even though the worst of the storm had passed. Richie made a gallant attempt to raise it over Bess's head and failed due to his short stature. Justin relieved him of the umbrella and urged Bess beneath it. He gave the door a good shove to shut it behind them.

Bess considered her students' condition. "You are very wet. Run ahead and change your clothes. We still have enough times to finish your sums, search the globe for Costa Rica and Cape Horn, and have a story before tea. Run along."

"Sums," muttered a glum Willy. "Stories," said a more cheerful Richie. Off they went, running so fast they seemed to slip between the raindrops.

Justin cleared his throat. "It would be more of my forcing you to marry. Bess, I have been plagued with urges and unseemly dreams that have only grown worse since we arrived here. Country air and exercise is not helping. I do not know how long I can contain myself before I take advantage of you."

"I've had the same dreams, feel the same urges, and do not regard them as unseemly, but beautiful and natural. If we should decide to act upon them, I trust you would take care not to get me with child."

They had reached the bottom of the slippery slope without tumbling and now walked around the large puddles lying in wait for them.

He'd taken her statement literally. "There is timely withdrawal. And French letters. I know James always carried a few. When I was rather young, I found them when poking about in his chamber at Bellevue House. James, being James and a Longleigh, told me that sheathing one's organ in a piece of animal intestine contained a man's seed and also prevented diseases. But I haven't used one myself. Prostitutes appear to know other methods, but that is women's business."

Her laughter, contained under the umbrella, rang out like one of the sweet ditties she so often practiced on the piano. "So serious, so earnest. I am glad to have the information, though. I will see what I can learn from the ladies. Just how to phrase it without giving us away."

"Bess, marrying you would take care of the problem."

"If it is a problem, then you don't really want to give up your way of life to be a husband or you would have spoken sooner. What would our lives be like if you did?"

"Oh, Papa would double my remittance to support a wife. We'd live here with the family much of the time and with Kate and Josh at Bellevue House during the Season. I could pursue my studies as some gentlemen do, but would lack interaction with other scholars and societies while staying here."

They'd reached the bottom of the marble steps and took them carefully, one slick step at a time. On the terrace, she asked, "What would my life be like?"

"The life of a lady, I suppose. Most people consider a female tutor absurd and to be one when married unthinkable."

"Even among the Longleighs?"

"Mama would have gotten her way and seen me married. I would not forbid your intellectual interests. Beyond that I cannot say."

They approached the garden doors. He slanted the umbrella, shielding them from more than the rain and took one last, long kiss meant to tide them over until the next.

Twenty-three

Bess saw Justin at breakfast where they exchanged covert glances across the table, but her duties in the nursery awaited. She excused herself from the table, yet failed to get out the door. The duchess delayed her with the raising of a hand.

"Stay a moment, Bess. Now that the household is sorted out, we are going to visit our nearest neighbors, the Earl of Edgemont and his countess. Their sons are of similar age to Willy and Richard. I want to take them along this afternoon to play with Trent's boys. So, no nature walks today."

Justin alerted at her words like a hound to a scent. Bess, trying not to seem excited at the prospect of being alone with him, said, "I will go over their morning lessons and see they are prepared for the visit. Will you need me or Sarah to watch over them?" Please, please, let her say no.

"I would like you to meet them personally. They have their own servants to keep an eye on the children. Justin, you will also attend. They have not seen you in ages. Though after performing the courtesies, you may go off with Edgemont and your father and do manly things whilst Kate and I share the latest gossip with Lucia, not that she cares for it, having been subjected to so much of it herself. They rarely go to the city, only pass through on their way to Swansdown or to see a play or two and buy books."

Bess had to admit her interest was piqued about a wealthy, titled couple who avoided society. It helped to allay her disappointment of being parted from Justin.

"Also, do wear one of your better gowns, Bess," the duchess said as if she needed to be told that.

"Shall I send Clement to do your hair?" Kate offered.

"Ah, no. I will contrive something myself." Rather than have the maid remind her again of what a pampered pet she was to the Longleighs.

"Perhaps you could wear it down," said Justin, a tad too eagerly.

Bess put on her most serious air as if correcting one of her students. "You know that would not be proper."

"You are right of course." But she could tell he was already running his fingers through her locks mentally.

"I will be ready after luncheon."

She went on her way and tried her best to concentrate on the lessons, but the boys were squirming with anticipation at being with their summer playmates again, and she wasn't much better, wondering if she would be snubbed by such grand people. In order to appear at her best, she dismissed her students an hour early and easily decided on the white frock with the rosebud trim as being the least like something a governess would wear. Her hair took longer as she brushed out her braids and gathered her crimped locks into a loose bun atop her head, allowing some blonde tendrils to escape in front of her ears. Of course, she would wear her locket to adorn her neck and one of the high-crowned bonnets. No need for a spencer or even her lacy shawl as the days continued to be warm and the houses stuffy, despite closed curtains to keep out the sun. London would have been much more intolerable.

The distance wasn't great, she'd been told, as Westbrook Park sat just on the other side of the post road. The men elected to ride, the women to take the carriage along with the two boys. In no time at all, they crossed the main road and entered a shady lane that gave way to a view of the country seat of the earls of Edgemont. Bess did not think it as grand as Bellevue Hall, but she might have been prejudiced. It certainly had two wide wings, three floors above the kitchen, and the requisite number of columns around the entry. A very proper butler allowed them immediate entry and escorted their party to the drawing room, where the imposingly tall countess with icy blue eyes and a full bosom rose to greet them from behind a tea table set with light refreshments of small custard and peach tarts with lemonade for the children who would have swarmed the treats if their mother had not held them back.

"Mind your manners," prompted Kate.

Emulating the duke, their father, and Justin, both offered a deep bow. "Good day, Lady Lucia. Are your sons at home?"

The former Lucia Stilwell offered them a smile that changed a very plain, strong-jawed face into a welcoming one. "They are out on the terrace with their father and have been waiting all day for your company. You know the way. Take a plate of the tarts with you."

They would have run, but balancing the plate slowed them down. "They are so like my own. Gentlemen, may I offer you tea?"

Out of sheer politeness, they took the offered cups and made a bit of small talk. Lady Lucia voiced the expected remarks about how the boys had grown and how impressed she was with Justin's position as a professor.

"Do you find it suits you?" she asked.

"Oh, very much—mostly." Justin's gaze shifted to Bess sitting beside Kate after an introduction had been made. She'd become Elizabeth Barton again, daughter of a don.

"And you, Miss Barton, tutor of young boys, and an extraordinary one at that. How marvelous. I must try to steal you for my rapscallions."

Though she mustered an appreciative smile, Bess could only think that if she took a position at Westbrook Park, she'd rarely if ever see Justin again. She put down her teacup and selected a tart to fill her mouth before she blurted out that she could never be tempted away for twice the money.

A light tapping sounded in the hallway. The door opened upon a beautiful child with golden curls and a delicate build, but her eyes—her eyes were clouded over, and she found her way with an ivory stick. The countess's expression warmed again.

"My stepdaughter, Ada. Come in, dear. Are your sisters with you?"

"Emily is bringing them."

"So good to see you again. You must tell us of your latest accomplishments," the duchess said.

Ada executed a graceful curtsy in the direction of her voice. "I have learned a new piece on the piano, Duchess, and would be pleased to play it for you."

The nursery maid entered with two girls about four and two in age clutching her hands. They wore little white gowns edged in lace. Neither could ever match Ada in beauty, but as Lord Edgemont's daughters, they would have an education, fine dowries, and great prospects regardless of their looks, Bess thought. Life was unfair that way. Why couldn't people simply fall in love and marry whom they wished without impediments put in their way?

"Ah, my youngest children, Florette and Dorothea," the countess introduced. "My first daughter is named for Lady Flora, who did so much to help me find happiness, and the second after my mother, who was jealous and kept saying Dorothea means gift from God. She also claims Dora resembles her and my sister. I suppose that is possible with her blonde hair and my shade of blue eyes."

"Perhaps a bit like dear Elinor, her other grandmother, also," the duchess said. For Bess's benefit, she added, "Edgemont's mother and my best friend before she passed away."

"Girls, greet the duchess," Lady Lucia prompted.

The elder managed a coltish bob. She would be tall, Bess guessed. The other was less accomplished. Her eyes stayed on the tarts. "Nice to see you, Duchess," the elder said.

"Very well. You may each take a tart, then off for your nap," Lady Lucia commanded.

"You have a great many children close in age and also your stepdaughter," Bess observed and then realized she'd made a gaffe of some kind by the silence in the room.

The duke saved her by booming out, "I said she was a breeder from my first sight of her."

"Yes, you were correct, my dear, but you do not have to keep repeating it," the duchess chided.

As for Lady Lucia, rather than stiffening with insult, she replied, "I am nothing if not prolific. Now we shall listen to Ada's new piece, not so very new, but one she has just learned from Trent. He is a wonderful pianist, not considered a masculine accomplishment, but one I cherish. He plays a selection, then places her hands on the keyboard, and she practices until she has perfected it. Proceed."

During the interval, Ada had made her way to the piano and taken a seat on the bench. She tested her fingers on the keyboard by sounding a few notes, then began an idyllic sonata that grew into a movement of clashing chords and then smoothed out again to an even stronger romantic theme.

When her hands came to rest again, the duke stood and declared, "Brava, brava! Is that not the song Edgemont composed for you, Lucia? We heard it so many times while he pined for you."

"Yes, it is. Ada heard it one day and wanted to learn it. Trent has given her music while I tutor her in all else. She can do maths on an abacus quite accurately. Though she cannot read except for some finger spelling in the palm of the hand, she is able to write on heavily ruled paper and learned using raised letters I made for her."

An earl had pined for this unlikely lady? This time, Bess did not inquire further but said, "Then you are a tutor for the blind. How wonderful. I would like to hear more about your methods."

"And I about yours in getting young lads to study."

The duke had remained on his feet and now clearing his voice, said, "Pleasant as this has been, I believe we will leave your company and allow you to have a nice chat. Where might we find Edgemont and the boys?"

"On the terrace, I am sure, clashing wooden swords, their favorite sport.

"Ah, I might be able to give some pointers. Josh, Justin, off we go."

Justin exited last and cast back one quick longing glance at Bess, telling her they would have no time alone this day. Her mind wandered as the duchess and Kate spoke of people and events she had no knowledge of or interest about. In the background, Ada played soft tunes until she paused to remind her stepmother she needed to change for riding.

"Yes, sweetheart, I lost track of the time. The groom will be bringing your white palfrey around any minute. You know the way."

"She can ride?" Bess asked with some amazement.

"Yes, and has a very good seat. If she wants to leave our grounds, she goes by a leading rein, but she and her mare have made a path around our meadow. Both of them know when to turn. If they go into the woods, she has only to give the mare her head to return to the stable. At thirteen, Ada is on the edge of womanhood. I want her to have all the confidence she can gather to face the wider world, though if I had my way, I would protect her from that forever, which is wrong of me."

"Never fear, Lucia, you will have my aid in introducing her to society when the time comes." That promise coming from the duchess carried great weight.

"Enough talk. Shall we get some exercise ourselves? Let's see how the men are faring." Lady Lucia waited upon the duchess, then fell in behind her.

Bess, now aware of precedence, followed Kate down the long hall to a terrace similar to the one at Bellevue Hall but possessing a stone wall across its front with steps leading down from either side. The middle was currently occupied by four boys vigorously crossing wooden swords and being prompted not to drop their guard and keep up a sideways stance. It appeared the men might have been demonstrating, since their jackets laid draped over the wall.

"Cease your mayhem for a moment and allow me to introduce you to Miss Barton, who tutors Willy and Richie. The duchess has come to visit as well. My sons, Galahad and Launcelot, or Gal and Lance. I know, I know. Ada named them. She is besotted with the knights of old. They are also Baron Eagleton and Viscount Westbrook. And of course, my husband, Trent Heaton, Earl of Edgemont."

Bess kept her composure at both the irregular names and astounding titles. She returned their bows with a curtsy. The eldest strongly resembled the earl, a tall man of rugged build and the face of outdoorsman and former soldier. No pallid pretty boy, but certainly a man that would draw the eyes of the ladies wherever he went. His were covered by smoked glasses. As he made his bow, he explained, "Strong sunlight still bothers me, but I am thankful I am no longer blind. I have my beloved wife to thank for giving me my independence when I could not see for a period of time. Now she does the same for Ada."

The adults looked over the edge of the terrace and watched Ada mounted on a dappled mare cantering effortlessly around the edge of the great lawn on a well-worn path. "Not a white palfrey, then," Bess questioned.

"It's a family jest. Ada asked for a white palfrey when very young. Of course, she received a white pony now living in luxurious retirement at Swansdown, Galahad's estate, except when we visit there with all the children, and she is put to use again. The dapple was bred here and trained up especially for Ada. In keeping with her obsession for ancient tales, she has named her mount Morgan le Fay, usually just called Fay," the countess answered.

"Does she understand what dappled means?"

"Yes, I made a cutout of a horse and put raised spots on its flanks for her to feel. Unlike most women, she tends to her own mount, brushing her down and such. She knows every part of a horse, and they seem to take to her gentleness."

A dog with even more spots appeared by the mare's side in complete companionship with the horse and rider. "An early gift from Trent, my dog Wayward. She realizes he is spotted, too, but did you know Dalmatians are born white?"

"No, another wonder of nature."

"Speaking of which, I know you are missing your nature hike today, but it has gotten too hot for me to stroll. Why don't Kate and I sit here in the shade while you and Lucia take a walk. Will you tell her your story, Lucy, as much as you care to share?" The duchess unleashed the fan always dangling from her wrist and swept it back and forth in front of her face.

"I would be glad to, Lady Flora. Take the left staircase down. It brings us to the kitchen garden, which is very pleasant, then out to the lime walk."

The countess showed her the way to a walled garden with espaliered fruit trees adorning the walls. While the pears remained green, the smell of the ripe peaches filled the air. The heat of the day brought out the scents of various herbs: basil, thyme, parsley, and rosemary. The neat rows of vegetables were as well-tended as a flower garden. They passed under a long grape arbor where the clusters of fruit were just turning from green to purple, enough to enjoy at the table and still make many pots of jam. From there, they went the short distance to the entry of the lime walk with its evenly spaced linden trees and here, the countess began her tale.

"I am a daughter of the gentry. My father has a thousand acres and a prosperous farm. When the time came for me to be offered for marriage, my mother sent me to an aunt with connections to be brought out. I found only cruelty and mockery about my appearance, but no husband. I earned the title of The Giraffe because of my height."

"But you wear it so well, Lady Lucia. You are regal," Bess insisted.

"Not then. Then I was awkward and known for treading on men's feet in the dance. I have grown into my height, thanks to Trent. Regardless, I was sent home to languish, and all efforts were put into my sister, Bella, who won Sir Guy Appleton in her first season. You will meet them as they live nearby. While we visited after the birth of Bella's first child, the duchess held a summer ball. There she sat me with the earl, blinded in the war and feeling very sorry for himself. I don't tolerate self-pity, but I had assisted our blind parish priest for several years. I challenged him to learn all his old skills as a gentleman."

Bess got ahead of the story. "You did, and he married you out of gratefulness."

"No, though I did teach him that he could ride, shoot, dance, play the piano, and play at cards with a special deck. I also hired a whore to visit his bedchamber and restore his confidence in that respect."

"Oh my!"

"There is much more. He returned to his chamber early while we were both hiding in his bathing chamber. Daisy, so pretty and petite, so accomplished in the ways of men, swung into action immediately saying she was a gift. And I—I watched. Like you, I had a great deal of curiosity, but this only led me to wanting more. I knew Trent would soon have no more need of me, so one night I presented myself as another gift. On several nights, actually. Finally, I knew what lovemaking was all about and could not stay. Trent would insist on marriage out of obligation if he knew who had come to his bed. I asked to return to Ferry Grange."

With the romantic tales of C.C. Leigh buzzing her head, Bess guessed, "He followed you home and begged you marry him out of love."

"No. He did accompany me on a short stay in London along the way. By then, I discovered his sight was returning, and he would soon see me as I was and am. I could not allow that. The world would open to him and offer him a huge selection of possible wives, all noble and lovely and accomplished unlike me, merely a landlord's daughter with a small dowry, a plain face, and a tart tongue—a very unequal and even dangerous match. The gossip had already reached the ton ahead of us that I'd stayed in his home without proper supervision and wore expensive clothes he'd bought me, that I was actually his ugly mistress. Within days, he challenged a man who insulted me and shot him dead. It could have been Trent. I turned down his offer of marriage and did go home, but he'd settled a huge sum of money on me, only making the rumors worse and attracting fortune hunters of all types. Even a good friend of his made an offer, thinking we'd get along well but all the while urging me to return to Trent."

Bess, running ahead again, said, "And you did!"

"No. I intended to use the money to start a small school for blind children."

"But you did not."

"When a forgotten spinster sits in the corner quietly amongst married women, she learns a great deal, and my maid Betsy confirmed my fear that I was with child. If Trent discovered this, he would insist we marry. I had to choose another husband and soon. Along came Baron Eagleton, ill with a loathsome disease and not long to live. In one of the few unselfish deeds of his life, he sought me out to provide a mother and guardian for Ada, cursed with blindness by one of his earlier ailments. I agreed to marry him and so briefly became a baroness in charge of a small but beautiful estate and a child who needed me."

"Not ideal but a good solution to your problem as becoming a tutor for the Longleighs is for me."

"Yes. Even better, Eagleton, having no heir, embraced my son as legitimate and had great satisfaction in shutting out an odious nephew. He also read and talked to Ada in his last days, all about the knights of the Round Table and put into her mind that one day Launcelot would come to watch over the boy. He did in the form of Edgemont, who at last convinced me to marry him and became a father to Galahad and Ada and the others to come. In fact, we might have started on another. I easily fatigue these days. Shall we turn around and rejoin the others?"

Bess nodded her assent. "So, the purpose of your story was to tell me to make love to the man I adore and get with child?"

"No, heavens no! Its purpose was to show that a match of unequals can be made to work if there is love on both sides. The two of you are fooling no one with your longing glances."

"Are we so obvious?"

"Absolutely. I'd never met you before today, and the last time I saw Justin, his mind was always in the clouds of academia. He seems to have tumbled to the earth over you."

"But I do not want him to give up his career for me and come to hate me later. In truth, I am also reluctant to give up tutoring. I seem to excel at it."

"I've heard you do. Both of you are very bright. Put your mind to it and you will come up with a solution."

"I will. Thank you for entrusting me with your story. I won't repeat it to anyone."

The countess threw back head to laugh, exposing her long neck without hesitation. "Oh, my dear child, though it is old gossip, everyone can tell that Galahad is Trent's son and Lance more resembles me. We stay in the country to spare them for now, and neither of us cares much for society anyway. I believe their titles will provide some protection from wagging tongues when they must go away to school, but for now, all is well. With the duchess and myself now a countess and no longer a country spinster, we will have the power to smooth their way."

They walked back in silence. Indeed, the countess had given her much to think about. A solution formed in her mind, one that would allow herself and Justin to act on their passions but not imperil his career at Oxford. There would be some sacrifice on her part, one she was willing to make.

Twenty-four

French letters, French letters, the words filled his mind day and night. He'd already searched the chambers where his brothers sometimes stayed, starting with James' night table, but no luck. When everyone else went out of doors, he crept into Joshua and Kate's bedchamber and found nothing there either—when Justin thought about it, not needed with Kate expecting another child. He had no other recourse than to make an excuse to ride into the village of Westbrook alone and approach the notorious House of the Mermaid with its red door and lascivious knocker.

He hesitated to raise the tail of the mermaid whose nipples had been rubbed flat and shiny by previous guests. Glancing around to see if any townspeople noticed, he finally let the tail fall. No one answered at once. What if his mother, who was out visiting, saw him standing there? Or his father had decided to come to town and have a pint at the pub as he sometimes did when he went out riding? The townspeople would only shrug and say there stood another young man sowing his wild oats before settling into marriage.

He'd nearly turned around when the door was opened by a young woman whose belly strained at the cloth of her uniform. She informed him that afternoons were extra because the ladies were taking their rest, but if he knew which one he wanted, she could awaken her, and he could proceed directly to her bed.

"No, no, no one special. I want to speak directly to the madam."

"In 'ere, then. She's only just finished her eating."

He followed the maid, who had reached the waddling stage of her pregnancy. She had a pretty face possessing large, dark eyes and surrounded by black ringlets. Once the child came into the world, he assumed she'd take her place among the other girls working in the house, another servant debauched by her master. What if he put Bess in the same position? No, never. French letters were the answer.

His guide left him in an ornate room where every decorative feature sought to stimulate the baser urges. The frieze over the fireplace depicted centaurs raping barely clad women while on the mantle two bronzes of Priapus, the god of fertility, faced each other as it they were about to duel with their erections. On an enormous rosewood desk, an inkwell depicted a satyr penetrating a nymph. The décor of red and black hinted at sins to come.

The floor creaked as a booming sound echoed in the hallway. Thud, thud, thud, thud. The door opened on a woman so large in build she filled the entire space as she moved forward using two stout canes carved with serpents. Though she wore black, her gown exposed a huge expanse of bosom accented with tassels that drew the eye. In her fat lobes, jet earrings wobbled and matched her dyed hair screwed into a topknot pierced with lethal looking hairpins. Jet necklaces ringed her neck. One might have assumed she was a rich widow, but he thought not.

Making her way behind the desk and sitting into a chair that creaked with warning that it might give way, she eyed him. "Madame Pansy, at your service. Generally, I nap after my meal, but it seems you have some sort of urgent lust you need to reveal to me. I assure you one of my girls will suit your purposes."

She did not offer him a seat in one of the wide chairs facing her. Instead, he stood, hat in hand, like a naughty schoolboy not knowing how to begin. So, he simply blurted it out.

"I've come seeking some French letters and thought you might have them."

"Ah, French letters. Do you know the Frogs call them English Riding Coats?" She chuckled deep in her throat. "I do keep some at hand for my more fastidious customers who fear disease, but my girls are examined monthly by a doctor and are also schooled in recognizing men with such maladies who are shown the door at once. Nothing to fear here, my boy."

"They—they are for personal use," he stammered and knew by the heat climbing up his neck that he blushed.

She laughed so heartily her chins trebled. "For an affair, then. You are one of the Longleigh sons, I can tell by your looks. Very disappointing clients as they seldom come here, if at all, though we do benefit from their house guests from time to time. Now the former earl of Edgemont knew how to enjoy himself and treated his friends often. But this one, never. No, no, he married the plainest woman I have ever laid my eyes on and appears content with his choice. She must know her tricks. Sorry I could not recruit her to my trade."

Hearing such foulness about Lady Lucia made him want to turn on his heels and leave, but he remained standing for Bess's sake. "About the French letters."

After she'd blotted her piggy eyes of the tears of laughter with a dainty handkerchief, she opened a drawer and drew out a handful of long, narrow cloth packages. "That will be five pounds if you please. No guarantees they will work."

"Five pounds for sheep intestines that may not do what they are supposed to do. That is outrageous."

She raised her fleshy shoulders in a shrug. "Take it or leave it. Ride to London where they might be cheaper. Or try some of the taverns the duke frequents. I am sure the barman will tell him what you've been about."

Ordinarily, this threat would not bother him as his father had schooled him in safe intercourse, but he would suspect Bess's involvement and demand marriage, upsetting all their plans, or rather Bess's plans, though no one would believe that. He found his purse, placed the five pounds on the desk, and scooped up the packets, stowing them away inside his jacket. At Bellevue Hall, he'd secrete them in James' unoccupied chamber.

Did one say thank you to such a person for such a transaction? No. He tipped his hat on the way out. Her deep-throated laughter followed him down the hall and out of the red door. He looked again for anyone who might know him, and seeing none, hastened back to Bellevue Hall.

Twenty-five

After the astounding trip to Westbrook Park, life fell back into its well-entrenched routine. Bess and Justin still did the nature walks together with the boys but had scant chance to be alone or talk at any length. Her plan grew in her mind, but she had no idea how to bring it about. A failure would disgrace her forever.

August dwindled away. Peaches gave way to pears in the garden. The grapes were harvested. Gantry began herding the tortoises back to the house by throwing cabbages some way ahead to encourage them to go in that direction as the winds grew brisker. That left only six weeks until Justin needed to leave for Oxford. No, make that five since several days were required to get him back to academia.

Certainly, they found time for passionate kisses when she sent the boys off to look for empty birds' nests or to see what fishes swam in the brook. A quick duck behind a tree, and they were at it until her students came charging back. As the weather grew colder, she had to don her spencer, just more cloth between the two of them, but he sometimes ran his cold hands under it and rested them on the warmth of her breasts. He had not made another attempt to raise her skirts. Sometimes, she wished he would simply get it over with, not a very romantic notion that.

October came and with it hunting parties and much visiting among the households before the snows. She'd met Lucia's sister some time ago at The Orchards. Though the duchess remarked that Bella grew stouter with each birth, three so far, she and Sir Guy Appleton were still a perfect match. All of the children, Jonathan, the heir, Isaac the spare, and four-year-old Eva, were fair and rosy-cheeked.

An invitation came to celebrate the first pressing of cider. As soon as they arrived, the boys ran off to climb trees and make themselves sick on too many apples while Eva, a perfect blonde and blue-eyed little miss preferred to sit quietly by her mother and eat small cakes. Bess offered to keep an eye on the lads and escaped the tea party. Justin had gone out with the men to sample the cider. He trailed behind, and she nodded toward the barn, quite small and not as occupied by either horses or stable hands as the one at Bellevue Hall. They ducked into a freshly bedded stall, its occupant currently out grazing before the fresh grass had gone brown with frost.

She invited his kisses and enjoyed them well, but finally pushed him away. "We must talk. Do you recall when I asked you about French letters?"

"Far too long ago."

"Were you able to obtain any?"

A blush crossed Justin's cheeks. "I did. I went to the Westbrook house of ill repute and paid quite a bit for them. Then was mocked for not wanting to try them out on any of the occupants. I did not succumb to temptation."

"I believe you. Would you be carrying one now?"

"Yes, I kept hoping we'd have a chance."

"Now we do. The groom is out, supposedly tending to the carriage horses and is asleep on the job. We have a fine bed of straw awaiting."

"I'd hope to do better by you."

"And you will someday." She took him by the shoulders and guided him downward, but he sat up immediately and fumbled in his jacket pocket.

"This takes some time to apply. I ruined one practicing." He turned his back and unbuttoned his flap. "Good thing your kisses made me ready. There now, all set. Close your eyes."

"But why?"

"I've heard the sight of a man's organ at full extension can be frightening to young ladies."

"I am not afraid."

"Even so, please close your eyes while I make sure you are also ready as I was taught. Sorry I am so rusty at this. We haven't the time to take any clothes off, more's the pity."

"I am glad you have gotten rusty. Proceed." She sounded sure but did startle a little when he found his way through her undergarments and inserted a finger inside of her, moving it in and out, in and out, a small pleasure once she let herself enjoy it. Even better when he thumbed a small part of her anatomy she didn't realize she had. A warmth spread through her, making her restless, thrusting her hips upward.

"I believe you are ready. The next is said to hurt."

"Then do it quickly."

He pushed into her, met her maidenhead, and broke through, not difficult for him, but he stopped when she gasped. "Shall I withdraw?"

"No, that wasn't nearly the horror some women claim. Stay, let me adjust, then begin again."

After that, conversation fell away; time lost its meaning. They were two as one, together at last, but not nearly long enough before they shuddered and ended the moment. Neither of them spoke at first.

Bess broke the silence. "If you are rusty, I can hardly wait until you hone your skills."

He seemed so pleased. "Next time, it will be better, and we will be naked in a bed, not in a barn, I promise."

"Anywhere with you is good enough."

"No, no, I must go to Papa and tell him we wish to marry. We must contact your father as well, and I need to resign my professorship, The madame at the whore house told me these devices sometimes fail. We should take no chances."

He'd turned away from her again to rid himself of the French letter, bury it in the corner of the stall, and button up.

She elbowed herself up. "No. I've thought of another way. I-I could be your mistress. I do not need jewels or fine clothes, only a small place to stay near Oxford with perhaps an outbuilding that would serve as my laboratory. I am not quite sure what mistresses do during the day, but I should not like to be idle. This way, you may keep doing what you love best."

"If you mean teaching, I think I've just found something better."

She could not tell him she feared this might be lust and not everlasting love, but she continued to lay out her plan, unsure if Fair Annet, Clement, or Lady Lucia had implanted the idea in her mind. "You must return to Oxford as you usually do, and after you have found a place to keep me, write saying my father is ill and needs me. I will resign as a tutor and come to you."

"Bess, you are giving up too much for me."

"That is my decision. Now help me up and make sure no straw remains on my garments to give us away."

He did that, but his hands lingered here and there, making her want to collapse again, even be caught, and forced to marry. But no, she could not do that to him. Voices sounded, coming nearer.

"Quick, out the back, and I will go out the front and into the orchard where the boys are playing. Hurry." She pushed him ahead, though he went with reluctance. There, she'd done it, solved their problem of being together.

Twenty-six

Joshua had come back with the small carriage at the end of September after a trip to London to see to his practice. Now, he prepared to stay at his wife's side until her delivery any time. Justin packed to return to Oxford for Michaelmas term. Weather permitting, his parents expected him home for Christmas. What excuse could he use to bring Bess along? Had her father recovered from his imaginary illness by then? They'd have to concoct a new lie. He put these thoughts aside and arranged his small trunk as usual with more formal clothes on the bottom and his academic garb on top.

The family stood on the doorsteps to bid him adieu, Sarah and Bess holding the hands of his nephews. He and Bess had managed a more passionate goodbye earlier, snatched after breakfast beneath the stairwell and broken up by the approach of a maid doing her duty. He rode away with his mind not filled with formulae and heavy reading but with the hope that the cottage he'd seen on one of his rides outside Oxford would still be for sale or rent if he could not afford the full price. His quarterly stipend from the duke should be in his bank account by now, shoring up all he'd spent on gowns for Bess and not regretted. Instead of studying, he worked out a budget with paper and pencil. It passed the time.

Mostly, he already missed her presence in the coach, at meals, and especially their daily walks together. He realized this had nothing to do with passion, that physical love was only part of this equation with no good solution. He'd do the best by her that he could.

Peterson dropped him off as usual by the entrance to the college and helped carry his box up the stairs. Then, the driver promptly turned the coach around and began the long way back to Bellevue Hall, hoping to put in a half day before bedding the team down for a night at a roadside inn. Justin stood in the quarters that had suited him so well and found them empty and wanting though they were exactly the same. No time to dwell on it.

While still dressed as a gentleman, he went out and hired a horse to take him to the outskirts of town and found the cottage still for sale. A few inquiries at the nearest pub got him the name of the owner and his direction not far away. He owned a butcher shop and came to the counter in a blood-spattered apron, his sleeves rolled up on brawny arms, his broad face curious about a gent interested in his granny's old house.

"She passed this summer and with my business in town and my wife not wanting to leave her friends for such isolation I have no use for it but more income. It's an old-fashioned sort of place with a sweet well in front and a necessary out the back. A small barn for your horse, sir, since she kept a cow to her dying day. Room enough for a kitchen garden. And I kept it in good repair, I did. My wife took what she wanted from the place. The rest of the furnishings go with it. Here now, I'll trust you with the key, and you can see for yourself. I can tell you're not the kind to steal from the likes of me."

He rode off again to do a closer inspection. He approved of the red brick exterior and slate roof, not wanting to put Bess in any house where the thatch might catch on fire. The front room possessed a large fireplace and two glass windows covered by homemade draperies to keep out the cold and the curious. Not exactly isolated, but it did sit back from the road and had a screen of tall trees in the yard. The far side of the living area held a large table, crude and full of knicks that told of many vegetables chopped in the making of meals and a single chair. He'd need a nicer table and seating for two. An abandoned tea kettle sat on the hearth, and a small cauldron, most likely the source of numerous soups and stews, hung on a cast iron arm. A set of tools to turn the logs remained behind as well. The simple mantle lay bare of the knick-knacks women liked to collect but did have a pair of pewter candlesticks. In an oven built into the fireplace, he discovered some baking pans, a small skillet and single pot.

To the rear, two bedchambers on either side of a short hall leading to the back of the place where the necessary sat along the path to the barn. Not much had been left behind but a large, sturdy bedframe, four-postered with curtains the old woman must have once embroidered with a pattern of leaves, but only the slats remained. He made a mental note to buy a feather mattress, and goose down pillows. His mother had supplied him with many blankets and quilts against drafty quarters. The other room contained a shallow bathtub behind a screen.

As for the barn, it had a clay floor and two large stalls whose stable doors could be opened for light and ventilation or closed against a storm. If he put up a wall, half the building might serve as a laboratory for Bess and the other for the keeping of his horse on overnight visits. He'd put in a potbellied stove to heat her side and allow her to boil any concoction she wanted. Yes, yes, this would work very well.

He returned to the butcher shop and struck a deal for a rental until the end of the year with an option to buy. The seller pressed a package of fresh cut chops upon him. He'd take them to the university dining hall and have them prepared for his dinner. Which brought up another problem. He knew Bess had not been taught to cook, but certainly could learn. In the meantime, he'd ask for extra food from the dining hall, and she'd eat much as she had when living with her father. He could hardly ask her to keep chickens and a cow, but a farmer dwelling further down the road might be paid to leave a regular order of eggs, milk, a crock of butter, and any produce they usually took to the town market on her doorstep a few times a week.

On his return, he spotted Barney Butts and his reliable 'Arry waiting for a fare just outside of the university. An idea occurred to him on how to make the cottage more hospitable for Bess. He pulled his mount alongside and asked, "Could 'Arry pull a wagon to transport some furnishings not a great distance from here?"

"He's a horse, now ain't he? Sure he could do that for you, milord."

"Meet me by the gate to the university in two days' time at nine. I must get some things taken care of before classes begin. I'd also like your assistance in buying a riding horse, nothing fancy, just a reliable mount for short excursions into the countryside."

Butts eyed the horse he sat upon. "I know this 'un. He'd do. The stable owner is me cousin. Mention me name. He'll give you a good price, especially if you board with him."

"I will be doing that."

That quickly, he became the owner of a bay horse named 'Enery so like in appearance to 'Arry except for a smudge of white on his forehead that he might also be a cousin. He left him at the stable and carried the chops directly to the university kitchen, leaving them with instructions that one was to be prepared for Professor Barton. That would open a conversation between them and grease the proposal that he be allowed to send Bess her rocking chair, writing desk, and bed to be used in the nursery at Bellevue Hall. His scheme worked well.

"I've kept her chamber as it was in case she deemed to visit, but now that she's out and about, I cannot see that happening, especially when she is far away in the north." He cut into his succulent meat and chewed thoughtfully. "I could reclaim that room as my study. But don't the duke and duchess have plenty of furniture of their own?"

"Yes, Bess has a nicely furnished bedchamber to herself as tutor. But there is room in the nursery for a few sentimental items to make her feel more at home."

Professor Barton sniffed and went on with his meal, pushing a mound of potatoes atop the chop. "Bess is she now, no longer Betsy. She's living in the lap of luxury and still wants those old things. You can have them taken away whenever you will."

"I'll see to it all."

"I don't suppose you've brought me a letter?"

"Ah, no. I am certain she will write soon and thank you for the furnishings." He had to remember to send her a post soon to cover that detail.

The next day he spent buying a fluffy feather tick and pillows, bed linens, a good supply of wax candles, additional candlesticks, lanterns and oil, more pots, pans, dishes, and cutlery, a small table and two chairs. Setting up a household was a great deal more work than most men knew, but at last, all including the furnishings were loaded into the wagon and transported by 'Arry to the cottage.

As Butts remarked when helping with the mattress and heavier items, "You setting up so far outside of town?"

"Yes, I find I need a peaceful and quiet place to reflect on my studies."

"Whatever you say, milord." He raised one end of the old table and backed it out to the barn with Justin heaving the other end.

The two beds were set up, the smaller by the bathtub, the rocker by the hearth, and the escritoire by a window. Since her father did not seem to care, he'd also taken the chamber pot and washstand with its mirror. How pleased Bess would be when she saw all he'd done. Had he forgotten any essentials? The French letters! He'd left three of them in James' night table. No matter. They'd be easy to find in a town serving hundreds of randy male students who made use of the pubs and the barmaids.

However, the thought passed through his mind that marrying her would have been easier. She'd have a luxurious life as part of his family, full of visiting, tea parties, and fetes. If snubbed by the ton, he doubted she would care. He'd have no need for French letters and if a child came along, she'd have the best of care. But would she soon grow bored of an idle life and look elsewhere, take a lover like so many women of the highest classes did? It did not bear thinking about.

Twenty-seven

The letter arrived two weeks after Justin's departure, a very long two weeks of trying to hide her true feelings and pretending to be entirely content with her status among the Longleighs. The day of his departure, the duchess and Kate had taken her aside and expressed their dismay that Justin had left her yet again.

"We did so hope he would remain by your side and propose. He's never stayed so long between terms," Kate said, hands resting on her full-term belly where the child kicked and turned, disturbing her sleep at night.

The duchess nodded. "The day of the great rain when the two of you took shelter in the tower, we thought perhaps something might happen to bring him around. I know my son would do the honorable thing by you, but he did not."

Bess kept her gaze on her hands knotted in her lap. He had told her they should marry more than once. It was she who refused to ruin his academic life. Now, she could hardly wait to be with him again, despite how kindly she'd been treated by these ladies.

"We merely took shelter from the rain. I thank you both for your good wishes and Fair Annet, too, if she is listening, but I am meant to be a tutor and am content with my lot."

Which was soon to change when Justin sent word. She would have his love, and he could keep his career. Perhaps, if she were very careful, she might find someone to tutor to fill her days. Teacher when the sun shone. Mistress when darkness fell. She only fretted that she could do the second as well as she did the first.

The first week of his absence, she managed not to lurk near the door when the afternoon post arrived. The second week was a challenge to stay away. When the missive did come, she fairly snatched it from Busby's hands as he sorted the mail in to bills, invitations, and family news from London. He arranged them on various silver salvers to be presented to the duke, the duchess, or Kate and Lord Joshua. With some embarrassment, she returned the letter addressed in Justin's hand, but to his mother, not her.

"I am so sorry, Busby. I-I expected a letter from my father."

He smiled only slightly. Servants observed everything. "I believe this one is for you." He plucked a letter from the bottom of the pile and placed it in her hands.

She rushed off to the privacy of her bedchamber to savor every word, knowing he could not write what he wanted to say. The duchess often asked others to share their letters and read them aloud.

Dear Bess,

I arrived safely at my destination and am preparing for the autumn lectures. I do hope to see you again at Christmas. Until then, stay well and keep stuffing knowledge into my nephews' heads.

I would write more but thought you should know at once that your father is in dire condition, brought low by a fever and unable to hold a pen. He bids you return to him and see him through this crisis as he has no one else. Your chamber is as you left it, waiting for your arrival. Should you need any assistance while in Oxford, I am at your service.

Yours, Justin

She held it up to the light of a candle to see if he might have written more in lemon juice, a ploy for sending secret messages. They had discussed this and decided against it because both the duchess and the duke had used the same device when Lady Flora had been captured by the Turks and held for ransom. Should the duchess become over curious, as she often did, any words of love they might have shared would be revealed. Nothing appeared on the sheet of paper. Now, she must affect distress over her father's condition and ask to be released to see to him. So many lies told to prevent Justin's life from being ruined as her father's had after marrying her mother.

She plucked out an eyelash or two, and the brief pain sent tears coursing down her cheeks. Taking the note with her, she sought out the duchess, who embroidered by a window on this rather gray day. An open letter lay on a nearby table. She glanced up, smiling until she noticed Bess's tears.

"Is something wrong, my dear child?"

"I had an upsetting letter from Justin who tells me my father is gravely ill and needs me." She offered it to Lady Flora and took the handkerchief from her sleeve to blot her eyes.

"I see. Then, you must go to him. But know you are welcome here at any time to resume your position as tutor. Kate will be so upset to hear this, but I won't bother her now with this. She ate only toast and tea this morning and is now back in bed resting. The babe has gone quiet in the womb. Mark my word as mother of ten, the child will be on its way within hours. I have summoned the midwife who birthed Justin, a woman of great experience, and asked her to stay in residence tonight. At least, you will still be here to see our Annette."

"I would like that so very much. I shall tell Sarah and the boys that I must leave for now and pack my trunks this afternoon. Perhaps I can ride the post coach down to Oxford. The rush of students returning will be over by now."

"Nonsense. Peterson shall take you and watch over you on the journey. He knows the best places to stop along the way where a woman will be safe. I will send orders to the kitchen to make up a hamper of food for both of you, and you can deliver some pots of strawberry jam to Justin to see him through to the Christmas holiday. The duke will provide a purse for your travel expenses."

"Please, that is not necessary. I have saved most of my salary."

"Doctors come dear when one is very ill. We want to help your father back to health in order to bring you home to us again. Here, this might cheer you, happier words from Justin than those he sent you." The duchess held out the letter she'd nearly snatched away from Busby.

"As you see, he has purchased a riding horse for exercise, though heaven knows why. He could have taken one of ours, Black Lightning perhaps, as he rode that one in London."

Bess managed a small smile. "He and Black Lightning were not the best of friends. I am sure Justin is only trying to live independently. Ah, his new mount is named 'Enery. It must be related to 'Arry, the horse who brought us halfway to London in the spring. How far I have come since then in so many ways. I will always be grateful to you and all the Longleighs."

The duchess waved her away. "As it cannot be helped, speak to Kate and the boys about your leaving. I shall notify Peterson and get a purse from the duke. Off with you before I cry, too."

She could not imagine the duchess shedding tears over a tutor but went on her way to scratch gently at Kate's door, not wanting to wake her if she slept. She found her pacing the carpet, not in bed, and wearing a dressing gown, her rich brown hair still in its night braid.

"Shouldn't you be resting?"

"The birth pangs have started but are not very strong yet. No use sending everyone, including my husband, into a tizzy as there is such a thing as false birth pangs. I expect that as this is my third, I won't be at it so very long if all goes well—six or eight hours at the most."

"Eight hours seems quite a long time to be in pain." Her own mother had died bringing a child into the world.

Kate's lovely laughter filled the room. "Willliam took twelve hours, which is not unusual. Of one thing I am certain, I want you to teach her as you do my sons."

Bess lowered her gaze to the carpet as if studying its complicated Persian paisley pattern. How she would have enjoyed giving a girl the same education as a boy. But she had to speak up. "I am afraid I will not be here to do that. My father has taken ill and summoned me back to Oxford to care for him. He is so weak that Justin had to write the letter."

Kate came close and enfolded her arms about her as well as she could with her belly in the way. "I am so sorry. We shall pray to make him well again. I know I will never find another tutor like you."

"Thank you. I know with Fair Annet watching over you, all will go well with the birth." She was not so sure she believed that, but if Kate did, all the better.

"Oh yes, she will be near, but she is so very disappointed that all her efforts to bring you and Justin together failed, all the dreams she planted in your minds. She felt sure they would come to fruition in the tower that rainy day. So did the duchess, for that matter. We expected you to return to the house wet but engaged."

"He—he restrained himself."

"All that academic training, I suppose. I did so want you as a sister, Bess."

"Nothing would have made me happier, but I must go." She returned the embrace. "I will tell the boys so you don't have to be bothered. Have a safe birthing, Kate."

Her next stop lay at the head of the stairs to the nursery where she'd instructed the boys only that morning. They sat at the table working on the sums she'd left for them. They looked up full of anticipation.

"Is it time for our nature walk?" asked Willy.

"We don't mind if it rains," said Richie.

"No, I am sorry to say I must return to Oxford as my father is ill and needs my care. I shall miss all of you so much. Sarah, I am leaving the primer we are working on right now and expect you to continue studying. If you have any difficulties, I am sure Lady Katherine will help you. Boys, do behave for your new tutor whenever he arrives."

"You are never coming back?" Richie asked with tear-filled eyes.

"I cannot say, but your education must not be set aside waiting for me to return. Soon, you will have a baby sister sharing the nursery. That will be wonderful."

"No," said Willy. "Maybe it won't be a girl. That would be better."

"Whatever, I expect you to listen to Sarah as she will be very busy with the baby and not as able to run after you."

While the boys nodded, she could already imagine schemes forming in their minds for escapades. How she would miss them. While Willy tried to offer her a manly handshake and bow in farewell, she hugged him and Richie tightly. Sarah startled at receiving the same from such a learned lady but did return it despite all the extra work her leaving would create once the baby arrived.

The duke waited in the library to give her the purse and say she'd be welcome to return at any time under any circumstances. Lord Joshua nodded in agreement and offered his bow. She went to her chamber to pack her belongings and found Clement already started as if eager to see her gone. One less person between her and the top of the ladder of servants. The maid left out her gray dress for travelling and turned on her heels to go without a word.

As the door to the hallway opened, Bess heard some low groans coming from Kate's room. Joshua's wife did not come down to dinner and afterward, he paced the drawing room restlessly as husbands had done from time immemorial. The mystery of birthing remained in the hands of women. After a time, the duchess rose and told him to sit. She would ascertain the progress of the birth. Bess played some soothing melodies as her contribution, though she would have been interested in witnessing a child coming into the world. As a mistress, she would not likely have children or be able to keep them if she did. That made her a trifle sad, but this was another sacrifice she made willingly for Justin.

The duchess reported back that it would not be very long now, and Kate handled the pangs bravely. Just before they lit their candles to take up to bed, a few sharp cries sounded, followed by the wail of an infant. Joshua did not wait but took the stairs two at a time only to be thwarted by the midwife who asked for a moment to clean the child, yes, a daughter, quite healthy and with a thick shock of dark hair, and set his wife to rights before entering. The others had arrived and glimpsed only the midwife's apprentice changing the sheets while the infant, still bloody and messy from birth, lay in Kate's arms. Joshua seemed to look beyond them and mouthed a thanks, perhaps to a guardian angel for watching over his wife, but the rest saw nothing. The midwife shut the door firmly and went about her tasks. Joshua stayed as a sentinel, and everyone else returned to the drawing room. After a time, they heard footfalls on the stairs, not the steps of the plump midwife, but of Joshua bearing his daughter in his arms and showing her around, very much the proud papa.

"Beautiful like her mother, our Annette. Kate is well but tired and will see you in the morning."

Bess, unused to babies, held the child briefly and then turned her over to the father again. The duke and duchess handled the babe with ease. What a privilege to be here on this night. She must tell Justin all about it—but perhaps not as it might make him fear he'd father a child of his own and be forced from the university. She went to bed with that thought in mind and woke ready to leave this life for one as a mistress to a brilliant, young professor, her choice after all.

Twenty-eight

A hastily written letter arrived by a messenger on a swift horse as he finished his morning lecture. The slower coach would arrive at the noon hour or a bit later and deposit Bess at the gate to the university. Professor Longleigh extracted himself from two young ladies forcing apples upon him, though he accepted both out of courtesy and left notice on the door that the afternoon lecture would be cancelled. With his black robe flying and his pace undignified, he raced to the gate and found Bess had not yet arrived. He sent a boy to summon Barney Butts and 'Arry, saying he'd pay for the man's time if he was not needed immediately. And to bring around 'Enery saddled as well.

Since the bell had rung for the afternoon meal, he stood in line for entrance to the dining hall but asked that two meals be packaged for him today as he was in a great hurry. That raised the eyebrows of the server, but the whims of the dons were not questioned. As soon as he had his basket of provisions, he was off to the gate again, pacing in anticipation and more elated than if he'd solved a difficult equation.

Butts arrived beforehand, a good thing, as Peterson might question his passenger's quick removal to another carriage. As he stowed the luncheon basket out of sight, he requested that the driver wait a discreet distance away, and just in time. The small Bellevue coach appeared and came to a stop by the gate. Before Peterson could tie the horses and attend to his passenger, Justin lowered the steps and handed her down—his Bess, dressed in his favorite blue gown with a becoming bonnet but beneath it, her golden hair was merely pulled back and worn loose as if she were still a maiden.

Peterson heaved her trunk to the ground. "Where shall I carry this?"

"No matter. I will see to it. Here, accept these vails for bringing her here safely and so promptly." He dug some coins from his waistcoat pocket.

"Your lordship, that is unnecessary as Miss Barton is a cherished member of the household. Speaking for all of us, we wish her father a fast recovery that will enable her to return to us soon."

"Yes, yes, of course. I know you must be eager to return to Bellevue Hall while the horses are still fresh. Away, then."

Peterson eyed him as if he might be a lunatic, but said, "As you wish, Lord Justinian." The carriage barely turned a corner before Barney's rig came to rest in its place.

"So nice to see you and 'Arry again," Bess said. "This must be 'Enery." She patted the saddled horse.

"No time for that. Get inside at once. Butts, come fetch the trunk before we attract the notice of the gatekeeper." He freed 'Enery from his leading rein and mounted. "To the cottage."

Butts gave him a knowing glance but said nothing. He remounted the box and clicked to 'Arry to walk on. Their pace increased once they cleared the town and passed into the nearby village and out into the countryside. 'Enery had made so many trips to the cottage, he turned in automatically and stopped. Looking right and left and seeing no one else on the road, Justin helped Bess down again and hurried her to the door, unlocked it, and fairly pushed her inside.

"What do you think?" He waited for her pronouncement. Had he missed anything? Only yesterday, he recalled he hadn't purchased tea, sugar, or salt and made a special trip to do so.

With a gentle smile, Bess said, "It is very like my grandmother's home—and oh, here is my rocker and my escritoire."

"The inkwell was dry. I have filled it. Your childhood bed is in the second bedchamber, but the other has the featherbed I promised you. If there is anything else you need, you have only to tell me."

Her hand went to his cheek. "Dear Justin." She leaned toward him.

"Ahem, where'd you want the trunk and this basket?"

"Oh, set the basket on the table and put her box in the larger bedchamber. Then you may be off—only will you stop by your cousin's farm and ask him to start leaving fresh viands three times a week." Again, he dug into his pocket to pay the fee and a bit extra. This time, it was not refused.

"Miss Barton, wishing you happiness here," Butts said as he left, but a touch of doubt tainted his words.

"I have dinner in the basket if you hunger. It might still be warm. I know how to make a cup of tea. Just let me light the fire and take the chill from the air."

"Justin, I have not come all this way for dinner. Tell me, does the featherbed have lots of blankets upon it?"

"It does."

"Then, the dinner and the fire can wait. Oh. how I wish I had invented those self-lighting splints. They would save so much time. I won't wait another minute for you to claim me again. It is all that has been on my mind for weeks."

"Mine as well. I am equipped." He pulled a handful of French letters from his waistcoat. "Quite easy to find in Oxford. I hope they are the same quality."

"As do I. Why don't we try one now."

"With pleasure, our pleasure."

It was. Two naked bodies on clean sheets, exploring each other under the comfort of a soft, light blanket. He suckled the pink tips of her breasts and found that spot she'd enjoyed so much before, tested her for readiness. As for himself, more than ready and in haste to get the preventative on and enter her wet warmth again. Her moans encouraged him, her hands against his hips pressing him on. It ended all too soon for both of them.

"Later we will take more time. Try new things you might like," he promised as she lay in his arms. Bess Barton's first day as a mistress had begun.

Twenty-nine

Justin had implored her to stay in the bed while he got the fire started, laborious with flint and steel and kindling as if they were camping in a forest. He'd bank it carefully in the evening in hopes that some coals would survive the night to be aroused in the morning. Gone an awfully long time, his side of the bed grew cold. Bess was about to put on her clothes again, when he reappeared balancing a tray with cup of tea and a nearly reheated dinner. Accustomed to the lukewarm meals her father had provided, she did not complain but found eating naked with the sheet tucked under her arms awkward. Perhaps, mistresses often dined this way, and she would become skilled at it. Justin did not eat with her but went out again to tend to the patient 'Enery who'd stood in the cold as they dallied and heat her laboratory set up in the other half of the stable.

Laboratory, one of the sweetest words in her vocabulary. She could not wait any longer to see it. Slipping from the bed, she dressed and scurried the short distance out the backdoor to the barn and found Justin on his knees coaxing a fire to life in a potbellied stove. He'd lit a lantern as it was truly too chilly to open the stall doors that served as windows. On the other side of a thin wall, she heard the shuffling of the horse who appeared to be enjoying his hay more than she had her meal in bed. A worn table with an equally ancient chair held a motley assortment of glass phials, beakers, and flasks. On a shelf, an array of chemicals in no special order awaited her touch. As if recalling their first meeting, he'd supplied a large barrel of water and set a wooden bucket at its side. She warmed at the memory.

The wood in the stove began to crackle. Justin rose to his feet. "I should have asked Butts to bring some coals, but my mind was entirely elsewhere. Did I forget anything else? I went into one of chemistry labs and made a list of all it contained. If you need more, do ask for it."

"Some texts to guide me, but otherwise, you have done well." In truth, she itched to begin some experiments and nearly wished he'd return to Oxford, but she didn't suppose mistresses demanded such things. Go back to your classroom and let me work. Not to be uttered.

He watched as she rearranged some of the items. Dusk settled in October early. He carefully banked the small fire and led her back to the house with the lantern in hand. There, he lit candles and placed the pewter holders on their table for two. Neither of them seemed to know what to do next.

"You haven't had any dinner. Let me set yours near the fire to heat, and we'll make fresh tea," she suggested. "We can—talk while you eat."

"That might be a good idea. I believe I should restore myself."

While the water and food heated, she went to the bedchamber and hung her gray dress on a peg in preparation for tomorrow. A warm wrapper joined it. It wasn't at all lacy or erotic but a pleasing shade of pale blue and easy to remove. Lacking a wardrobe, she left the rest of her clothes in her trunk, removing only four sealed crocks of strawberry jam sent by the duchess to her son. These she carried into the front room where Justin stared into the fire, his mind not on the food which had begun to bubble on one side but not elsewhere.

She turned the plate and poured the water that had come to a boil into the teapot still half full but with some life left in the tea leaves. No sense in wasting what had already been done.

"Rags, we shall need some clean rags for lifting pots and other chores." She'd brought her own for her courses but no need to mention that yet. Justin had many sisters and must know of the monthlies, but it wasn't a subject to be discussed. After all, her father had turned her over to the housekeeper when she thought she'd bleed to death and not remarked on the subject again. Women who had given birth and nursed their babes did not have their courses, nor did those who were very ill. She did not expect either to befall her.

"What an oversight. Rags, of course you need rags." He appeared embarrassed but did not need to be. They'd always been able to talk freely. Now ordinary conversation seemed awkward.

She brought him a cup of tea and his dinner, sat with him while he ate. "Oh, news from the Hall. Kate birthed a baby girl the day before I left. Both are well as far as I know. She has named her Annette after her ghostly helper and is joyful to have a daughter. Willy and Richie are not as delighted to share the nursery." There, she'd delivered that information as casually as possible.

"I am glad. To be truthful, I prefer her to my own sisters. Her obsession with Fair Annet is eccentric, but not harmful, though men other than Joshua might have her committed. Otherwise, she is most sensible and intelligent, not to mention courageous when she was incarcerated in a tower and left to starve. That is where she discovered Fair Annet who helped her survive. Has she told you of that ordeal?"

"Not directly. I suspect she doesn't want to remember it. But it seems that C.C. Leigh used her story as a plot in *The Haunted Tower*."

"You've been reading the twins' novels? That is an education in itself."

"You have read them too?"

"Only brief portions when I was much younger and found them shocking. Not so much anymore. Some men might forbid their wives from reading them."

"A good thing I am not a wife, then. As for Fair Annet, I cannot discount the dreams I had at Bellevue Hall that Kate claimed were sent by her ghostly friend. They were so arousing."

"I had the same. Torment to be with you every day and not be able to act on them," He finished eating and laid down his cutlery decisively. "We can act on them now. If you are willing."

"I am at your complete disposal." *Now that was something a mistress would say.*

Thirty

They had made love all night long. He'd encouraged her to ride atop until she convulsed over him and made him do the same beneath her, and later satisfied her by lapping at that oh so sensitive place between her legs while he recovered. Shockingly wonderful. Early in the morning, she'd learned the difference between urgent intercourse and slow and lazy lovemaking. All so good.

He'd wanted her to stay in bed again while he roused the fire and started tea, but she refused to do so. Because farmers rose early, they found a small crate with a jug of milk, a crock of butter, six eggs, and a loaf made by the farmer's wife. Breakfast! Easy enough to boil a few eggs and slather the bread with fresh butter and strawberry preserves. He ate in his shirtsleeves and pantaloons while she stayed in her wrapper, her feet warmed by slippers Kate had made for her.

He told her he would start the fire in the laboratory when he went to the stable to saddle 'Enery for the return to Oxford. "I scheduled my Michaelmas lectures to suit our arrangement, one the hour before noon and the other at two. That way I can return to you each evening and bring whatever else you might need. If I must stay to consult with a student or have a meeting with my colleagues, my arrival times might vary, but I shall always come to you."

"I would like to say all that I need is you—but toasting forks and a simple cookery book might be put to good use. After all, cooking is basically chemistry. I am sure I can master some simple dishes."

"There is no need. I can set up an account at the chop house to deliver a meal and will bring more from the dining hall."

"To be honest, I am not sure how I will fill my days without two little boys to tutor and would like to try my hand at things other than chemistry."

"Whatever will make you happy. And now I must go." He kissed her deeply enough to last all day, but of course it did not.

She spent her morning in her cozy lab making her favorite precipitates for the fun of it, scrambled some eggs in a buttered pan over the fire, adding a touch of milk and pinch of salt, easy enough to do. They made a good egg sandwich. She ate one of the apples Justin had left on the table the previous evening and speculated there might be more of them arriving tonight.

Missing her daily walk, she grew restless after the meal. The sun shone with October brightness on the changing leaves of the trees in the front yard. The air had warmed enough that her spencer over her gray gown should be warm enough for a stroll. Putting on her bonnet, she ventured outside.

No one on the road, but she took a side path, perhaps one made by deer or cows returning to a barn. For lack of flowers from a garden, she plucked some small branches bearing yellow and red leaves to brighten her house. The path did end at a pasture gate enclosing some very contented looking brown cows who turned to face the stranger approaching them. Beyond them sat a tidy farmhouse with numerous outbuildings and laundry hanging on a line to dry, no finery but sturdy clothes meant for the fields and household. As she stood by the fence, a long-haired black and white dog began barking and summoned a stout farm wife from the side of the house.

"Who be you upsetting my cows?" she shouted.

The cows did not appear upset, but she replied, "Only a neighbor out for a walk. So sorry to bother you. I'll be going now."

"You the young lass being set up by the gentleman next house down. Anything else you need? He's paying well for your keep." The woman came closer, examining her every inch with small brown eyes almost black in color as she wiped off soapy arms on an apron. A white cap kept her gray-streaked dark hair from falling in her face. She looked incapable of smiling, all hard lines and deep grooves.

Bess strained to think of something. "Perhaps a small cheese. Your bread was very tasty."

"Happy you found it so. I'm Mrs. Uriah Butts—and you?"

"Elizabeth Barton." What more to say? "Perhaps some vegetables might be added to the box or fruit."

"Not much in the garden this time of year but cabbages and onions. I'll see what I can do. Leave the box outside your door once you have emptied it." No invitation to sit and chat, but then she'd interrupted the woman's washing. Washing—she'd need to find someone to clean her clothes and especially their sheets.

"Thank you. I'll be on my way. A pleasure to meet you." She retreated down the path and to the main road, followed that back to her house. Hoofbeats sounded coming from behind her, so not Justin returning early. Instead, a lady mounted on a white horse cantered along as if she'd just ridden from the pages of a C.C. Leigh novel. Her hair of gold, her eyes of blue, her face porcelain, though as she came closer, Bess thought she might have rouged her cheeks and lips and was not quite as young as she appeared from a distance. However, her riding habit spoke of quality and style. She pulled up her mount beside Bess.

"Welcome to this dreary little town. I suppose you are the other one all the gossips have been nattering about."

"Other what?"

"A kept woman. I'm Daisy Churchill and pleased to have your company." She spoke as well and graciously as any member of the ton.

"Elizabeth Barton." No use in denying her status.

"It's a great nuisance getting onto a side saddle, so I will just walk Moonshine alongside of you and we can converse."

"My house isn't far. Would you care to come inside? I only have tea, bread, and jam to offer but would be pleased to share it." The idea of company appealed to her. Perhaps she could get some pointers from this experienced beauty on being a mistress. Close up now, she knew the courtesan must be well into her twenties.

"I believe I would enjoy that."

Upon arrival, Daisy threw her leg over the saddle horn and slid gracefully to the ground. "Where shall I put my horse? Around the back would be better. People will talk."

"I have a stall behind my laboratory. Let me show you."

"A laboratory. How interesting."

Bess threw open the stall door for Moonshine and left the upper half open to give the mare some air. A bit of hay remained in the manger, and she was welcome to it.

Bess showed Daisy around the front to her lab and explained some of the precipitants she'd created that morning while putting water in a beaker to sustain her autumn leaves. Her companion didn't seem all that interested in chemistry but did appear impressed that a woman might do such remarkable things.

They went into the house with Daisy peering into both bedchambers with great curiosity. She took the offered seat at the table while Bess made tea and sliced bread, buttered it thickly, and offered the jam. Her guest dabbed on just a tiny bit.

"I must watch my figure at all times. That is how I managed to convince Walter I needed to learn to ride and required a horse for exercise. You should ask the same of your young man. How I envy you to have one so handsome and eager. I've seen him riding by from my window often as he made a place for you. He never once looked my way." Daisy sighed. "I must be content with what I have, a man of middle age, moderate wealth, and with few demands of me except the usual. According to him, his wife locked him out of her bedchamber after their seventh child was born, and a man has needs. That's what they all say, but he visited Madame Pansy's house often enough before that whenever he came through Westbrook in the autumn to buy cider to distribute to various inns and taprooms in Oxford and London. He manufactures his own high quality ale as well. Hence, his wealth. Regardless, he always asked for me if I was not otherwise occupied."

"Westbook, you say. I've just come from there. I was a tutor to two of the Longleigh children." Perhaps she shouldn't have divulged so much but Daisy had been very open with her.

"Ah, I see. The youngest son debauched you. I thought he had the look of the duke's sons, not that any were frequent visitors to the House of the Mermaid. Only when young and wanting to provide some entertainment for visiting friends. At least he is taking care of you. I cannot tell you how many of Madame Pansy girls were previously servants gotten with child by their masters. They did the laundry and housework until the babe came, all the while learning the trade by watching through the peepholes or being taught by the older women. Then, it was off to the church steps for the child and paying Madame Pansy back for their elocution lessons and new gowns once their figures returned."

"How harsh."

"Not at all. Where were they to go with no reference and a big belly? Most were in service to send money to large families left behind. They could not burden them with two more mouths to feed. As for myself, my pig of a father, actually a swineherd, sold me to Madame Pansy at the age of fourteen. I owe all to her. Especially, that I am living very well now and not wed to a lout and spewing out infants that die in poverty."

"I see. But what if you should conceive a child now?" Her mouth became very dry. Bess took a swallow of her tea. "I mean, we are using French letters, but I understand they sometimes fail."

Daisy waved a soft and scented hand in the air. "Oh, la. There are ways to bring off infants, ways to stop them from coming at all, the French secret being just one. Some mistresses believe you should have at least one child by your keeper in order to have a better hold on him, but that is not for me. Midwives know how to bring off a child with their potions. I have not had to resort to that because I am very careful. I always insert a sponge soaked in honey before entertaining Walter. He likes the taste. And afterwards a douche of vinegar and warm water once he sleeps."

So much she did not know. "I should get pencil and paper and note these ideas."

Daisy let forth a practiced laugh like the trill of a bird. "These methods are passed by mouth from woman to woman and always have been. A good thing as most of us can neither read nor write. Madame Pansy often read to us but considered educating women like us to be dangerous."

Curiosity aroused, Bess asked, "Whatever did she read to you?"

"Oh, not that boring Jane Austen. We very much liked *Fanny Hill: Memoirs of a Woman of Pleasure*. I still have not entertained a dwarf but enjoyed hearing about it. They are supposed to possess very large organs. *Tom Jones* was also amusing. I'd like to have a lover like him."

"Would you want to learn to read? I'd gladly teach you. Perhaps in return, you could instruct me in riding Moonshine."

Daisy cocked her head in a very engaging way. "Let me think. I usually sleep until noon, have a light meal, and then prepare myself to receive Walter or go riding if he is not expected. A mistress must always look her best. But I admit, that does not fill my day. I do miss the girls at Madame Pansy's house. We would talk and trade tales. If a client treated one of us badly, we would go to Madame and insist she not admit him again. Generally, she would shrug all her fat and say her business would never lack for men. She'd have our evening doorman expel any we objected to. Here, I can go shopping along the main street. The storekeepers are glad for my custom, but not my company. So yes, I will ride here Monday through Thursday as Walter is not likely to visit then until the evening. You will have the mornings to work in your laboratory, then ride a bit, and afterwards teach me my letters. How does that sound?"

"Perfect," said Bess.

~ * ~

Justin arrived after dark, giving her lots of time to change into a becoming gown and loosen her hair from the braid she wore in the laboratory to give it a good brushing. She had the fire glowing and the candles lit on the table where she reread from her aunt's book of fairy tales. She left a lantern by the door which he picked up to guide his way to the stable, not that 'Enery would have any trouble finding it and a ration of oats. As he unsaddled the horse and got him settled for the night, she started the tea. By the time he came in the rear door, she ran to greet him with a kiss. He suggested they eat first and set the food by fire to warm.

He'd brought her two chemistry books and one of cookery, two toasting forks, the wooden bowl from his lodging and two more apples. For the rest, he'd stuffed his saddlebags with rags. No need to burn her hands this evening turning dishes. As they waited for their dinner, she told him of her day.

"I went for a walk to the farmer's house and met Mrs. Uriah Butts, who was not very cordial but did promise to supply a cheese and what vegetables and fruits she might be able to find."

"I suppose that did no harm but be careful when going about alone."

"I will, but I later made a new friend in the same circumstances as I am. We plan to shop together, and I am going to teach her to write. Her name is Daisy, and she is the most glorious creature, formerly of the House of the Mermaid in Westbrook. Isn't that a coincidence? Have you heard of her?"

"Perhaps a mention or two among men but I assure you I never made use of her services. I am not certain you should be seen together."

"Why not when we are both kept women?"

"I don't want you to think of yourself in that way. I do not keep you for my pleasure but because I love you, Bess, and would have it no other way."

She took his hand, and they abandoned dinner, only returning later to eat slices of a raisin-studded pudding with cold tea before returning to bed again.

A fresh box of provisions sat on the doorstep in the morning, this one with the additions of a small cheese, two onions, and a cabbage. She was not sure what to do with the vegetables, but supposed the cookery book might have some suggestions. They sat side by side toasting bread and boiling eggs for their breakfast, perfectly happy without kippers or deviled kidneys. When Justin rose to leave for Oxford, he asked what more she needed and said he'd leave orders for the chop house to deliver her a meal in the afternoon because he'd forgotten to do so earlier.

As for her needs, she asked for honey, vinegar, and a sponge.

Thirty-one

One thing Bess did not miss was having to be fully dressed in a day gown to go to breakfast each morning. She enjoyed toasting bread with Justin in nothing but a shift and her wrapper. After his departure, she put on one of her tutor's gowns and a leather apron to work in her lab. In the afternoon, a lad from the chop house delivered a meal of pork and potatoes which she ate at the table as she perused the cookery book. *Hmm, cooking cabbage, not too difficult.*

She heated a pan, greased it well with butter and loaded in the chopped cabbage, one sliced onion, salt, and pepper. Watching it bubble down to half its size did remind her of some of her experiments. Before long, she had a side dish to go with her pork chop. A taste told her it was good enough to serve at dinner to Justin. She put the pan aside to reheat later.

Now, to prepare an alphabet for Daisy. How she regretted leaving her primer behind, though Sarah would make good use of it. It amused her to make comical drawings for each letter, A for apple of course, B for a stick figure boy, C for a cow, D for a spotted dog, and so on. Since Daisy slept until noon and then had to primp far more than she did, it passed the time until her student's arrival.

Daisy breezed in the back door. "Are you ready to ride?"

"As ready as I will ever be."

"You must ask for a proper habit and boots, but I suppose your half boots will do for now and there is no one about to think you immodest if you show some leg or ankle, but we will need a mounting block of some kind." Daisy wrinkled her nose. "Whatever is that smell?"

"Some cabbage I have cooked. It's quite good and still warm. Would you like some?"

"No! It gives me the horrors—and flatulence. That is barely all my mother cooked before I was sold to Madame Pansy, though we did have pork and ham to go with it at times. Another lesson about being a mistress. Your lodging should never stink—of anything—and certainly not cabbage. Air out this room at once and if you have perfume, use it. A man should think of sweet scents when he thinks of you—lavender, attar of roses, scented soap. If you lack these things, do not hesitate to ask for them. You want to stay pretty for him. That always works."

Bess put a lid on her cabbage and opened the windows, grateful that the autumn afternoon had turned mild. She'd learned another mistress lesson, but it squelched her pride in her cooked cabbage. They went out back where Moonshine was tethered and took a log from the woodpile to help her mount with one leg slung awkwardly over the horn, her bottom barely on the saddle, and the reins clutched in her nervous hands.

"Now, give her the order to walk along with a touch of your heel and a loosening of the reins."

The well-trained mare flicked her ears back to receive the order and paced slowly forward.

"To turn her, pull on the rein in the direction you want to go and turn her head. That's right. When you want her to stop, pull back on both reins, don't jerk them. See how easy this is."

"Yes, but I am still a long way from the ground."

"Moonshine is an Arabian and quite small for a horse. My advice is not to look down and, if you feel yourself falling, simply let yourself go."

Bess did not fall. For a time, she walked the mare around the barn, around the house and back again, but felt some relief when the lesson ended. She still felt the horse under her even when her feet were on the ground. On to something she was good at—teaching.

Daisy did take her lesson seriously, repeating the alphabet over and over and mouthing its sounds much as Bess had ridden in circles. After all this exertion, Bess again offered tea, bread, and jam, and they settled in to talk. She could tell this experienced woman anything without shocking her.

Shyly, she confessed, "Justin has encouraged me to take the upper position and ride upon him as I did on Moonshine."

Daisy's laughter trilled out again. "I hope not sidesaddle, as that would be very uncomfortable."

"Oh, no, astride. We both enjoyed it very much."

"Well, it is a lazy man's position when they don't want to make the effort to be on top. That, and when have you take their rod in your mouth."

"He has done something similar to me, and I confess, I loved it."

"You have a rare gentleman. Usually, it is all about them and their pleasure. They do so love having their genitals fondled and their organ sucked to completion."

Bess concealed her shock. Mistresses must do this sort of thing all the time. She should get used to the idea.

"I must be going. I need to wash and perfume myself in case Walter comes."

"Every night?"

"It is best to be prepared at all times. You have so much to learn—as do I about the written word. Until tomorrow."

That night, she had some surprises for Justin and not just cooked cabbage, though they ate first, and he declared it as good as something Monsieur Pepin might concoct if he ever served cabbage. Probably untrue, but she accepted the lovely compliment. After tea and biscuits, they adjourned to the bedchamber as usual and disrobed, sliding beneath the covers onto the cold sheets.

Bess shivered in his arms. "Perhaps we need a bedwarmer."

"That is why I am here." He reached to draw her close, but as he turned, she allowed her hand to stray to his genitals and begin fondling them, loose balls in a furry sack beneath a limp shaft that flipped in surprise. She moved her hand to it and caressed it to fullness.

"Do you enjoy this?"

"I believe every man does, but I must get my preventative on."

"Not necessarily." She ducked under the covers, applied her lips to the head of his cock, and began to suck.

Even muffled by the covers, she heard his gasp. His hand moved down and drew her up. "Please don't do this."

"Did I do it wrong? It gave you no pleasure?"

"It is pleasurable, but degrading for you because you derive no pleasure of your own from it. I don't want you to do this."

"It is not degrading if I want to do it."

"Loose women are paid to do this in alleys. You are not like them."

"You mean your parents or Kate and Joshua would never do this to each other?"

"I cannot speak to that—though I would not put much past my parents. I've overheard talk of a feather torture more than once."

"That sounds interesting. I must ask Daisy about it."

"Please stop taking her advice. You are nothing like her either." He held her close to his chest.

Though she tried to suppress it, her chin began to wobble, and her eyes filled with tears. "I think I am failing at being a mistress. I made you cabbage, and the house stank of it."

"Barely noticed it. My mind was on other things. You may touch me down there any time you want." He moved her hand to cover him. "See, still aroused, despite all this talk. We are both learning. Only yesterday, I was told the French letters can be rinsed out and used again. Considering how many we are going through, that would be an economy. But here."

He reached beneath his pillow and handed one to her. "Would you like to put it on me?"

"Yes." She opened the packet and considered its narrow width. "Are you sure it will fit?"

"It is very snug, as it should be. Be sure to roll it all the way to the top."

Less adept than he was, she finally got on the sack of animal intestine. Her efforts helped sustain him.

He asked, "Would you prefer to be on top or bottom this evening?"

"No matter what Daisy says, I'd like to be on top. It's much better than riding a real horse."

"Ride on, my love, ride on."

Thirty-two

The days continued to grow shorter, the nights longer and colder. Justin rode with his sword cane to use against any who might note his route and attempt to waylay him. He asked Bess to keep the doors bolted when he could not be there, but she left them open to Daisy, her only visitor who never stayed until darkness.

Bess bothered Mrs. Butts for more vegetables and oats, mastering a creamy porridge, mashed turnips, baked swedes, and best of all, the French omelet that the cookery book claimed had been served at the court of Napoleon. Since her meal from the chop house always consisted of a slab of meat whether beef, mutton, or pork and potatoes, she often saved the remains. The potatoes could be sliced and fried, the meat chopped and added to her omelets, along with cheese and onion and some parsley that Mrs. Butts did not begrudge her. She provided Justin with hearty breakfasts before he went on his way in the morning.

Changing raw foods into cooked, fascinating, oats and milk turning into porridge, eggs from nearly liquid to a solid.

Her riding skills increased. Moonshine took her on gentle canters along the road while Daisy studied spelling lists and practiced with chalk and slate to form letters. Such an eager student, she learned rapidly and had presented Bess with a new alphabetical chart with naughty drawings such as P is for penis with a sketch to match and B for balls that were not kiddie toys. No, not like teaching little boys, though they would have snickered over it. Justin did not know of the riding lessons. She planned to surprise him one Sunday when they had the whole day to themselves by asking him to let her ride 'Enery. She suspected Daisy did not reveal her new accomplishment to Walter either.

They continued to end their visits with tea, bread, jam, and talk. Bess boasted to Daisy that she had mastered three new sexual positions to which the courtesan replied, "Oh, there are an infinite number of those. I do hope you are keeping up your appearance and asking for French undergarments. I see you in the same gowns all the time. You need more and better or at least warmer with winter coming on."

"Why, when we barely keep our clothes on at all?"

"For the allure—and fine clothes and silk and lace shifts might be sold if you are ever in need of money."

"Justin supplies all that I need."

Daisy let her eyes stray around the simple furnishings, the total lack of luxury. "My dear, you possess an entire house which is impressive, but I have the complete third floor of the local boarding house and even that is adorned with oriental rugs and velvet settees. Think of your future. I intend to leave this life at some point and buy a cottage in the country or on the seaside like Fanny Hill. You must think of your future."

"My future is Justin."

"Poor child to think so. When they tire of us, we are discarded like clothes only fit for rags. Let me see your nightdress."

Bess fetched the modest white cotton garment with a small frill of lace top and bottom. Whenever it or one of her gowns needed washing, she promised Mrs. Butts extra to take special care of them.

"Oh my, that shall not do. I will bring you one of my French shifts to entice him and encourage him to buy you more. Of course, one doesn't always need alluring clothes. If you appeared before him naked except for the leather apron you wear in your laboratory, that would certainly gain his attention."

Would Justin desert her one day and leave her with nothing? "The house is only rented until the end of the year."

"Then you must get more out of him before then."

"But we are happy as things are,'

"That is the answer of all ruined governesses for a time."

She did not divulge to Daisy that she had six-hundred pounds being held as her dowry. However, she could hardly ask her father to release it with no marriage forthcoming. A problem for another day. She put that aside. On the other hand, if Justin needed more variety, appearing in only her leather apron cost nothing, and it would stir memories of his heroic rescue. She would put that plan in place very soon.

One very dark and dreary night, she stoked the stove in the laboratory with an extra log, carefully removed her work in progress to safety, and left a note on the stable door to meet her in her lab. She had something special to show him. When he arrived and put 'Enery in his stall for the night, she undressed and tied on just the leather apron. She waited, leaning against the old table in a languorous way. When he entered, she saw the astonishment on his face. In a C.C. Leigh novel, his next move would have been to sweep her flasks and beakers aside and take her on the tabletop.

"My God, you will catch your death of cold! I thought you had s scientific breakthrough to show me."

"Only myself." She dropped the apron.

He did rush forward, shedding his woolen riding coat as he came. She leaned farther back on the table offering herself. He gathered her into his arms, wrapping the coat that smelled of him and horse around her.

"We must get you into bed before you contract pleurisy."

He set off carrying her in his arms to the house and placed her in the bed, added two blankets, and rushed off to make tea to warm her. At first, she thought it was part of the game, but no. He returned to the laboratory to bank the fire, and retrieve the lantern, then served her the reheated dinner in bed while he sat beside her in one of the kitchen chairs and asked about her experiments. She had to admit that Justin hadn't a romantic bone in his scholarly body. No bonbons, bouquets, or jewels from him. His last gift had been a packet of raisins to add to the porridge or to eat if she pleased.

"Tell me about your research," he asked.

"I am attempting to precipitate aluminum by chemical reduction, with little luck so far."

"Each attempt eliminates what did not work and brings the outcome closer."

"Yes, you are right." She would not use the leather apron again for anything but work.

"If you are nicely warmed now, perhaps I could slip in beside you and make sure you are perfectly recovered."

She was. But he insisted she take the bottom position so as not to overexert herself.

Telling Daisy of her failure made the woman laugh again. "What you have is a husband, not a lover."

"Oh, he is an excellent lover and always puts my preferences first."

"A rare man indeed. I brought along one of my French shifts. Try covering it with a dressing gown in a warm room this time."

"It will do no good now. I started my November monthlies and would not want to ruin it. I must tell him I am on the rag for a week and do not know how to handle that."

"Dear child, it is the man who must decide. Some like sauce with their pleasure. Others insist that you use your mouth or hands on them. Some simply wait it out. I suspect yours will be among the last."

He was, insisting she stay in bed and bringing her hot water in a metal container wrapped in flannel to lay on her abdomen and ease her cramps. As soon as he left for the day, she was up and about, dressed and working in her lab. He didn't seem to realize that only wealthy women could afford to lie abed at this time of the month. Others had to get up and care for children and their chores.

She recalled that Lady Flora had told her the Shawnee had a separate hut for menstrual women. They were brough food and drink and spent their time making moccasins and gossiping. Sometimes their suitors would play the flute outside the hut, as had the duke when she was a captive, despite his lack of musical talent. Bess thought this a wonderful idea to make such a time a pleasant rest rather than a dreaded ordeal, but doubted this would ever become popular in England.

At least Daisy visited. She brought along a gift she had made with her own hands, a large, warm shawl in a mix of bright colors: red, green, and yellow, each set of strands knotted off into a fringe. As she had nothing to offer in return, she tried to give it back.

"Many of the girls did needlework or knitting to pass the time and taught me. You can't keep wearing that light, lacy shawl that belonged to your mother at this season of the year. I, like your lover, am afraid you will die of a lung ailment. Besides, you have given me the gift of reading, which is worth so much more."

Of course, Justin noticed the shawl immediately. "Did you buy it? Are you cold? I should have seen about getting you winter garments by now."

"Daisy made it for me. I have a bit of my last salary left and some of the travel money the duke gave me, and I try to use it frugally, but I do want to purchase something for Daisy as her reading is coming along so very well. Could you find a set of C.C. Leigh books? I think she would enjoy them?"

"Your last request is easy and won't cost a cent. My mother keeps stacks of them in the guestrooms for female visitors. She hides them discreetly under the Jane Austens, Maria Edgeworths, and the Fanny Burney novels. I will send to Mrs. Crump for a set. I should have given you an allowance. I am so sorry. I will take one of your gowns to a seamstress in Oxford and have some made in woolen fabrics."

He showed up that evening with a long, blue hooded cloak with matching lined gloves for her outdoor walks—and her riding, though he had no idea of that. The dresses came one a time, long-sleeved and made of fine woolen cloth in a pale gray, a dark green, and deep blue, all lightly embellished at the neckline and hems.

Daisy regarded them with exasperation. "Serviceable and pleasant like you, but at least you won't freeze."

She'd hung her own cloak, red and fur-lined, on a peg. Despite the left-handed compliment about her dresses, Bess was pleased to present the package of books. She could tell Daisy yearned to read them as she fondled the red covers and lingered over the sometimes lurid frontispieces picturing women with their clothes half ripped off and shirtless heroes. She picked out a few words from the pages.

"I will cherish them, Bess."

"Just enjoy them when you feel you are ready to read longer passages. They are fun and outrageous. But not Jane Austen."

"Oh, thank heaven for that!"

Thirty-three

On an idle Sunday late in November, Bess decided to delight Justin with her skill at riding. "Do you think I might ride 'Enery?"

"I believe anyone could ride 'Enery. You will always end up at a warm barn where a bag of oats awaits. But certainly. Let me lift you up and lead you around."

"Not what I had in mind. Give me the reins."

"Be careful, Bess. He won't bolt, but you could easily slip off sitting sideways on the saddle."

She gave him a merry glance and 'Enery an authoritative kick and order to walk. Once around the barn, she moved the horse into a trot and on the third turn to a canter, then slowing down in front of an astounded Justin to ask, "What do you think? Daisy taught me on her Arabian mare."

He helped her to the ground, but did not return her enthusiasm. Taking her shoulders in hand, he stared directly into her eyes. "I suppose now you will want an expensive riding habit and a white horse to go parading around town when I am not here. I know she does."

"I have never done that."

"Nor will you. Bess, I have run through my quarterly allowance buying you clothes and paying the rent. Married family members get twice as much and my salary is not adequate to support another person. If you had consented to be my wife, we would not be in this predicament."

"I only wished to make you happy, having both your academic career and me."

"Do you think I am happy when I spend all day worrying about you living here alone and how I will be able to feed and clothe you properly when down to my last penny? Even if I try to rest in my old lodging, I cannot, because I miss you beside me. I am in agony."

"I've brought you no pleasure?"

"Certainly you have, but it only lasts until I leave you for the day. I cannot concentrate on my lectures or research with you on my mind."

He moved his hands from her shoulders to cup her face. "Has *she* been telling you that you are so beautiful you could do better than a poor professor?"

"No, she said you are more a husband than a lover. I told her you were a fine lover and very considerate of me. Then, she replied that you are a rare man indeed."

His hands dropped away. "I am not sure if that is a compliment, but it does not matter. Michaelmas term ends shortly. We must go to Bellevue Hall for the Christmas holidays and spend the month, which will save our paying Mrs. Butts for food and laundry and the chop house for your dinners. I have already sent the letter saying that your father is much better but unable to travel. However, he insisted you visit your friends rather than sit in his quarters minding him. My mother has written often that she's had no word of you since you left. It would have helped if you'd sent her a note now and then, but I replied that taking care of your father consumes all your time. By January, I will be solvent again, but we must be careful with our money."

"Your money. I gave you all that I had to give, and it is not enough. You tell me you are miserable. I do not see how this can work in the future—too many lies, too much expense. Perhaps I can ask Kate to take me back as a tutor. She need not know I am utterly ruined and completely devastated." Her tears flowed. No holding them back this time.

"This was your scheme and now you must live with it. I told you I would have more money the first of the year. Pardon me if it is not enough. Did *she* teach you to cry when you don't get what you want?"

"N-no, Daisy is my only friend and might care for me more than you do."

"Then enjoy her company. I am returning to the university now. My students are studying for their examinations, and I must administer them before we can leave."

'Enery seemed puzzled when his master mounted and turned his head toward Oxford so early in the day. No rest for him evidently. But yes, oats and a stall at the other end.

He left her without a kiss or words of love. The perfect day of crisp, sharp light shattered. The cold wind hit her wet face like small shards of glass. She went inside, wondering if and when he would return, and that night slept alone for the first time since entering the cottage. Now they were both miserable.

~ * ~

Daisy did not visit on Sundays. Walter came to her after attending church with his wife and family and consuming a fine meal. Then, as he told his spouse, he needed fresh air and exercise, at least of the kind his mistress provided. She arrived at her usual time in mid-afternoon to find Bess with a swollen, tear-stained face and in search of guidance.

"He said I'd made his life a misery and used all of his money. This had been my idea and now I must live with it. That much is true. I did not want him to have to choose between me and his life in academia. Now I know which he loves more. We have never quarreled before this."

"Ah, dear girl, a mistress should never fall in love with her keeper. Far better to consider it a business deal, our services for his support."

"What do you do when you quarrel with Walter?"

"We do not quarrel. Walter is always right, and I let him believe so. So it is with most men, but it is rather good to know that Justin isn't perfect after all."

"What should I do?"

"You could try the French shift I brought you to win him around again."

"I think if he saw me in that, he'd accuse me of wanting to buy more."

"It always works for me when Walter is out of sorts." She offered one of her nonchalant shrugs, lifting her delicate shoulders and relaxing them again.

"What if it is over? I cannot return to my father and live at the university. The Longleighs might take me back as a tutor, but then, I would see Justin often. I don't know if I could bear that." Bess offered the bread, butter, and jam and poured their tea as if this were any other visit.

"If you are returning to Westbrook, I can guarantee that Madame Pansy would take you on immediately. No need of elocution lessons, and you are well broken in when it comes to bed sports. You lack only a more alluring wardrobe."

Bess felt the heat rise in her face, probably the color of the strawberry jam she spread on her bread. "I am not sure I could be with many men—and what if someone came from Bellevue Hall or Westbook Park and recognized me?"

"Ah, Westbrook Park, the seat of the earl of Edgemont. I visited him once when he was still blind, a gift to restore his confidence. Now there was a man. Such a pity he could not see me. Perhaps he would have chosen me over that very plain woman he wed. Yet, somehow she went on to marry a baron and give that man an heir, and later came back as a widow to wed Edgemont and give him a son. Lots of gossip at the House of the Mermaid about that, I might say. I always wondered what quality she had that I lacked. How did she do it?"

"Lady Flora says she has a strong character. The duke admires her fertility. Lady Lucia has given Edgemont three children so far and most believe the baron's son is his also. When you see them together, they are certain."

"Not what men look for in a mistress. Just the opposite. Regardless, Walter is taking me down to London directly after Christmas with his family. We shall see the sights, shop at the Burlington Arcade, and drink champagne, perhaps see a play if it is a comedy. I will keep my ears open for vacancies at the better houses of ill repute or any men who might suit you better than what you've got."

"I know you will enjoy the arcade. That is where Justin purchased my summer clothes, though no one was to know except Lady Katherine. I probably emptied his bank account then also. No, I think I will return to tutoring. The Longleighs will give me a reference. We leave at the end of the term."

"In that case, keep the French shift, my Christmas gift to you along with my best wishes for your future. I don't know if our paths will cross again once you leave."

"And I wish you a cottage by the sea. Here, take this jar of strawberry preserves. It is all I have to offer."

"That and your friendship is quite enough."

~ * ~

He'd left her in tears, shivering even though she wore the blue cloak. He'd said despicable words to her, all brought about by worry over his finances and resentment of Daisy, who knew more about the ways of the world than either of them. Where else was Bess to find a friend as a fallen woman? He'd taken away the support of Kate and the duchess, while he still had his colleagues and students surrounding him.

Now, when he wanted to go back and apologize despite the truth of the matter, he could not escape the young men fishing for hints as to what his final exam would contain. All that he told them was each ended with a command to explain and demonstrate one of Newton's laws, and they would not be the same on each test so they should study them well. The young ladies who had no excuse to stay for the examinations doubled their gifts of apples and hinted that if he had no place to celebrate Christmas, their families would be glad to have him.

Darkness had fallen several hours ago, later than his usual time to point 'Enery toward the cottage. He took it as a good sign that Bess had left the lantern outside the front door as usual. First, he must see to the faithful 'Enery, who had unwittingly started their argument, and then make it up with Bess, though he had nothing to offer but apples and himself. He opened the door to the big box stall and found it already occupied, not by an Arabian mare but a muscular black.

A tall man broad in the shoulders stepped from the shadows. Justin drew his sword cane. "Who are you and what are you doing here?"

Had Bess taken a new lover so soon? Or worse, had this man forced himself upon her in this lonely cottage?

"Put that down before you hurt someone, baby brother."

"James? Why? How?

"On horseback obviously. Why—Mama of course. Exactly how long did you think you could get away with playing house with Bess before she figured it out? Why don't you tend to your rather sad horse while I explain. I am sure there is enough room for him to share with Black Lightning."

As Justin removed the saddle and gave his loyal steed a quick brushing, James went on, nonchalantly leaning against barn wall. "The devil is in the details, as we all know. It seems a letter came for Bess a fortnight ago written in a firm scholarly hand and from her father, who asked if she'd received her furnishings in good condition, and being the man he is, hinted that she might ask if he could spend Christmas with her at the Hall. As Mama, who had no qualms about opening it said, not a mention of illness or of Bess's arrival in Oxford."

Justin pulled down some hay for the horses and made sure the water buckets were full as he contemplated his error in failing to have Bess write her father about the arrival of the furniture. Excited as he was to see her, it had entirely slipped his mind. No use fretting over it now.

"Does Bess know you are here?"

"No. Not a sign of life when I got here at least an hour ago, both doors locked. No lanterns burning inside. Rather than startle her, I waited here. I've been observing your comings and goings for a week now from that small woods between here and the farmhouse. Naughty, naughty Justinian. Not to mention that you left her in such a state on Sunday, I considered going to comfort her but thought the better of it. I am not good with weeping women."

"Nor am I." Visions that Bess might have harmed herself over their argument or gone to stay with Daisy raced through his mind. "We should go inside at once."

As they walked past the deserted laboratory and down the path to the house, matched stride for stride, James continued. "I had newly returned from Scotland, excellent salmon fishing and good red deer hunting, but Phemie's brood of children give a man no rest in his own castle. Mama insisted I ride here and discover what had happened to Bess. Easy enough to do. I waited for you to leave the campus and followed. The locals had much to say as well about the kept women living in their midst. Would the whole town soon be nothing but a brothel? I wrote a report saying that you had set Bess up as your mistress and sent it by special messenger the same day. This morning, I received my orders to bring the both of you home, delivered by a man on a well-lathered horse. Peterson is on the way with the carriage."

Justin unlocked the rear door but hesitated. Would he find Bess undressed, attempting to mend their quarrel or worse if she'd harmed herself. "Perhaps I should go in first and prepare her."

"I've got all night as I will be staying here. It's late to return to the inn."

Justin nodded, thinking for a moment of his highly masculine brother curled up in Bess's childhood bed with its canopy of butterflies right across the hall from their bedchamber. Even if Bess forgave him, there would be no bed sports tonight. He entered, calling softly, "Bess, I am home."

She did not rush into his arms or answer. He lifted the lantern from the barn and saw the main room empty, the door to the bedchamber closed. He turned the knob and found her in bed with the covers pulled nearly over her head. Was she breathing? A chemist would know how to bring about a peaceful death. A few paces brought him to her side. "Bess, I am home."

She sat up so abruptly they nearly knocked heads. "A good mistress would have greeted you beautifully dressed—or naked, but I am not a good enough mistress, am I?"

She swung her legs over the side of the bed, and he could see she wore her nightdress. Her cornsilk hair lay snarled about her shoulders. The lamplight did little to flatter, exposing dark circles under her eyes.

"I went to bed early as I did not sleep well last night."

Nor had he. "Have you eaten? I left our meal in the barn but will go get it."

"I had the remains of my mid-day meal from the chop house which I paid for myself. Whatever you brought from the university is all yours to reheat by yourself. You no longer need to take care of me. I shall ask Kate for a reference and seek employment as a tutor again."

"Bess, please, not now. We have a guest."

"A guest?"

"James, my brother James."

"Then we have been found out."

"To say the least. Please dress. He has much to tell us."

"Go get the food and offer it to him while I prepare myself."

As soon as he got to the door, she closed it behind him.

He let James inside and escorted him to the table. "I left our dinner in the barn and will be right back. Bess is making herself presentable."

"Naked?"

"No, asleep and in her nightdress. Do not expect to see her at her best."

"That does not bode well in a mistress."

"Don't call her that! She is the woman I love."

"Too bad you did not realize that sooner." James stretched out his long legs in the direction of the low burning fire.

Bess had not appeared when he returned with their meal, and after stirring the coals and adding a log, he set the food on the hearth to warm and waited. She made an entrance in the dark blue gown he preferred and wore her hair loose, simply pulled back with a ribbon. He missed the brightness he usually saw in her blue eyes when he appeared, the welcome on her face. She turned toward James, who rose to greet her and sat beside him, leaving Justin to put the kettle on for tea.

"James, what a pleasure to see you again. Or is it?"

He offered one of his arch smiles. "That may depend on how you look at it."

"Might we just get on with it," Justin snapped, his jealousy of his brother rising like the flames in the fireplace.

"Since I am here, you must know that your arrangement has been discovered. I am to take both of you back to Bellevue Hall as soon as possible. But here. A letter from the duke to Justinian. As you can see, he has ripped the paper with nib of his pen and blotted much of the address. I'd say he is not in the best of moods."

Justin accepted the mauled missive and cracked the ducal seal on its back. He unfolded the letter which went on for two pages and began without niceties:

To my youngest son,

I cannot believe that you of all my children who cared only for the life of the mind has given yourself over to the lure of the flesh by seducing and debauching a young woman under my protection. You will make this right for her. We have announced your engagement and the first of the banns about your intent to marry have been published this past Sunday in the village church. You will wed Elizabeth Barton on the week before Christmas. Turn in your resignation to the university, as you will not be returning.

I have written to Professor Barton who appears to know naught as he sent a letter asking to spend Christmas with Bess at Bellevue Hall. He shall. We will not reveal his daughter's shame but have merely asked for his blessing on the match and his presence at the wedding. I am certain he will agree.

Close up your bawdyhouse and send along anything you wish to keep from it. My banker has contacted me out of concern with the information that you have already expended your quarterly allowance, spent on household items and female garments. A woman, of course, but I did not think it could be our beloved Bess. Your mother knew better. We sent James to see what he would discover—that you have been living together without the benefit of clergy. That will soon change.

Defy me, and you will be cut off without a cent.
Your father,
Pearce Longleigh, Duke of Bellevue.

The smell of burning issued from the hearth. Justin rushed to save his meal and forgetting to use a rag, singed his fingers. The water for tea steamed. Bess did not rise to take care of it. He poured it into the waiting pot. His life with Bess was in shambles and still they must eat.

James eyed the plain surroundings. "Hardly a bawdyhouse, more of a cozy love nest. If only you had offered for her in London, all of this could have been avoided."

Bess studied her hands resting calmly in her lap. "At that time, I had some hope but knew then he would not give up academia for me. Justinian is not to blame. The scheme was mine, a plan for us to be together without his losing what he loved best. I seduced him. He told me we should marry several times while at Bellevue Hall, but I refused. The blame is mine."

James's dark brows rose. "Extraordinary. Perhaps I should have offered for you myself, but Mama insisted I merely make Justin jealous enough to propose out of a strong belief that Bess was meant for you only, my brother."

Bess who had been pale as the frost forming on the rooftops, flushed slightly. "I know you only showed interest in me at your mother's behest."

"At first, but I did find your company charming and your curiosity in all things appealing. I so enjoyed annoying Justinian, the genius who could not figure out he was in love despite his skill with mathematics."

Justin placed the platter on table. He put two slightly squashed bread rolls he'd carried in his waistcoat beside it. "Won't you eat, Bess?"

"I've told you I paid for my own meal."

"Since I've been waiting in the cold for your arrival, I'd appreciate a meal." James ripped a leg off half a chicken and raised it to his mouth.

"We do have plates and dinnerware." Justin rose to get them, though he and Bess had often eaten from the same dish, each offering the other the best tidbits. "Do you want tea?"

"Considering the circumstances, I'd like something stronger."

He went to the writing desk and revealed his decanter of brandy. He'd moved almost everything he'd had to the cottage, including the battered chair that still smelled of his father's pipe smoke, where a nearly naked Bess had once sheltered. The level in the bottle had hardly changed since the day he'd given it out to calm Professor Barton. He poured some into the teacup and slapped it down in front of his brother. "There."

James took a sip. "Ah, Papa's finest. You want to take that along with you to the Hall. What else? Make a list so we can get on with it." He helped himself to the mashed potatoes and gravy, the glazed carrots, and a roll. "Much better than what I was served in the dining hall as a student. The dons always ate like the king."

Justin poured tea for Bess and himself. At least she accepted that and warmed her hands around the cup. He placed the packet chocolate biscuits he'd brought as a peace offering because she liked them so, but she didn't reach for one.

Instead, she began her list. "My rocking chair, the escritoire, my childhood bed. The rest should fit in my trunk. Also, the contents of my laboratory must be carefully packed. I am hoping the duke might find a place for me to continue my experiments once he is over his anger with me."

"About that. I'd advise you to say nothing and let Justin take the blame as a gentleman should. Our father wants to believe no wrong of his daughters and considers you as one of those."

"Forcing Justin to marry me was not what I wanted."

"Don't concern yourself about it. The duke forced Valls to propose to Iris as he lay on the floor with a sword to his throat. You'd be too young to know about that, Justin. He vowed to make Phemie a widow when her Scottish laird kidnapped her and did a handfasting. As for the twins, their escapade determined me to leave for Europe. All of them seem entirely happy, as Mama predicted. She would say it is not how it begins but how it ends. My biggest regret in all this is that now she will set her sights on making me happily wed as she has run out of other children."

"I think the family has given up on you. With Joshua having the two boys, the line is assured. You should be safe now." Justin replaced his tea with a measure of brandy.

"No one is safe from her matchmaking ever. Well, it's been a long, cold day for me. I shall turn in. By the way, you will be sharing your bed with me, my brother, and Bess will use the one from her childhood. No sharing of a chamber on the road home either. Our parents want no accidents between now and then, unless it is already too late. You left these behind in my night table drawer." He withdrew the French letters from a pocket.

"We have been careful. I am not with child," Bess said.

"Be sure to add that when begging the duke for his forgiveness, Justin. It might count for something."

James rose, stretched, and entered their bedchamber. Bess said nothing more as she went to sleep in the bed of her childhood. Justin was left to clean up the mess from dinner.

Thirty-four

He wrote his letter of resignation as a professor of physics at the escritoire and handed it to the chancellor the next day, giving as his reason his intent to marry.

"Who is the fortunate young woman that has lured you from your studies?"

"Professor Barton's daughter, Elizabeth."

Although obviously astounded as he must have expected one of the young misses who haunted his classes to be the bride, the chancellor tried to make light of it. "Then we lose a prime professor, but our laboratories are safe from destruction. My best wishes to both of you."

He oversaw the examinations for his students without mentioning a word of his retirement from academia. He had no desire to hear Betsy Boom jests at his expense that might raise his temper to make gestures more foolish than once challenging his brother to a duel.

Professor Barton could not have been happier. "From misfit to tutor to a marriage into the family of the Duke of Bellevue. However did this come about with you here and she so far away?"

"I expressed my love in letters and asked for her hand."

"Of course. Will I be taking the carriage back with you for the wedding now that the term has ended?"

"I am riding home with my brother on horseback. The carriage will be sent for you later." Lies and more lies. How complicated his life had become.

As for what he wanted to take to Bellevue Hall, his books and the blankets and sheets his mother had given him, the apple bowl for sentimental reasons, and the academic robes he would not wear again. When he told James that he also wanted to take 'Enery, the man had laughed.

"You can have the pick of anything in the duke's stable and you want this nag. Sell him back to the man who sold him to you. I am sure you paid too much in the first place and won't get that back, but it will put some coins in your empty purse."

"I have little else to give Bess as a Christmas gift. 'Enery is reliable and loyal and would never throw her or brush her off. She does not ride as well as she thinks. Her friend's Arabian mare is so well-trained anyone could ride her."

"Her friend being the other fancy woman upsetting the locals. Now that is a mistress. I observed her practicing her letters as Bess went riding. Kind of Bess to teach her to read and write."

"Bess loves teaching, as did I. But that is over with. The butcher we lease the house from has agreed to take the table and chairs, the dishes and pots and pans in lieu of our December rent, but I do want the feather tick. Cost a fortune. I believe I shall put it on my bed at the Hall for now."

"Yes, very comfortable, indeed."

His brother grinned in a way that made him want to punch his teeth in, but that would upset Mama who still fretted about the small scar James had on his cheek. The last few nights lying beside his muscular and always naked brother who gave off heat like a house afire made him miss Bess more than he thought possible. Oh, to be able to turn over and take her in his arms again rather than getting an elbow in his side if he took up too much room on the mattress.

In the end, the last of his university stipend paid off the chop house and Mrs. Butts. Penniless, he mounted the coach with Bess sitting across from him and 'Enery being led behind, which slowed their travel some but not enough. Spectacles in place, Bess read from one of her books. He studied some scientific papers he'd been meaning to peruse.

James rode alongside, rarely in the coach. He suggested strongly that this would be a good time to make it up with Bess. "Whatever you quarreled about that Sunday."

"I told her our arrangement was making me miserable and that I'd run out of money to keep her. She misunderstood and took it personally."

"What a way with women you have. I had a mistress for only a short time when I thought all men were expected to have one. She was greedy and demanding, but did I say so when we parted? No, I thanked her for a delightful sojourn and gave her one last purse to tide her over until the next man came along."

"Bess was neither greedy nor demanding. Every moment with her was a wonder until that argument."

"Then tell her what you really meant."

"If only I knew."

The miles passed and on the last day of travel he tried his best to apologize. "You do know that I love you and want to marry you."

"Having been forced to the altar. You will come to hate me as my father did my mother and me for robbing you of your career."

"We will manage to make some sort of new life together, never fear." He had no idea what that might be.

When at last the coach turned into the gates of Bellevue Hall and came to a stop at the front steps, he no sooner helped Bess down than she ran into the open arms of Kate and began to cry. The servants who had assembled to welcome her home murmured, "Did her father die?"

"No, no. Tears of joy to be back among us and for her upcoming nuptials. Back to your duties," the duchess said, waving them away, all but Sarah trying to remove Willy and Richie from their clutch on Bess's legs and already reciting their grievances about the new baby sister.

"She cries at night and only eats and sleeps."

Bess kneeled to hug them. "She will become more amusing with time. I am ready to resume our nature walks if the weather allows."

Kate, one arm around Bess's shoulders, escorted all of them inside, past the duke standing with his arms folded at the head of the stairs. "Justin, with me to the library."

James gave him a slap on the back. "Good luck, I do mean that. I'll see 'Enery has a warm stall and some oats. I am amazed he survived the trip."

His father turned and expected to be followed. Inside the library with its tall shelves of knowledge towering over them, the duke took a large chair made especially for him. He did not grant his son permission to sit. A fire burnt with enough heat to send the sweat coursing down Justin's back, or perhaps it was only fear of what was to come. He waited for his father to speak.

"Explain yourself."

He'd been going over and over a proper speech on the way home. Most of it fled from his mind at his father's forbidding, black gaze.

Clearing his throat, he began. "I wanted the best of both worlds—academia, and Bess—whom I do love. She—I thought we could live happily as if we were married, and I would take care of her. She loved me so she was willing to do this. She was not forced, but I failed her in so many ways. I am glad we were found out and will marry.'

"No plans to desert her at the altar and run off to France or elsewhere."

"None. I want to make Bess my wife, no matter what the price."

The duke rose and paced to one of the tall windows that allowed light for reading. Today, with the heat of the fire inside and the cold pressing against the glass, tears of moisture streaked the panes. He gazed out at the wooded hills of his estate, not its exquisite garden and fountain drained and turned off for the winter. How often Justin had seen him scatter tobacco in the forest, an offering to the spirits of the earth and the animals, always a pagan at heart.

"I gave up a life of freedom among the Shawnee to assume the responsibility of a huge estate and a large family for love of your mother. An extraordinary woman demands extraordinary sacrifices."

"Bess is certainly not ordinary."

"Is she, as the women put it so delicately, *enceinte?* Why they cannot simply say with child, I do not know."

"No, Papa. We were very cautious."

"Good, I taught you well."

Justin bit the tip of hits tongue, this coming from a man who had fathered ten children and showed very little restraint when it came to his wife. He remained silent.

"I will be doubling your remittance to allow you to support a wife. Make sure you treat her well."

"For the rest of her life." He meant that pledge.

"Go to the drawing room. Your mother wants her turn with you."

He left his father still staring at the forest and approached the door behind which his mother waited. She sat alone, close to the fire, no Bess, no Kate nearby. She patted the settee to indicate he should sit by her.

"You have brought about the ending I wanted for the both of you, but not in the way I would have liked. Still, we shall celebrate this wedding with a pretty gown and a fine wedding breakfast. Most of the family will be here for it and of course, our closest neighbors. But why Bess's tears?"

"I told her the way we were living was making me miserable, not her, only the circumstances. I told her often we should marry before we left Bellevue for Oxford. She would not agree."

"Ah, you told her. You did not ask her. Have you said I love you?"

"Over and over, every day. I do mean it, but she has this idea that I will come to resent her for taking away my career and that is why she mistook my words."

The duchess retrieved a large box from a side table. "I suggest you propose to her properly as you should have done in London. Here, choose a ring to offer and go down on one knee in front of all who are gathered here this evening. I think that will help to mend things, but you must reassure her." She opened the box which sparkled with gems like a pirate's chest.

He selected a large sapphire ringed with small diamonds. "Like the blue of her eyes and the sparkle of her smile."

"Very good. I would work that into your proposal. I had that stone as a gift from the Bashaw of Tripoli when Thalia and I were captives in his harem. So, a good tale to go with it and pass along to your children."

"Are you sure it does not have sentimental value to you?"

"I rarely wear it, a gift from a tyrant. It will be a pleasure to see it on Bess's hand. Do it tonight after dinner. Two of the banns have been published now and only two weeks remain until the wedding. The plans for the breakfast are well in hand and invitations already sent to The Orchards and Westbrook Park.

The family will be assembling for Christmas. We will welcome Bess as a Longleigh."

"Thank you, Mama." He gave her powdery cheek a kiss.

~ * ~

Kate sat beside Bess holding her hand. The tears had stopped, and the story started tumbling from her mouth. "Downstairs Justin is taking all the blame, while I deserve it. It was my suggestion that we live together, and I become his mistress. We were so desperate to be together those last days in September, and I did not want to ruin his life. As it turns out, I only made him miserable."

Kate patted her hand. "I bear some responsibility as well. I prompted Fair Annet to inflame your desires to bring about a proposal. I fear she overdid it."

Bess eyed all four corners of the room. "Is she here now?"

"No. She tends to stay in the nursery hovering over little Annette, keeping her from harm. I can only say my daughter's future suitors had better treat her well."

"Do you think Justin will use our dreams as an excuse?"

"I highly doubt it. It wouldn't be a manly excuse. Now rest, sleep, come to dinner refreshed and lovely. Let Justin see the beautiful woman who will be his wife. We will start preparing what you shall wear for your wedding."

"Oh, I already know. In the bottom of my trunk just above my books is a silk evening gown that Justin purchased for me last spring. I have not worn it, but it is beautiful, a rather plain white underdress overlaid with gold. When I first saw it, I imagined being married in it. Now that has come to pass whether we are ready or not."

Kate went to the chest and carefully removed the gown. "Oh, yes. Perfect. I shall send it to be pressed. Clement will do your hair. You shall be the most beautiful bride."

When she turned to Bess again, she saw that fatigue and emotions had taken their toll. The next Longleigh bride slept.

When Bess awoke, she washed her face and combed out her hair, which she braided and knotted at her nape. Putting on the green gown and peering in the mirror, she saw not a mistress nor a bride but a tutor once more, which she could never be again. In an act of defiance only Justin would recognize, she wore the gaudy shawl Daisy had made for her against the chill of the house and went down to join the family.

~ * ~

Bess appeared in the drawing room shortly before the gong sounded for dinner. She wore the dark green gown he'd bought and had arranged her hair into braids coiled at her nape. With the exception of the locket at her throat, she seemed to emulate her tutoring days. But then there was that shawl, a reproach to him for failing to clothe her for the winter, he thought.

"Did you take up knitting while caring for your father?" Kate asked for the benefit of the servants around them.

"No, a friend made it for me. It might not be stylish but is warm."

"With just the family here, we are all dressed more for comfort than for style," the duchess said. "It is not necessary to impress the ton in one's own home."

With no guests to be accommodated, the duke took the arm of his duchess, Joshua escorted Kate, and just to annoy him, James claimed Bess and let Justin straggle behind. He heard his brother's murmurs of how lovely she looked and began to wonder if he'd have the audacity to propose to Bess himself.

That worried him throughout a rather basic meal of soup, fish, game, roast, and side dishes of winter vegetables, cauliflower in a cheese sauce, glazed beets, and potatoes browned in butter. Bess's cabbage would have outshone them all. The usual nuts, cheeses, and puddings followed, but at the end the duchess proposed the men bring their port to the drawing room and join the ladies immediately for tea and coffee. He threw her a grateful glance that she'd shortened the time until the proposal.

When she asked Bess to play the piano, he realized she recreated the evening when he'd declared Bess should be a tutor. The duke and duchess sat next to each other, their faces filled with expectation. Kate clutched Joshua's hand. James lounged with a slight smirk on his lips. Bess took her seat on the bench, remarking as she did so, "I did miss playing music."

That moved him to stumble to her side and say, "I wanted to buy you a piano, but now you will never be without music again." Not how he'd wanted to begin, but that is what came out.

Before he could make more of a botch of it, he dropped to one knee and declared, "Elizabeth Barton, I am asking you to be my wife and hope you will consent. Know that I shall put you before all else in my life, now and forever. Please accept this family ring with a sapphire the color of your eyes and diamonds that sparkle like your smile. You will make my life a joy because my love for you is boundless."

As had happened the first time, she appeared to be speechless and had to gather herself for a moment. He feared what her answer might be. Would she be the one to refuse and run away? It seemed as if no one in the room breathed and for a moment, he thought he saw a young woman in white standing behind her mouthing, "Say yes."

"Justin, whatever comes, we will face it together. You have all my love. Yes, I will be your wife." He slipped the ring on her finger and rose up to take her in his arms.

James applauded. "Well done, as good as our poet Jason could have composed. He will be jealous when we write to him about it. I hear he proposed to Miranda while sitting in the sand at the back end of a turtle with nary a poem in his pocket."

Kate surrounded both of them with a hug while Joshua preferred to shake the groom-to-be's hand. The duke called for champagne, which coincidentally arrived already chilling in a bucket of snow. The duchess said, "We must dance. Kate will play, then I shall take a turn. Only roll up the rug, since our group is so small. No need to move the furniture."

Amazing how long seven people could dance. Justin looked forward to lying on his new feather bed with Bess at his side, but when at last they took their candles to light their way to rest, James tailed them.

"I am really sorry, but Mama has said you are not to sleep together until after the wedding. Only two more weeks. Have patience, brother. You have found true love. I almost envy you."

Fine for him to say who had never experienced love's turmoil.

Thirty-five

The numerous members of the Longleigh family, once nearly extinct but now flourishing thanks to the current duke, began to assemble the week of the wedding. They filled the family rooms and all of the guest wing. The servants doubled up with the excess of valets, ladies' maids, and nannies. The smallest grandchildren took over the nursery while the older ones were placed two or four sideways in a bedchamber near to their parents. Willy and Richie were thrilled to be paired with their Aunt Phemie's two oldest boys who were full of Scottish mischief. The duchess declared no meals in bed as it put a strain on the kitchen staff. They were family, not guests, and could come down to the large dining room for the breakfast buffet 'to be kept warm and renewed most of the morning. The same with the afternoon repast. Once the children were abed, they could eat a regular meal and have adult conversations.

Bess did her best to help with the chaos and calm her own nerves before the wedding. She led groups of children on a daily nature walk, once to the meadow to identify what animals had passed in the scrim of snow covering the grass: the roe buck and smaller fallow deer, rabbits, and pheasants, the large imprints of crows and smaller birds, as well as the sheep still grazing and growing their coats of wool until the snow deepened. The duke came along and impressed upon his grandchildren that being able to track sometimes meant the difference between having food or not, or more important, scouting for the enemy. Not the message she'd meant to convey about the variety of nature, but he did so love sharing his stories of life among the Shawnee and the boys and girls adored them.

Atalanta, Pandora's daughter, raised her hand and asked, "I am named for a great huntress, Grandpapa. Will you teach me with the bow and arrow?"

"Girls don't hunt," Thalia's second son, Piers said.

"As soon as you can string a bow," the duke replied, putting an end to that question.

"I know, let's play Indians and enemies and see who is captured first," shouted Phemie's oldest of the red-gold hair and light freckles. "Captives will be held in the wigwam." He grabbed Atalanta's arm and attempted to drag her toward the wigwam. She did not go quietly.

The other children scattered with the duke calling after them, "Be in by teatime or sooner. We cannot track you in the dark if you get lost."

"I am so sorry. I did not see that happening."

"They need to run and play as well as learn. Come, we will go back to the house."

Before they reached the steps, Justin appeared on 'Enery, adding hoof marks to the snow. The duke went ahead and left them alone now that they were properly engaged.

"He needed exercise, I thought."

The horse nudged Bess. "I am so sorry, but I have no apple for you today. I'll bring one to you tomorrow." She'd earned

'Enery's undying love by feeding him the apples Justin accumulated from the lovelorn maidens who pretended an interest in physics. At least, her interest had been sincere.

"Should I sweep you up and carry you off as Leo did Phemie?" he asked.

"I am not sure he could carry two of us and get very far."

"As far as the wigwam, I'd bet."

"Not a good idea today. The children are putting their captives in there at the moment."

"Thwarted wherever we turn in this crowd." He leaned down to kiss her, and she rose to meet his lips. This would have to do for now.

~ * ~

The next day, she took the children to visit the tortoises in the conservatory where they basked in the heat and enjoyed the small pool in their enclosure kept immaculate by Amos Gantry who, like his charges, had moved inside to the servants' quarters for the winter. Eager hands offered the turtles cabbage leaves until the two got tired of the attention and retreated into their shells. Mostly, the grandchildren wanted to know when the pair would make eggs again and vied to be put on a list for a baby turtle of their own, though their parents already possessed one. Those reserved for James and Justin had found homes at Westbrook Park when it became obvious that neither would have a place to keep them.

"That is up to the duchess," he told them.

Out of the blue, Helena Erickson asked, "Where do babies come from, Mr. Gantry? Are they truly found in cabbage patches or brought by storks? Neither seems likely." She would have been too young to recall her mother's fourth pregnancy, which brought her third brother, Harald, into the world and none of her aunts was obviously expecting this year.

"You must ask your mam that one."

Bess herded them toward the door. "Stay on the pathways. Do not tread on the plants. Thank you for your time, Mr. Gantry."

"Time is all I've got, Miss Barton. Until this crush lets up, I'll sling my hammock between two palms and spend the night in here with old Duncan, minding the fire."

Bess crossed another trysting place from her list. Nothing to do but wait for Saturday to come. Meanwhile, she'd have the children gather holly, laurel, hawthorn, and other greenery to make the wreaths for Christmas Eve decorations, as well as mistletoe for kissing balls pulled down by the men who'd come along to help, Justin among them always ready to steal kiss beneath every tree. She helped Kate, the duchess, and the other ladies prepare the Christmas stockings, a major undertaking with nineteen of the twenty-two grandchildren in residence. Each child would find one hanging on their bedpost Christmas morning as there was hardly enough mantel room for these gifts from St. Nicholas in the house.

Patience—her wedding day would come.

~ * ~

Yet when it did, it seemed too sudden. She awoke early to wash in rose scented water in the duchess's bathing chamber. Barely dried and in her undergarments, she was assailed by Clement, who attacked her hair, combing and pulling it into a shape that would accommodate a small lace cap to be held in place by a circlet of gold.

"You certainly played your cards right. Got him in the end. Some wonder if your father was really ailing."

Bess realized she owed Clement no explanation. "If you pull my hair one more time, I shall tell Lady Katherine and have you dismissed."

She wouldn't of course, but she did enjoy seeing Clement clamp her mouth shut and apply a gentler brush. Oh, the power of becoming a Longleigh. Yet, she knew that servants were often dismissed on a whim by the wealthy and some of them ended up in the brothels. She would not condemn even Clement to that.

Kate and the duchess came into the room as the wedding gown was draped over her shoulders and fluttered to her feet to be followed by the golden overlay. She wanted to wear only her mother's locket as an adornment, but the duchess had one final embellishment to add, a gold opera cloak to keep her warm on the way to the church.

"Do you recall this cloak and the use you made of it, Kate?" the duchess said.

"Oh, yes. My improper use of it at Almack's resulted in both Pandora and Phemie being ejected from the ballroom as well as myself, all to attract the attention of a man."

Her mind distracted from the imminent wedding, Bess asked, "Joshua?"

"Oh, no, we'd made that bet that I could not gain a proposal from the best catch of the season, at that time Viscount Astin, as I told you. I did succeed without setting another foot in Almack's, but it came at a great price."

"Yet you married Joshua."

"The man I loved. The men and the rest of the family are at the church already. Our carriage awaits."

So silly that her knees wobbled on her way down the long staircase. She supposed it was one thing to be a mistress and another to make a lifelong commitment—or perhaps the lack of a breakfast.

Just before leaving wrapped in the golden cloak, she was handed a small bouquet by the duchess. "A bride should have flowers and there are few this time of year, but my conservatory has produced this spray of orchids for you."

Bess accepted the bouquet of exotic blooms tied up with ivy and white ribbons. The thoughtfulness after her transgressions brought tears to her eyes.

"There, there. None of that," the duchess prompted.

She blinked them away and went out into the cold for the ride to the village church. With all the Longleigh children and their spouses, plus Edgemont, Lady Lucia, and the Appletons, but minus the grandchildren who might disrupt the solemnity of the occasion, the priest had a larger congregation than he did on most Sundays. Her father, imported only a day ago from Oxford but planning to spend Christmas, helped her off with the cloak while the duchess and Kate moved to the front of the church to take their seats. Beyond them, Justin stood awaiting her, his gray eyes bright with anticipation. James stood up with him, jesting that he needed to prevent the groom from running off, but Justin showed none of his bride's nervousness.

Her father offered his arm. He'd turned down an offer from the duchess to supply him with proper morning wear and wore his best academic gown and mortarboard instead. She had no objection to that other than a reminder of what Justin had given up for her. The aisle was short, and the traditional service over by half nine. Somewhere, a slim gold ring had been found and now rested on her finger. She left the church as Lady Elizabeth Longleigh, and the throng of her new family followed behind in a variety of coaches.

No need to wait very long to break their fast. Yet another leaf had been added to the vast table in the dining room to accommodate the wedding feast: platters of ham and sausage, eggs prepared in serval ways, mounds of breads still warm from the oven and toast, coffee, tea, and hot chocolate, and bottles of champagne for toasts to the couple. A large white frosted cake dominated the center, where the bride and groom sat before its grandeur. When all had filled their plates, they took their seats with Edgemont and Lady Lucia seated to the duke's right and left while the duchess endured Professor Barton and the priest. The rest of the family arranged themselves more by age than rank, though they counted a marchioness and several viscountesses among them.

The duke offered the expected toast to their happiness and health, ending lightly with the suggestion he had only twenty-two grandchildren and needed more. Then, Professor Barton rose and withdrew something from inside his robe.

"I have here a bank note for my daughter's dowry of six hundred pounds which I have kept safe for her. Now, it is yours, young man, though you probably have no need of it." He handed it over to Justin.

Silence fell at this gauche display. Such matters were done in private and settled before the wedding. Bess cringed. But Justin stepped up to accept the bank note. He in turn handed it to his bride. "To do with as you wish."

"As it should be," Pandora shouted, to be joined by rest of the women. The awkward moment passed, the meal progressed, and the cake was cut to expose an interior rich with currants, almonds, candied fruit, and redolent of brandy.

If only they could leave now as most of the newly wed did to begin a wedding trip or travel to the groom's home. She and Justin had no such relief, though several of the couples including the duke and duchess hinted that because of the early hour of rising and heavy meal, they might lie down for a while.

"Shall we?" Bess asked her husband.

But her father interrupted. "I've barely seen this place. Would you give me the tour, my daughter?"

She could not refuse. They viewed the many antiquities, visited the conservatory and the tortoises, and then bundled up once she'd shed her finery to visit the follies. At last, her father said he'd have a lie down before tea. By then, that was all Bess wanted, too.

"But my love, it's been so long," Justin whispered in her ear. "Our feather tick is on my bed awaiting you." They'd passed several bedchambers where people obviously weren't sleeping.

"Tonight, I promise." What was wrong with her? They were married now and could delight in each other any time they wanted, as the duke and duchess proved. She returned to her original chamber and found there a linen nightdress, cut low and embroidered on the hem and yoke. She recognized the duchess's work but did not think she'd wear it tonight. She took out Daisy's gift of red silk bordered with black lace and no longer than her knees. Tucking it under her pillow, she slept well.

But then, there was tea and a lengthy dinner, card games, and dancing in the ballroom, heated for the occasion, half of which had been turned into a playroom for the grandchildren, but the toy soldiers, dolls, balls. and checkers were pushed aside to make room. They left the best toy of all: the miniature railroad which grew larger every year with the addition of new stations and wooden livestock to load, including sheep with real wool and horses with manes and tails made of hair. More tiny people had appeared to ride on the passenger cars, many resembling family members, and a whole contingent of army men. Each child was allowed to push it along the tracks a certain distance before having to relinquish it to another. Some of them made numerous stops to load passengers or livestock in order to extend their possession. A few of the adults played with it now.

So many of the women were skilled at the piano, even Edgemont taking a turn when he wasn't joining his wife five months with child in a waltz, that no one had to play for very long. The dancing went on and on, endless into the night until at last the party wore down in the small hours. How tired she was, yet she could not disappoint Justin again. She accepted Clement's services to take down her hair and help her into the white gown but declined having her locks braided as Justin liked them free. The maid had been careful with the comb but now protested that her fine hair would be a rat's nest by morning.

"Then, I shall brush it myself. Go!"

As the maid's footsteps disappeared toward the servants' staircase, she shed the white gown and donned the red, hiding it beneath a dressing gown as she tiptoed down the corridor to her husband's chamber and found him already in bed and naked.

"I feared you weren't coming."

"I keep my promises."

She hadn't meant it as criticism, but he winced and said, "Let me make it up to you."

Bess revealed the French shift. "Yes, a gift from Daisy, and I do not need any more of them, just for you tonight." She slid under the covers and reached below the blankets. "I see you appreciate it."

"I appreciate every inch of you." He ran his hands under the shift and suckled her breasts through the sheer cloth. By the time he'd reached down and found the place that gave her the most joy, the naughty French undergarment lay tangled in the bedclothes.

They were not new to this or each other. "Top or bottom?" he asked when she rose against his hand.

"Bottom," she answered, and he drove into her eagerly and sustained their passion as long as he could. When they lay in each other's arms, he remarked, "It is better without a preventative, but we will do whatever you wish in the future."

"I'll think about it, but right now I am glad we got a head start on the wedding night."

Thirty-six

The next morning, she started her monthlies. Drat it! It wasn't Justin who brought her a container of hot water wrapped in flannel for her belly but a young maid, who also helped her arrange her rags. When another light rap came on the door, she assumed more cosseting, but it was Justin, tray in hand with hot tea and a breakfast plate. He sat beside her as she ate, then kissed her hand.

"It will be over by Christmas."

She made a point of getting up and putting on her dark blue dress which drew a commendation from the duchess. "We should not allow these trifling women's problems to dominate our lives."

Fine for her to say as she hadn't had to deal with the mess for many years now. Kate leaned toward her as they still worked on filling the stockings: an orange from the conservatory in each toe, packets of sweets, yoyos, and Jacob's ladders, hair ribbons, and small wooden animals that when paired could be marched into the Noah's ark in the play area.

"I haven't had mine since Annette was born, but then there is the other consequence of childbirth that can go on for six weeks."

Perhaps they should continue using the preventatives. But as Justin said, it was over by Christmas day.

The children rallied early and raced to the ballroom to dump the contents of their stockings on the floor between their legs, sucking on oranges and spoiling any breakfast by eating sweets. The adults prepared for church, even the duke who seldom attended, and with that out of the way, the Christmas feast began with an enormous roast goose and a boar's head provided by the duke and his huntsman earlier in the week. They ate their way through the abundance of food until the Christmas pudding was brought out topped by a sprig of holly and soused with brandy that went up in a blaze of blue flame.

After that, the singing of carols while a huge yule log dragged in from the forest warmed the ballroom and released the fragrance from the wreaths bedecked with small apples, oranges, and ribbons hung the previous day. Since all but James were married, couples kissed shamelessly beneath the balls of mistletoe that appeared to be hung in every doorway. That night Bess and Justin resumed relations, though she asked him to use the French letters again.

On boxing day, the servants received small purses of coins and clothes being discarded by those they served, and they were given the day off. The duke rode out with James, Joshua, and Justin distributing gifts of holiday food to the cottagers and returned with an odd assortment of presents in return: a cabbage, a clump of turnips, a suckling pig tucked in Joshua's saddlebag. To refuse such modest offerings would have been an insult to proud people. As for their own family, plenty of trays of cold collations had been prepared, along with an abundance of the remaining mince pies and other puddings.

The Appletons hosted a house party and Lord Edgemont and his lady a ball on New Year's Eve. The duke opened the front door to let out the old year and welcome in the new. Bess, whose holidays had consisted of the quiet of the university between terms and a small gift or two from her father, usually writing paper or a new book, felt fatigued and overwhelmed by it all, even after her father had been sent back to Oxford by the duchess directly after Christmas with a hamper full of delicacies and a firm farewell.

But that would soon pass once Twelfth Night arrived and the vast Longleigh family members prepared to depart, weather and roads permitting. A snowfall on New Year's Day helped ease the passage of time for Bess until Epiphany. She went outside to watch the children at play making snow forts and firing off compacted balls of snow at each other. The girls favored falling backward and creating angels by moving their hands and legs back and forth. Since boys will be boys, they shoved ice down the back of their sisters and cousins, and being Longleigh women in the making, the girls shoved snow in their faces. Soon, they would all go inside, change from their wet clothes, and drink cups of chocolate while eating slabs of gingerbread. Enjoying their frolic, Bess reconsidered having children, only not just yet.

Justin joined her on the terrace, which had been cleared of snow and ice. He studied her face framed by the hood of her blue cloak.

"You seem glum. Is it my turn to make *you* miserable?"

"Not you, never you."

"Has anyone been unkind to you?"

"No. Your family is most accepting. Well, there is Clement, but I have put her in her place and expect no more trouble."

"Good for you. Why Kate tolerates her I do not know. Then what is it?"

'I don't fit in here with all these people, the balls, the feasts, the finery, the visiting. My upbringing was so eccentric and yours so privileged."

"Ha!" A single sharp syllable denied what she'd said. "In case you haven't noticed, all the Longleighs are eccentric in their own ways. Pandora with her passion for women's equity, the twins with their books, even gentle Phemie, who has gone full Scottish wearing her husband's tartan across her gowns on every occasion. I could go on and on. I barely took my nose out of a book to wonder about any of it. You are perfect for this family, and for me. Only give us some time. Why, after Twelfth Night, they will all depart, and we will have solitude once more."

A terrible thought occurred to her. "Everyone? Kate as well?"

"Yes, the baby has been judged strong enough to travel, and Joshua must resume his practice of law. He has been gone far too long and traveled hither and yon several times this autumn. Her other babes were born at her parents' estate closer to London, but the duchess pressed for this one to be born at Bellevue, and Josh and Kate obliged her."

"My best of friends gone, no children to teach, no laboratory. I am totally useless."

"Not to me."

He cupped her fair cheeks reddened by the cold. She did the same to him. A kiss would have been forthcoming had not a snowball hit them squarely on the side of their faces.

"You," shouted Justin, not exactly sure which child he meant as they were all so bundled. Justin vaulted over the terrace wall into a drift of snow and waded out of it to pursue the fleeing boy. Once the culprit was caught, he had his face scrubbed in the snow. Justin made his way back to her, up the slippery stairs.

"What do you say we steal their treats, drink their chocolate, and eat their gingerbread?"

"A perfect revenge, I think." She rubbed her cheek which still stung from the onslaught.

He had comforted her, even made her laugh at his vengeance against a nephew, but she remained troubled.

~ * ~

Gifts were exchanged on Twelfth Night in honor of those given to the Christ child by the Magi. The women of the household had been sewing small items to exchange or went shopping to see what Westbrook village could supply. Bess still had little money, though Justin's doubled allowance had been reinstated at the first of the year. The duke, teaching him a lesson in squandering funds, had not allowed him an advance. As she had been the cause of this, she didn't want to ask for more. As for sewing gifts, she wouldn't desire anything she made with needle and thread as a present her skills were so poor.

But an idea had occurred to her on the snowy terrace. What was snow but crystals. She knew how to make crystals of many kinds, but her cookery book had suggested that a wonderful treat could be made from sugar called rock candy. That very afternoon, she swept into the kitchen and braved Monsieur Pepin's glare, which disappeared quickly as he recalled she was now Lady Elizabeth Longleigh.

"I shall need twenty-four glass canning jars and a great deal of sugar finely ground from sugar loafs as you would for baking."

She learned he had a supply of this but would need more and two kitchen maids were set to work with mortars and pestles. "And boiling water, a large pot of it. Also a table where my experiments can remain undisturbed. Have you any wooden skewers?"

Of course, he did. "*Mais oui*, Lady Elizabeth. My kitchen 'as many." He watched with curiosity as she tied two skewers at right angles after rolling one damped with cold water in the granulated sugar and popping it into a jar as if she thought to dip candles.

Next, she directed her kitchen helpers, their arms well worn out already, to place three cups of sugar in a large bowl with one cup of boiling water and stir until not a trace of the sugar remained. She had two bowls made up to be certain she had enough of the solution and began adding it carefully to each jar

273

by herself. Several fingers were cut, and other accidents occurred as the rest of the staff kept stealing glances.

"We only have to let them set for five days and watch the crystals grow. You have made a very fine solution," she told her helpers.

"A solution to what?" asked the bolder one.

"Not to a problem. A solution in chemistry is dissolving solid matter in liquid until it disappears. But you have assisted me in making my Twelfth Night gifts, so yes, a solution to a problem as well. Do not touch the jars, but you may look at them daily and see the changes."

"Is it magic?" the shyer one said.

"No, chemistry. Cookery is chemistry."

"Back to your duties." The chef ordered the kitchen maids to work with a flick of his hand. "Cookery is an art learned over a long period of time, not science.

"The ingredients you add, the precise time of roasting or baking is chemistry. When you add something new hoping for a certain effect, that is an experiment. However, I admire you as both a master of the kitchen and a very fine chemist."

"As you say, madame."

Despite his terse answer, she knew he was pleased. As was she when, after five days, she returned to see each jar had produced a stick covered thickly in chunky crystals of sugar. She removed each one carefully, sometimes having to break a thin layer of sweet crust on the top and laid them out to dry.

"Do not worry, Monsieur Pepin. Wash the jars thoroughly in very hot water and they will be ready for the making of marmalade."

"We did watch them grow," said one of her assistants.

The other whispered. "It was magic. Nothing in those jars but a stick and now these appear."

"Only sugar in another form—chemistry," Bess assured her.

She gathered her offerings in a pretty box just before Twelfth Night, and as she had made extra in case of any failing, gave one each to the kitchen maids and a large one to Chef Pepin. The girls immediately began to suck on theirs. "Sweets!" they cried.

Monsieur Pepin set his aside. "For later when I am not so busy with ze Twelfth Night dinner."

"They can be stored for a year if kept dry."

"I might try one day ze experiment myself."

"That is a great compliment, indeed." Again, she thought he might have almost smiled.

After the large dinner was completed, the family assembled for the exchange of gifts. Bess had expected jewels and rare perfumes but found that most had been made by hand. Iris and her husband had been quietly sketching throughout the holidays and now gave each set of parents pencil drawings of their children with a collection of all of them for the duke and duchess and portraits of Justin and Bess together and James by himself. They would be treasured.

Pandora received a letter indicating a large donation in her name had been given to the Abolitionist Society from her husband, Daniel, who had once owned slaves. "We are getting closer to seeing slavery ended in England and all the colonies. If only giving women the right to vote weren't so far behind."

The twins distributed their latest novel, cleverly covered in a tartan pattern and embossed in gold lettering *A Lion in the Heather*. "Thanks be to God, I am not the hero of this one," James said as he skimmed the opening which featured a tall Scot with long flowing hair and fine legs in a kilt abducting a young woman with dark curls.

His sister, Clio, stood on her tiptoes to pat his cheek. "I am afraid you have gotten to be too old and gray to be a hero, brother."

"I have not!"

"Oh, I see one gray hair here and another there," said Callie, joining in the teasing.

"Yes, we had so hoped Leo McLaughlin would wear his kilt this year."

"Too drafty," the man in question said, his arm around his once abducted wife, Phemie, his red-gold hair cropped short. "I've brought new parts for the train set. Heaven knows, I make more money off that patent than I do from my real engines and couplings. Why, we have employed a whole village in making them, and Scotland badly needs new enterprises. That toy is a gift to all."

Bess presented her treats, the largest for the duke who was known to have a sweet tooth. "It is called rock candy, and I made them by using a chemical solution…"

"Explain the chemistry later," her husband prompted. "We have many other gifts to be distributed, but these are a fine surprise."

"The real surprise is that Monsieur Pepin allowed you in his kitchen," said Pandora.

"I explained that cookery is chemistry and vice versa. He took it very well and might make them next year."

"Now that is a gift that will continue to give." Despite her usual dignity, Thalia, who had received piles of new sheet music, had taken a lick or two. "The children would love these."

"They could make them as chemistry lesson, too," Bess added. She'd received several lacy fichus and beautifully embroidered scarves from her new female relatives who knew her wardrobe was lacking. Kate gave Bess her black pearl hairpins to keep.

Phemie had given all the ladies tartan shawls woven by the women of castle McLaughlin but had a special gift for her papa. She patted her stomach, "Your twenty-third grandchild is due in June."

"Dear God, that is number five," muttered Pandora who had only two and by various means intended to keep it that way. "Little Rory up in the nursery is only a year old."

The gift giving approached its end, but one large box remained. It ended up passed from hand to hand into Bess's lap.

"From myself and the duke. It is not new as I had only the village seamstress to work with, but she cut it to your measurements."

Bess drew out a stylish riding habit that included a fetching small hat. "I am so grateful. I do want to do more riding."

"And you shall. You have not seen my gift to you yet," Justin said.

"Toasting forks?" she teased.

"Better."

He led the way to the front door and opened it. At the base of the steps stood 'Enery, never looking better with his bay coat sleek and his black mane and tail bedecked with ribbons. On his back he patiently bore a sidesaddle. He nickered at the sight of Bess who had kept up a steady supply of apples to his stall.

"He is yours now," Justin said.

"But I do not want to ride without you."

James stood on his other side. "My gift to Justin is having persuaded Papa to give him Black Lightning. He is far too spirited to be a carriage horse. I have broken him of his bad habits. He will not throw you or scrape you off if you just keep a firm hand."

"Thank you, I think."

"Although 'Enery has made a fine presentation, I suggest all of us come in from the cold, including him before we all catch our deaths," the duchess commanded.

No one objected. The party had ended and most of the family would depart at various times in the morning, Phemie and her family back to Scotland, actually the shortest trip, and Thalia and her family taking another route to Yorkshire. The twins headed to their castle on the eastern coast with a short stop on the way in

London where Pandora and Iris resided much of the year. They planned to travel together if the snow held off and the roads stayed frozen. Footmen had been sent out and reported that the post coaches had broken the way.

Kate and Joshua sat up a bit longer with the duke and duchess, James and Justin and Bess. "I've had a thought. The boys miss Bess so terribly I thought she and Justin might come and stay with us. She could tutor them if she wishes, and Justin will be near the great minds of England who accept many gentlemen scholars into their midst. In fact, the two of them might want to start a small school together, the Longleigh Day School, if a proper building can be found."

Pandora had left something behind and caught the end of the conversation. "Would they accept girls and give them a real education? I would enroll Atalanta. Then you could call it the Longleigh Progressive Day School."

The first time since her marriage, Bess's heart beat with excitement unconnected to Justin. "I will put my dowry into it and provide all the laboratory supplies I have in storage."

The duke nodded. "I might invest in such an idea, provide desks and such, whatever is needed."

"I doubt the ton will wish to send their children. They will cleave to the old ways, but I believe the citizens of London will fight to get their children educated by a former Oxford don," the duchess concurred.

Though Justin had not said a word about the loss of his career since his resignation, his face shone with the idea. "Let's do it, Bess."

James sighed. "Only myself and my mummy will be left behind. I have found no place to unwrap him."

"How could I forget." The duchess sorted through the clutter left by the party and found a letter which she handed to her eldest son. "I had written to some of my London friends with a more intellectual bent about the unwrapping, and this one responded.

Let me tell you about her. She is Miss Athena Harcourt, granddaughter of the late Admiral Harcourt, who left her a large inheritance as his only heir. You see, his daughter ran off with her music instructor and later died in childbirth, an old, old story when a proper matchmaker is not involved. The admiral and his wife raised the child, educating her far beyond normal and always teaching her to beware of men. Hence, she did not marry."

Bess couldn't help but give a little shudder. The tale sounded similar to her own.

But James broke in. "Are you trying to pair me off again?"

"Oh dear, no. Miss Harcourt is twenty-nine and thoroughly on the shelf. However, she holds a monthly salon of bluestockings which hosts interesting speakers. As you can see from her correspondence, she is very excited by your mummy."

"I had hoped Iris might offer her salon for the unwrapping if I could find no other."

"Her salon caters to artists, poets, writers, and musicians. Half would faint at a mummy unwrapping, but Miss Harcourt's group is made of sterner types. The lectures are open to both women and men, no membership required. One can never tell who one might meet there. I attended when they brought Mary Anning up from Lyme Regis to speak about the fossil creatures she has discovered."

Pandora had lingered. "I heard her speak as well. She was denied membership in the Geological Society of London due to her sex, but Miss Harcourt welcomed her."

James scanned the letter. "She does seem very interested in the mummy and does not gush or pay false compliments to me. She suggests we set a date in April when more of her group will be in town. Sensible."

"She is that. You and the mummy can stay the winter with us. Your dear papa is aging and could use your help in running the estate. We see so little of you ordinarily," the duchess said.

"I am not aging and need no help with…" A rap of her fan on his knuckles stopped the duke's protest. "Ahem, I would be glad of your company, James."

~ * ~

Because of the sudden change in plans, the carriage carrying Kate, her boys, and baby plus Bess left a day later than the others. They would travel at a slower pace because of the babe and 'Enery in tow. Joshua and Justin, astride Black Lightning, went on horseback. Their last view of the family was of the duke with the duchess tucked snugly against his warmth, waving them off to a new life while James stood rather glumly behind them.

"We are about to begin a great endeavor," Bess whispered to Justin as she mounted the coach.

"Together," he answered.

Epilogue

Busby entered the drawing room where the duchess and her eldest son sat while Lady Flora with her many lists plotted their return to London for the Season and James fidgeted to be gone. He'd packed his belongings, secured the mummy and had naught left to do.

"The post has arrived, Your Grace. Two for your ladyship and one for Lord James." The butler offered them the contents on the silver salver he carried and returned to his duties.

"Ah, news from London and a packet from Ariel Island. Let's see, which first," she debated, as if choosing a bonbon. "The one that has come the farthest. Do look, James, Miranda has included small watercolors of their daughters, all beauties. I think Nerissa favors Jason with her dark hair and eyes. Portia remains fair and green-eyed while Jessica is a combination of the two with her black hair and light eyes."

James gave the paintings a passing glance. He had little interest in his many nieces and nephews, especially those living half a world away off the coast of Georgia.

"Jason reports that their island resort is thriving with guests from the north in winter and those more local hoping to catch the sea breezes and go on turtle watching expeditions with Miranda in the summer. He sends some of his latest poems. We must read them aloud after dinner."

James had opened his own message and hardly listened to his mother go on and on until she said, "Where is the duke? He will want to see these."

"The portraits, yes, the poetry, no. You know he could never abide Jason's poems. Regardless, he has gone out to say farewell to his woodlands prior to leaving for London. I believe he would rather stay here year-round like Edgemont."

"Edgemont has his own reasons for avoiding London, but your father and I agreed when we married that I should have six months of culture and company and he six months of hunting and fishing. It works out very well for us."

"Yes, marriage requires sacrifice. Look at what Justin gave up for Bess."

"The second letter is from him. They have found a suitable building in which to house their school. There is a kitchen, two large rooms which were once the dining and drawing rooms and will serve for classes, above the stairs a large bedchamber that will become their sitting room and three more to use as they wish. Best of all, a brick storage building will be transformed into Bess's laboratory. 'Enery and Black Lightning have a stable in the mews, and they will hire a stable boy to tend to them. They plan on finding a woman of all work to cook and clean, though Bess wishes to continue practicing her kitchen chemistry. He says her French omelets surpass those of Monsieur Pepin, but not to tell him. How charming. No mention of a child on the way."

James cleared his throat. "There are ways of preventing that, Mama."

"Yes, I realize that, but each of you should know the joy of having children."

"I've always thought we were a great deal of trouble."

"In an interesting way. What does your letter say? Another from Miss Harcourt, I assume."

"Yes, we have settled on a date in April and a special guest list for the unwrapping of the mummy. She has obtained what I asked for, a device for rolling up the bandages as we go along. Of course, I will lecture first on the burial customs of the ancient Egyptians. Once I am in London, I shall go to her salon to approve the room. She seems very efficient—like you, Mama."

"Yes, we have much in common."

"But not as beautiful, I'd wager." He knew his beloved mother did appreciate such a compliment.

"Oh my, no. At twenty-nine, she is a dried-out husk much like your mummy, but very, very intelligent."

So was his mother. If Miss Harcourt's letters had not been so businesslike, he might have suspected Lady Flora of matchmaking again. No, he would never set a toe in the parson's mousetrap.

Meet Lynn Shurr

Lynn Shurr grew up in Pennsylvania Dutch country, but left to wander the world shortly after getting a degree in English Literature. After living in several states and Europe, she picked up a degree in librarianship. Her first reference job brought her to the Cajun Country of Louisiana. Eventually, she became director of a library system. For her the old saying, "Once you've tasted bayou water, you will always remain here," came true. She raised three children near the banks of the Bayou Teche and lives there still with her astronomer husband, where she writes, paints, studies history, and roots for the LSU Tigers and the New Orleans Saints.

Works From The Pen Of Lynn Shurr

A Taste of Bayou Water – a prequel to *Blessings and Curses*
When Celine Landry refuses to leave Cajun country to marry billionaire Jonathan Hartz, what else can a brilliant techno-geek do but try to become Cajun?

Blessings and Curses – Adrienne and Pete: is their love real or are they the victims of an old traiteur's love potion?

The Courville Rose – Can four souls find love in two bodies?

A Place Apart - Jacob Day is a mentally wounded warrior who seeks solitude on a deserted Maine island call No Hope. Diana Mayfield is a society girl who has trashed her reputation and wants to build a private haven on Jake's island. Once they had a past together, but can they learn to share No Hope? Sparks fly!

The Longleigh Chronicles

Lady Flora's Rescue: Book One of the Longleigh Chronicles - When an English Lady desires a half-Shawnee Lord who wants to return to the wilderness, love must go to war with freedom

The Perfect Daughter: Book Two of the Longleigh Chronicles - When a fascinating gentleman rejects perfection, what must a young lady do to gain his love? Perhaps, seduction.

Daughter of the Rainbow: Book Three of the Longleigh Chronicles – The Tale of Iris Longleigh - Shy but lovely Lady Iris Longleigh is passionate about only two things—painting and Lord Valls.

The Double Dilemma: Book Four of the Longleigh Chronicles - What is Lady Flora to do when her twins demand to marry only another set of twins and none are at hand?

Dear reader,

I hope you've enjoyed reading this ninth in the
series of *The Longleigh Chronicles.*

Your opinion is valuable to other
readers like you,
who may be looking for books like mine.

Please consider taking a few minutes to post a
review, however brief,
on the site where you purchased this book or
on the Wings ePress web page.

You may also want to visit my author page at
the Wings' website where you can find the
other eight books in this delightful series that
traces the adventures of the children of Lady
Flora and Lord Pearce Longleigh.

Thank you!

Lynn Shurr

Visit Our Website

For The Full Inventory
Of Quality Books:

<u>Wings ePress, Inc</u>

Quality trade paperbacks and downloads
in multiple formats,
in genres ranging from light romantic comedy to general
fiction and horror.
Wings has something for every reader's taste.
Visit the website, then bookmark it.
We add new titles each month!

Wings ePress, Inc.
3000 N. Rock Road
Newton, KS 67114

* 9 7 9 8 8 9 1 9 7 9 8 9 5 *